the

martin
chronicles

john fried

GRAND CENTRAL
PUBLISHING

NEW YORK   BOSTON

This book is a work of fiction. Names, characters, places, and incidents are the product of the author's imagination or are used fictitiously. Any resemblance to actual events, locales, or persons, living or dead, is coincidental.

Copyright © 2019 by John Fried

Cover design and illustration by Elizabeth Connor
Cover copyright © 2020 by Hachette Book Group, Inc.

Hachette Book Group supports the right to free expression and the value of copyright. The purpose of copyright is to encourage writers and artists to produce the creative works that enrich our culture.

The scanning, uploading, and distribution of this book without permission is a theft of the author's intellectual property. If you would like permission to use material from the book (other than for review purposes), please contact permissions@hbgusa.com. Thank you for your support of the author's rights.

Grand Central Publishing
Hachette Book Group
1290 Avenue of the Americas, New York, NY 10104
grandcentralpublishing.com
twitter.com/grandcentralpub

Originally published in hardcover and ebook by Grand Central Publishing in January 2019
First Trade Paperback Edition: January 2020

Grand Central Publishing is a division of Hachette Book Group, Inc. The Grand Central Publishing name and logo is a trademark of Hachette Book Group, Inc.

The publisher is not responsible for websites (or their content) that are not owned by the publisher.

The Hachette Speakers Bureau provides a wide range of authors for speaking events. To find out more, go to www.hachettespeakersbureau.com or call (866) 376-6591.

Parts of this novel were previously published as the short story "Birthday Season" in issue 45 of *Columbia: A Journal of Literature and Art*.
The chapter "Destroy All Monsters" was originally published in the *Blue Penny Quarterly*.
The chapter "Nueve" was originally published in the *North American Review*.

Library of Congress Cataloging-in-Publication Data

Names: Fried, John, author.
Title: The Martin chronicles / John Fried.
Description: First edition. | New York : Grand Central Publishing, 2019.
Identifiers: LCCN 2018003658| ISBN 9781538729830 (hardcover) | ISBN 9781549195266 (audio download) | ISBN 9781538729854 (ebook)
Subjects: | GSAFD: Bildungsromans.
Classification: LCC PS3606.R545 M37 2019 | DDC 813/.6—dc23
LC record available at https://lccn.loc.gov/2018003658

ISBN: 978-1-5387-2983-0 (hardcover), 978-1-5387-2985-4 (ebook), 978-1-5387-2984-7 (trade paperback)

Printed in the United States of America

LSC-C

10 9 8 7 6 5 4 3 2 1

PRAISE FOR

the

martin

chronicles

"John Fried's debut is a funny, tender, honest coming-of-age story, brimming with heart. *The Martin Chronicles* is about first love and family and loss, but also, set on the Upper West Side of Manhattan in the '80s, it's a nostalgic look into the past and, in the end, a love story about that specific place and time."

—Julianna Baggott, nationally bestselling author
of *The Seventh Book of Wonders*

"Fried's lighthearted humor shines through...offers playful moments and an evocative atmosphere."   —*Publishers Weekly*

"Fried infuses every page with warmth and wonder."

—*Booklist*

"Poignant and funny."   —*New York Post*

for Laura

contents

the

martin
chronicles

destroy all monsters

GIRLS INVADED OUR SCHOOL a month into sixth grade. We watched from the window of Mr. Harding's second-floor classroom, craning our necks to catch a glimpse of them, but their school bus, pristine and glowing orange against dark dirty brownstones, blocked our view. We could only hear their high-pitched voices vibrating outside the entrance of our school. As the sound grew closer, all of us ran to the door of the classroom, waiting to see what appeared at the top of the stairs.

"How long are they staying?" my friend Dave asked. All we had been told was that they were from our sister school across town and that there had been some kind of water-main break. Most of us didn't even know we had a sister school.

"I heard they're going to be here months," my friend Max, the perennial exaggerator, said. "Maybe all year."

"That's okay with me," Alan Oates, the classroom Casanova, said with a smirk. Alan wore his blazer with the sleeves pushed to his elbows, and his tie dangled loosely around his collar. Rumor was that he had made it to first base with a girl and got thrown out stretching it into a double, but most of us weren't even sure what that meant.

"Boys!" Mr. Harding, our sixth grade homeroom teacher, shouted. "Back to your seats, *tout de suite!*" Mr. Harding was also the middle school language teacher, English teacher, and math teacher, a compact man who wore oversized corduroy blazers and had a long beard that made his mouth vanish when he wasn't speaking.

We ran back to our seats, mine the last in the back row, a choice spot for keeping a low profile. I was a decent student, but I preferred to stay away from the action, particularly from Mr. Harding, who marched in front of the class, calling on random students. Kids in the front row, the easiest targets, often looked beaten up by the end of the day.

Mr. Harding shuffled to the door, his sneakers slapping against the linoleum floor. From the hallway, we could hear a woman's voice shouting out names, sending the girls to different rooms, including our own. When they appeared, Mr. Harding opened the door with a grand flourish, and said, "*Bienvenue! Willkommen! Benvenuto!*" The girls filed in, gathering by the blackboard. Like us, they were in matching uniforms—white dress shirts and plaid jumpers—but they looked very different from one another, some as tall as Mr. Harding while others were as small as lower school kids. The boys in my class all looked the same, small and childlike, our hair cut neatly close to our heads, our skin untouched by acne. It was hard to believe we shared anything in common with these girls.

Mr. Harding asked the girls to introduce themselves and they gave typical girl names. When they were done, he was about to say something when another girl came running into the room. Boys started to laugh, whispering to one another. This girl had bright red hair and a face full of freckles, but that wasn't what had set them off. It was the wire mouth gear circling her face from ear to ear and strapped around her head like a catcher's mask. "*Silencio!!*" Mr. Harding shouted.

I recognized the mouth gear immediately. I had worn one last year every night. I hated the way the retainer dug into my mouth, the straps pulling at my skin and hair as I slept. Wearing it during the day seemed like torture. Everyone continued to laugh, even me.

"Boys!" Mr. Harding shouted, and we quieted down. He turned to the new girl and said, "Welcome, my dear. What's your name?"

She said, "Alice Jakantowicz."

Her name sounded as jumbled as the tangle of metal in her mouth.

"Nice to meet you, Miss Jakantowicz. Now, boys," he said, returning to us, "it's your turn for introductions. And please offer these young ladies more than your name, rank, and serial number. An interesting fact about yourself perhaps."

Daniel Ashford started, announcing that his cat's name was Itchy. That set the trend. Peter Barson had a rabbit named Ruben. Alan Oates had a pair of guinea pigs named Peanut Butter and Jelly. Dave had a dog named Zipper.

"I'm Marty," I said, when it was my turn. "Martin Kelso. Eleven years old. I don't have a pet."

"What else, Martin?" Mr. Harding's tone was impatient. "Why don't you tell our guests something about our fine institution?"

All I could think about was food. Lunch was less than an hour away. "Today's lunch is meatloaf," I said. Mr. Harding pressed me with his eyes. "This means tomorrow's lunch will be hamburgers because no one eats the meatloaf. Which means the next day's lunch will be sloppy joes because they have to finish the meat. They're good. The sloppy joes." Mr. Harding raised his hand as if to change the topic, but I was rolling. "The next day it'll be something different because they can't do much with sloppy joes, although someone once said the chili dogs are just hot dogs with sloppy joe on them. Basically a hot dog with meatloaf on it." I paused. "Stay away from *them*. The chili dogs, I mean."

The boys around me nodded their heads. The girls looked bewildered. "Fascinating," Mr. Harding said, tugging on his beard. We finished introductions and then Mr. Harding said he would find places for the girls to sit. He looked around the room and pointed at the girl with the mouth gear. "Miss…" he said. "Miss…"

"Brace Face," I whispered to myself, but evidently it was loud enough for everyone to hear. I couldn't believe I had said it. I was just thinking about what I had been called when I first got braces, the way I had been teased for weeks until two other boys came in with braces and what had seemed so strange became normal. When I said it, all the boys started to laugh again, even some of the girls.

"Mr. Kelso," my teacher said. "Your first demerit. *Che buona fortuna.*"

Demerits were these bright yellow note cards teachers handed out when kids did something wrong. Max got them for talking in class. Alan Oates collected them for wearing his shirt untucked. Even Dave, who never got in trouble, got one once for picking his nose in the middle of class. They really didn't mean anything unless you got three, because then you had to get the demerit signed by your parents. I hadn't gotten any so far this year. In fact, I had never gotten a demerit. It was a point of pride for me, like being the Attendance Iron Man (only three absences since kindergarten) or the Times Table Titan in third grade. But the day the girls arrived, I got my first demerit. It had to be their fault.

I didn't want to look at Brace Face and she clearly didn't want to look at me, but as she walked to her seat, our eyes met. She didn't look defeated or upset. Her expression was determined, almost fierce, as if she were prepared to attack. I turned away and tried my best not to look at her again the whole class.

Girls were invading my life at home as well. My mom's sister Beth was visiting for a few days with her daughter, Evie. Aunt Beth lived in upstate New York, but she was thinking about moving to the city and had pulled Evie out of school so they could look at apartments. They were sleeping in the guest room, which shared the bath off my room. I spent every trip to the bathroom holding the door closed with my foot.

When I walked into our apartment that afternoon, I found my mom and Aunt Beth in a smoky kitchen, shouting above the sound of the fire alarm. Evie was sitting at the kitchen table, turning pages of a magazine, as if nothing was going on around her.

"What's that smell?" I said.

"It's cassoulet," my mom said, standing on a chair to get to the alarm. Aunt Beth stirred a large pot on the stove. "It's been cooking since this morning," she added.

Ever since Uncle Karl died, Aunt Beth was always into something new. Two visits ago it was hairstyling, and when she left, my dad and I both had crooked haircuts. The last time she visited, it was palm reading. One evening she looked at my hand and told me I needed to stay away from alcohol and drugs and that she saw a career in either watercoloring or gynecology.

The alarm finally stopped. "It's French," my mom added, battery in hand. I nodded and turned to leave.

"Marty," my mom called. "You didn't say hello to your cousin."

I turned and looked at Evie, her eyes still locked on her magazine. For years our families had rented a house together every summer on Cape Cod. Evie and I had been inseparable. She was four years older than me and had ordered me around, but I didn't mind. She taught me how to snorkel and catch tadpoles in the tidal pool. Every night we would play hide-and-seek until bedtime. Evie was a master at squeezing into small cabinets and tiny crawl spaces of the dusty bungalow. I often gave up, wandering the house and shouting her name until she came out. Once a week, we would make our parents order pizza. Evie told me that the proper way to eat pizza was to rip off the crust first, then dab it over the surface to collect the oil. I followed her dutifully.

After her dad died two years ago, we didn't take the Cape trip again. We mostly saw them on holidays. It didn't matter, because Evie seemed to have changed, growing sullen and quiet. I knew that her dad's death had shaken her up, but it was also clear that she wanted nothing to do with me anymore. The four-year difference in our age had become insurmountable and only confirmed my theory that girls were creatures from an alien planet. "Hey," I said, and waved at her.

"Hey," Evie said, her expression blank, as if she barely knew me at all.

———

The next day, the girls were back at school. It had rained all morning and the hooks where we hung our dark blue school ponchos were covered with red and yellow and pink raincoats, the floor beneath them lined with matching boots. Mr. Harding rearranged the classroom alphabetically, which meant I was in the second row, way too close to the action. Brace Face sat in front of me. I stared at the back of her head, the strap of the brace caging the top of her skull. Her red hair, fiery in the fluorescent light, spilled out below the straps, draping over the back of the chair. I was about to reach out and touch it, when I realized Mr. Harding was calling my name.

"*Attention*, Mr. Kelso?"

"Yeah?" I said. "I mean, yes?"

Mr. Harding walked over to my desk, his beard hanging over me. "Can you tell me what a homonym is?"

"A homo-what?" I said.

Several boys snickered. Mr. Harding cleared his throat. "A homonym."

We had started a lesson about homonyms the day before the girls had gotten there, but I didn't remember any of it. My stomach gurgled, still digesting what little of the cassoulet I had managed to get down. "I don't know."

"You may not *know*," he said, with added emphasis, "but you just used one."

"I did?"

"Does anyone *know*," he said, pausing dramatically, "what homonym Mr. Kelso just used?" Again, silence. Brace Face's hand shot up.

"Ms. Jakantowicz," Mr. Harding said.

"Homonyms are words that sound the same but are spelled different. I mean, differently. *Know*, K-N-O-W, and *no*, N-O."

"Excellent," he said.

"We did that last year," she added, and all the girls around her nodded. Dave looked over at me and curled his lip into a snarl directed at Brace Face.

In the afternoon, we had music class with Mrs. Ablethorpe. Usually she had us listening to music from different cultures and marching around the room shaking tambourines and gourds, but with the girls visiting, Mrs. Ablethorpe wanted us to sing. "It'll be so nice to have the different pitches, the tonal variations," she said, her hands folded in front of her with delight. She read our names, arranging us alphabetically in a tight semicircle, shoulder to shoulder. "Alice Jakantowicz?" she called out.

"Coming," Brace Face said, as she stuffed something into her book bag. When she stood up and took her place, I almost didn't recognize her. She wasn't wearing her mouth gear. Her face was immediately rounder, almost softer, as if the brace had been contorting it into odd shapes. I hadn't noticed her eyes before, but now I couldn't stop looking at them—a bright, translucent candy green. Mrs. Ablethorpe called my name and I went to stand next to Brace Face.

"Hey," I said, but she ignored me.

We started out singing "De Colores," a Mexican folk song we had butchered all through fourth and fifth grade. Today wasn't much better. Alan Oates was on one side of me, booming out verse after verse, his voice as flat as the floor. It didn't matter. I was listening to Brace Face. It wasn't that her voice was so good, but rather that as she sang, I could not only hear her voice, but feel it resonating through our touching shoulders and down into my body. This closeness was a little unnerving at first, but after a few verses I started to enjoy it. I stopped singing just to feel her voice inside me. It was like nothing I had ever experienced before. When the song ended and she stopped singing, I felt empty, as if I had been given something wonderful and then had it abruptly taken away. Brace Face turned to me and said, "You're not singing."

"Yes, I am," I said.

"No," she said. "You're moving your mouth, but nothing is coming out."

I didn't know what to say. "Shut up, Brace Face."

Her hand shot up.

"Yes? Ms. Jakantowicz?" the music teacher asked.

"Martin isn't singing," she said.

"Martin?" Mrs. Ablethorpe said, walking over to stand in front of me, her expression grave. "Is this true?"

"I'm singing," I said.

Mrs. Ablethorpe raised an eyebrow. "I hope so."

We started a new song, rounds of "The Erie Canal." Again, I mouthed the words, letting the sound of Brace Face's voice pour through me. I closed my eyes, losing myself in the hum of her voice vibrating across my skin. Halfway through the song, I heard a cough in front of me, and when I opened my eyes, there was Mrs. Ablethorpe, still conducting with one hand and waving a yellow note card with the other. A demerit. Next to me, Brace

Face scooted away. Even with the space between us, I could still feel the heat from her shoulder on mine.

———

That afternoon, Dave came over to my house to watch *Destroy All Monsters*, one of our favorite afternoon monster movies. In the movie, a band of alien moon women used mind control to get the monsters to destroy major cities around the world. We had seen it dozens of times, but it never got old. Our favorite part was when the newscaster announced, "Godzilla is now in New York City! The city's been invaded by Godzilla!" People ran through the streets, screaming in terror. We would say the line and stomp around the living room carrying old toy trucks and police cars we never played with anymore, bashing down pretend buildings like a pair of Godzillas invading our own city. After, we sat in my room running through our favorite Godzilla battles: Godzilla versus Mothra. Godzilla versus King Ghidorah. Godzilla versus Mechagodzilla. Finally I said, "Who would win in a battle between Godzilla and Brace Face?"

"She'd be toast," Dave said. "He'd fry her with his atomic breath."

"I don't know," I said. "Brace Face might bite through him with her grill."

I got up and pretended to be a crazed monster, marching through the room. "I have to take a leak," I said, heading for the bathroom. As I opened the door, I saw my cousin Evie sitting on the toilet, bringing a wad of toilet paper from between her legs. Our eyes met, her expression as startled as mine. My gaze slipped to the shadowy space between her legs and she snapped her thighs together, covering herself with her hands. I stepped back into my room and shut the door.

Dave's head snapped up. "That was fast."

I didn't move, my hand still on the doorknob. "I just saw my cousin on the toilet."

Dave looked at me, awestruck. "Did you see anything?"

I leaned toward him, whispering, "I think I saw her vagina."

There was a pause as he considered this information, and then he said, "What'd it look like?"

I hadn't really seen anything, just a flash of thigh, but I'd put it out there. "Like Mothra when it gets really angry." Dave nodded, as if it all made sense.

At dinner that night, I avoided eye contact with Evie. Aunt Beth had made something called borscht, this purplish thick liquid that looked like the blood of one of the monsters from a Godzilla movie. She and my parents were talking about where to look for apartments, my mom suggesting a few neighborhoods and then my dad reminding her how expensive the rents were in those places. Evie was pushing a potato through her soup, not eating any of it. Finally, Aunt Beth took a sip of her soup and said, "This needs pepper." She looked at me. "Don't you think, Marty? Pepper might give it a kick in the pants."

I shrugged.

And then, out of nowhere, Evie said, "This tastes like shit." It was true, but I couldn't believe she said it.

"Evie!" Aunt Beth said. "Watch your language!"

"This is awful, Mom," she said, throwing down her spoon. She pushed her chair out from the table, as if she was going to flip the whole thing over. I hadn't been able to look at her all evening and now I couldn't take my eyes off her. Her face turned red, her lips clenched in anger. She was like a monster, lying dormant for millions of years, suddenly set free again. "I don't even know why you try," Evie added.

"That's enough," Aunt Beth shouted, her voice angrier than I had ever heard. Her mouth trembled and I couldn't tell if she was going to scream or cry. She took a deep breath, resting her hands on the table as if she was trying to steady herself. "If you can't be civil, you can go to our room."

Evie got up and marched out of the dining room. Aunt Beth looked at my mom and dad. "I'm sorry," she said, rising and walking to the kitchen. My mom ran after her. My dad looked at me. "It's all right, buddy," he said. "Evie's having a rough time. I'm not sure she wants to move." I nodded, but I didn't get it. I couldn't imagine living upstate, where they were now. Way too quiet. My dad looked at the bowl of chunky liquid in front of him, raising his eyebrows suspiciously, before pushing his chair back and following my mother into the kitchen. I sat there, in silence, wondering if I was supposed to wait or I was excused.

———

At school the next day, Mr. Harding spent the morning reviewing homonyms for a quiz, but I couldn't get Evie's explosion out of my head. I wondered if it was all because I had walked in on her in the bathroom. Part of me wanted to tell her that I hadn't seen anything, but that would have meant talking to her, and I wasn't going to do that.

At lunch, I sat with a bunch of my friends while the girls clustered together at another table next to ours. It was sloppy joe day, the heavy smell of meat sauce all around us. I stared at Brace Face. She wasn't wearing her mouth gear and seemed to smile more without it. Someone at my table dared Alan Oates to go sit with the girls. He flipped up the collar of his blazer and walked to their table. I couldn't hear what he said, but a few moments later all the girls stood up and cleared out. "They said they were done," he told us when he returned. "Their loss."

I watched the girls clear their trays at the cleaning station and then hurry out the door. Alan started boasting about some girl he had met from another school who taught him how to French-kiss. I got up and took my tray over to the cleaning station.

That's when I saw it.

Nestled on a tray between a half-eaten sloppy joe and a crushed milk carton was Alice Jakantowicz's retainer box. You couldn't miss it, this round, bright blue container glowing in the pile of trash on her tray. In the cafeteria light, I could make out the outline of the retainer sitting inside, like a creature resting in its cave. There was no one behind me, so I grabbed the container and stuffed it into my jacket. Outside, in the hallway, I jammed the box into my book bag just before Brace Face reappeared, running toward the cafeteria. She looked at me for a moment, her expression worried, and then darted inside.

It took no time for news about the missing retainer to make it around our grade. Max came into the library and found Dave and me doing our search assignment, trying to find a book on giraffes by using the card catalogue. "Guess what," Max said. "Brace Face lost her grill."

I tried to look surprised.

"She's down at the dumpsters searching for it," he added.

I thought about telling them. They were my best friends. Still,

I decided against it. Max was incapable of keeping a secret and I wasn't ready to tell Dave. Not yet. For some reason, I didn't want anyone to know. This was just between me and Brace Face.

Back in class, we were working on a math lesson, subtracting six-digit numbers. Brad Yost raised his hand to ask how that would ever be useful, and Mr. Harding dropped a demerit on Brad's desk. Fifteen minutes later, Brace Face returned to the room. Her hair was a tangled mess, her jumper and white shirt covered in stains. Her eyes were puffy and red, as if she had been crying. The boys in the class started giggling and Mr. Harding was having a difficult time quieting them down. Finally, he whispered something in her ear and she turned to leave. She looked devastated. I knew the feeling. I had lost several retainers myself in exactly the same way and had spent a few afternoons rummaging through garbage cans behind the school, only to come up empty-handed. I wanted to tell her I understood, but I just smiled at her, thoroughly delighted, not because I had the retainer, not because she was a mess, but because there was a connection between us that hadn't been there before. She looked back at me, her eyes suspicious, as if I alone was responsible for her losing it.

That night at dinner, I couldn't wait to be excused. Aunt Beth had made moussaka, which looked a lot like lasagna but tasted nothing like it. Evie wasn't feeling well so she stayed in her room. My dad worked at his food with the slow precision of a surgeon and a troubled expression on his face. My mom and Aunt Beth, though, seemed oddly chipper, telling stories about when they were younger, one after the other. The time Aunt Beth stuck an acorn up her nose. The time my mom crashed her dad's car. They kept telling the stories, laughing all the way through, even though they hardly seemed like the kinds of things you wanted to remember. Evie was the closest thing I had to a sibling, but I couldn't imagine we'd ever be as comfortable as my mom and Aunt Beth seemed with each other.

After dinner, I shut my door and retrieved the case from my book bag. I sat on my bed and put the blue case on a pillow in front of me. Rain was coming down, the sky outside the window so gray it felt as if our building was caught inside a cloud. I snapped open the box and a familiar mint scent drifted to my nose. I held my breath as I opened the box completely and saw it—a flimsy piece of pink plastic with a silver wire, the black strap balled up beside it. The whole thing looked exactly like the one I had worn last year, only smaller, more fragile.

I lay down on my back and held the retainer to the light, dragging my finger along the plastic. One side was smooth, but the other was covered with bumps and ridges, a mold of the top of Brace Face's mouth. It was strange to feel the terrain of the retainer as if I were touching the inside of her mouth. For a moment I wondered if maybe she could feel it too.

I sat up and tried to fit the strap around my head. It was too small for me, barely reaching all the way from one ear to the other, but I was able to stretch the strap, attaching each end to the retainer and fitting it into my mouth. I knew the drill. The retainer itself was small and didn't sit right, but I moved it with my thumb, forcing it into place. The rough side of the plastic tore into the flesh on the top of my mouth, but I didn't care. I rolled over onto my stomach and started to move my hips, rubbing against the bed. The plastic continued to give me trouble, catching the inside of my mouth on its rough finish. Outside, the rain fell, hammering my air conditioner like a drumroll.

I didn't hear the door open.

"What the hell are you doing?" Evie said, startling me.

I turned and saw her standing in the doorway.

"What are you wearing?" she said, and started to laugh. Her eyes drifted down to my pants, tented at my hips. "Gross!"

I turned away from her. "Evie!" I shouted. "Get out!"

"Oh, I see. It's okay if you walk in on me, but not the other way around?"

My heart raced. "Evie," I said, "please."

She didn't say anything for a moment, and then I heard the door close. I quickly took off the brace, stuffed it into its box, and buried it in the deepest corner of my closet.

———

The next day, Mr. Harding gave us our homonym quiz. He wrote a series of words on the board. *Dear/Deer. Pail/Pale. Bear/Bare. Know/No. Tail/Tale.* Each person had to go up and write a sentence or two that used both words. Dave got the first and wrote, *Dear Diary, I shot a deer today with my rifle.*

"Very creative, Mr. Pearson," Mr. Harding said, sitting in the back row. "The NRA would be proud. Next, why don't we have Mademoiselle Papoochis."

This girl we called "Pooch" stood and wrote, *The pail was filled with pale water.*

"Excellent," Mr. Harding said. "Almost poetic." He searched the room. "How about Mr. Kelso."

I walked up to the board and looked at my words. *Bear/Bare.* For some reason, I couldn't focus, as if the words weren't English. The incident with Evie lingered in my head, clouding my thoughts. I brought the chalk to the board to write some-thing, but stopped short.

Mr. Harding said, "In this lifetime, Mr. Kelso."

Finally I wrote, *I saw a bear in the woods*. I knew this was right, but I couldn't think of anything to do with *bare*. At that moment, I didn't even know what it meant.

"While Mr. Kelso is brooding, let's have someone else," Mr. Harding said. He searched the room. "Ms. Jakantowicz?"

Brace Face took her position next to me. *Know/No.* Those were her words. It seemed completely unfair, as that was the homonym she had used earlier in the week. She could just write the same thing if she wanted. But when she got up to the board, she didn't do anything, just stared at me as if I was the problem she had to solve. Mr. Harding cleared his throat and said, "Ms. Jakantowicz? Is something amiss?"

She continued to stare. I turned and faced her. She was cleaned up, no food stains, no retainer. She looked pretty. "What's your problem?" I said.

Finally, she moved to the blackboard and began writing. People started whispering. I turned to see what she had written: *I know Martin stole my retainer. He can't say no.*

The noise in the classroom grew louder. Brace Face walked closer to me, saying, "I know it was you. I know it was you."

Mr. Harding leapt up, his shoes slapping the floor with a loud crack. "Now see here, Ms. Jakantowicz. We don't just go making uninformed accusations…"

But Brace Face kept repeating the words, "I know it was you. I know it was you." Tears began to stream down her cheeks, and she kept saying, "I know it was you," as if she could actually prove it. She was glorious, like one of the monsters in the movie ransacking the city, knocking down buildings as if that was what she was born to do.

If I had stayed quiet, the whole thing might have passed over. She would have gotten in trouble and I might not have needed to finish the quiz. I was the victim, she was the monster. But Brace Face was accusing me, the anger in her eyes like the look Evie had given her mother at dinner the other night. I said the first thing that came into my head.

"Godzilla is now in New York City! The city is being invaded by Godzilla!"

Students started laughing uncontrollably. "Godzilla is in New York City!" I said, repeating the words over and over. Harding was shouting at us to be quiet in multiple languages, but even he couldn't stop it. At last, he picked up a ruler and slapped it across the blackboard. The room fell silent. "Take your seats!" he yelled. "Everyone pull out a sheet of paper and write new sentences for each of these homonyms. Absolutely no talking." There was a general moan before he slapped the blackboard again, shouting, "Enough!"

I walked to my chair, my mind racing. I couldn't figure out how she knew. Had she seen me put it in my bag? Why didn't she stop me? Had Evie told her? How could she know Evie? Did all girls know each other? My thoughts swirled. In front of me, Brace Face slipped into her seat, her back heaving with sobs. Harding walked the aisle, handing her a demerit. She took it without a word. He was about to walk away when he turned and handed me one as well.

"She started it!" I said. "That's not fair!"

Mr. Harding's eyes, weary and desperate, searched the room, until he caught himself and looked back at me, this time with a familiar intensity. "Life," he said, "is not fair, Mr. Kelso. I believe this is your third demerit." He walked toward the front of the room, but not before adding, "Have your parents sign it."

I took the yellow note card, staring at the line where my parents would have to sign, my heart beating so intensely I could feel my whole chair shake.

That night, I wasn't hungry, despite the fact that Evie and Aunt Beth were out looking at apartments and my mom had made dinner. "You love spaghetti," she said, her expression concerned when I didn't eat.

"Is something wrong, bud?" my dad said.

"No," I said. The demerit was in my pocket. My whole body felt depleted, as if I hadn't slept for a long time.

"Is it about Evie?" my mom said. It wasn't, but I couldn't tell them. I nodded. My mom reached over and took my hand. "She's going through a tough time."

I pushed the noodles around the plate. "Can I be excused?"

My mom turned to my dad, as if she wanted him to do something. "I don't see why not," my dad said. My mom shook her head, before adding, "Honey, if you want to talk, we're here, okay?"

"I know," I said, and headed to my room.

I sat in bed, trying to think what to do. I had never really gotten in trouble, and at that moment everything seemed to be coming down around me. I had a stolen retainer sitting at the bottom of my closet. I had to get my parents' signature on a demerit. Alice Jakantowicz hated me. My cousin hated me.

I woke the next morning with a plan of how to fix at least one thing. I decided I would bring the retainer back to school and tell Harding I had found it by the garbage. Alice Jakantowicz would have her grill back. I would be the hero. Maybe Harding would let me forget the last demerit. Maybe Brace Face and I would be friends. Everything would return to normal. Maybe for the better.

The moment I got to school that day, everything had changed. The extra chairs had been removed. A row of dark blue ponchos lined the coatracks. My seat was back in the last row.

The girls were gone.

"Where'd they go?" Alan Oates asked.

"The water main was repaired," Mr. Harding said. "They're back at their own school. Perhaps now we can get back to some degree of normalcy."

The room was quiet, as if we all were waiting for something else to happen. No one said a word. When the girls had been there, I had wanted them to leave. Now the classroom felt smaller without them.

No one was home when I got back that afternoon. I watched television for a while, because the afternoon special was a replay of *Destroy All Monsters*. I tried to get into it, but for the first time, I actually felt sorry for the monsters, as if they were the ones who suffered, getting ordered around by the moon women and attacked by armies. It wasn't their fault.

Finally, I turned it off and went to my room. I jammed one shoe under the door and another under my bathroom door. No one was getting in. I pulled the retainer out of my bag and set it on the floor. My whole body tensed as I looked at it. This sad little piece of plastic and metal wire had caused me nothing but problems. I picked up a big toy truck Dave and I used when we pretended to be Godzilla, and started hitting the retainer, gently at first, just tapping at it. When it didn't break, I put all my strength into it, smashing the truck against the retainer and the floor. I was making a ton of noise. It didn't break at first, although the wire started to bend and the plastic flattened out. I would probably never see Alice Jakantowicz again, but at that moment, I wanted to destroy any trace of her. The pink plastic started to give, large cracks veining across its surface until the whole thing shattered, scattering across the floor.

There was a knock at the door and I leapt up. "What are you doing?" Evie said, pushing the door open enough to get her head in.

"Just playing," I said, out of breath.

"Uh-huh," she said, her eyes searching the room. "Look, our parents went out to dinner. They left me money for pizza."

"I'm not hungry," I said.

"Whatever," she said. "I already ordered it. I'm going to eat in the kitchen. Come in if you want some."

I cleaned up the broken pieces of the retainer and threw everything—shattered retainer, strap, case—down the garbage chute. I walked into the kitchen and sat down at the table with Evie, who was once again reading a magazine. Her mom had decided they couldn't afford to live in New York, so now they were thinking about New Jersey, or maybe somewhere just a little ways away from where they lived now. I started to think the whole moving thing would probably never happen, that it was just another idea Aunt Beth was trying out. We sat there in silence until Evie looked up and said, "What's wrong with you?"

"Nothing," I said.

She smirked and said, "Is it a girl?"

"No," I said, sinking into my chair.

Evie went back to her magazine. "You look heartbroken."

"I'm not," I said, but at that moment I knew that wasn't true. I hadn't been able to destroy the memory of Alice Jakantowicz. I could feel it, this heaviness, like I was still wearing my backpack. Truth was, I didn't know if I wanted the feeling to disappear.

Finally I said, "I'm in trouble."

She sighed, looking up from her magazine. "Like you know what trouble is."

I didn't say a thing. She put down the magazine and looked across the table at me. "Okay. What happened?"

I pulled out the demerit form and laid it on the table. Evie picked it up and read it. "This is it? A teacher's slip?"

I nodded. "I've got to get it signed by a parent. They're going to kill me."

Evie laughed. "You got a pen?"

"Why?" I said.

"Give me a pen," Evie said. I took one out of the kitchen drawer and handed it to her. She sat straight up in her chair and signed the note card like there was nothing to it.

"You can't do that," I said.

"I just did," she said.

I looked at the demerit. There it was: *Sarah Kelso*. My mom's name. The problem seemed to be solved.

The doorbell rang.

"Let's eat," she said. I stuffed the signed note card back into my pocket. Evie got us sodas and paper plates. She handed me a slice of pizza and set one down in front of herself.

"Everything's going to be fine," she said, pushing her hair behind her ears and sighing. At that moment, I understood she needed to believe this as much as I did. "Yeah, it is," I said.

Evie ripped off a piece of crust and dipped it into the grease on top of the cheese. I did the same, following her lead, though I couldn't remember why I had ever liked it better that way.

safe

DAVE TACKLED ME, BRINGING me to the floor. He emptied my pockets, pulling out everything he could find—gloves, a pack of gum, a bag of pennies, a New York Knicks stapler. Max was on me as well, but he was single-minded, only interested in the safe cradled in my arms. He dug his hands between mine and the gray metal box, trying to pry off my arm. It wasn't going to happen. They could take anything—my wallet, my backpack, even my clothes—but they weren't getting the safe.

The game was called Mugger. The rules were simple: Get from one side of my bedroom to the bathroom door on the other side while two muggers tried to steal everything you had. We took turns playing the victim and the muggers. Before each round, the victim packed his pockets with randomness—Matchbox cars, pens, rolled-up socks, soap bars, keys, flashlights—whatever we could find around my room. It was almost tough to walk with your hands full and pockets overflowing, but that was the point: You were basically begging to be mugged.

We each carried one special item, the real prize if you got it away from someone. Max carried a small portable radio that didn't work. Dave had an old leather wallet packed with colorful

Monopoly money. I had my safe, this small gray metal box, the size of a shoebox and as light as a football, which I hugged across my chest. The muggers could do whatever they needed to do—tickling, grabbing, full tackles—although above the neck was off-limits. I had already had to explain one scratch on my cheek to my parents, who looked at me suspiciously when I told them it was from a game with my friends.

That afternoon, even with my friends all over me, I was still able to drag myself across the room, my feet digging into the carpet for traction. When I got close to the bathroom, I stretched out my arm and touched the door, shouting, "Base!"

Max fell off me, leaning against a dresser, catching his breath. "Damn, Marty," he said, pointing at the safe. "You never give that thing up."

Dave said, "What's in there, anyway?"

"Nothing important," I said, which was the truth, more or less. It was packed with things I had collected for years: A complete set of 1982 New York Mets baseball cards—a thoroughly forgettable team. A supposedly authentic piece of moon rock given to me by a neighbor for my eighth birthday. A bunch of vacation photos from Cape Cod with my cousin Evie. Nothing special. The only thing I cared about was what I had discovered inside the safe when I found it in the attic at my grandfather's house: a bullet. It was small, this short little stub, half the size of a crayon, with a dull yellow case and dark gray tip. The whole idea of having it made me feel powerful, a little dangerous.

When I found the safe at my grandfather's house it was locked, but after several weeks of working on it, I'd figured out how to open the door. There was something so satisfying about doing it—feeling for the clicks, the snap of things slipping into place, the door swinging open. Later that week, I was supposed to give a presentation for Mr. James's public speaking class, where we walked the class through the process of something we knew how to do well. I was going to bring in the safe and open it with my eyes blindfolded, maybe show off the bullet.

"Who's next?" Max said, standing up.

"I think it's me," Dave said, pulling out his wallet filled with red, green, and blue fake money, and stuffing it into his pants. I started stripping out of my extra clothes, throwing everything to the floor in a pile, eager for the next round to begin.

It had all started in March, when Principal Conrad announced at assembly that several kids from Welton, a super rich private school across town, had been mugged walking home. We were told to be on alert, but I didn't think much of it. Welton was on the East Side, a world away from where I lived and went to school. They might as well have been mugged on the moon.

A week later, though, Willy Maffert, a boy in the third grade, three grades below me at my school, was mugged in the park. The mugger took his wallet and his Casio calculator watch. We all wanted the watch because you could play *Space Invaders* on it. The numbers fell down the screen like rain.

Two more boys at my school went down soon after, fourth graders, mugged playing video games at the Twin Donut only a few blocks away. The muggers stole their backpacks and all their quarters.

Then the first middle schooler fell. Fifth grader Jason Slocum. He was mugged around the corner from school, waiting for the bus home. It was school fair day and there were plenty of people milling around, but the muggers had still managed to get Jason, taking his backpack, his bus pass, even the Strat-O-Matic Baseball game he had bought at the fair. It was as if a storm had been creeping closer and closer for weeks, and it was now upon us.

Rumors swirled about the muggings. At first, I'd heard that it was a kid my age, but soon there were other versions circulating around the school. It was a gang from the Bronx that had moved into Manhattan after they mugged everyone in their neighborhood. It was a grown-up, alone, someone who had escaped from prison. Sometimes the mugger was black, sometimes white, even Dominican or Chinese. He had a gun. He had a knife. He had an extra finger. The story was never the same. The muggers were like ghosts, everywhere and nowhere, constantly changing. I wasn't scared. I was in sixth grade, after all, and so far the muggers had gone after younger kids. Still, there was this nervous energy pulsing through the school, people constantly talking about the muggings. I'd seen a few kids bawling after school assembly—one third grader supposedly pissed in his pants—but my friends and I delighted in any news, eager to know who had gone down next. That's when we invented Mugger, the game. We thought we would be prepared if it ever happened to one of us, although none of us believed we would ever get mugged. Fact was, the game was fun, like playing cops and robbers, or cowboys and Indians, only better, more like real life.

"We should play this afternoon," Dave said to Max and me on our way to gym the next day. We were changed out of our school uniforms and into gym clothes, these team-colored shirts and floppy gray shorts. They were both on the blue team. I was on purple, although Mr. Regan, the gym teacher, insisted we call it maroon.

"I can't," Max said. "Hebrew school." Twice a week, Max went to a synagogue on the East Side. His bar mitzvah was less than a year away.

"Tomorrow," Max said. We agreed. Then he added, "Did you hear the latest?"

Max's mother worked at our school as a secretary, and his brother was in the tenth grade. He got all the good gossip before anyone else.

We shook our heads. "Another victim," he said, smiling.

"Who?" Dave said.

Max leaned in closer and then whispered. "Sasha Duberoff," he said. I knew Sasha. He was on the red team. "Happened yesterday. After school."

"No way," Dave said.

Max nodded. "And get this," he added. "They stole his money and his shoes. His freaking shoes!"

I looked down at my sneakers, ratty old Adidas I couldn't imagine anyone would want.

My friends and I stopped in front of the gym. This week we were playing dodgeball, my least favorite sport. You weren't supposed to throw at people's heads, but I had caught one in the face the day before. My nose was still sore. Through the closed door I could hear the squeak of sneakers against the floor, balls bouncing against the ground, and kids screaming. If you didn't know better, you would have thought there was a war going on inside.

At dinner that night, my parents told me the principal's office had called everyone about the muggings.

"Do you want one of us to pick you up after school?" my dad said.

I shook my head. "Dave and I walk home together."

"Should we get Richie to walk you?" my mom asked.

"No way," I said. Richie Shandberg, aka the Knish, was this eleventh grader who lived in my building and went to my school. He was a big kid, doughy and baby-faced, but everyone called him the Knish because he walked to the lunch truck every day to buy a knish. You could set your watch by him arriving back from the truck at noon, mustard smeared across his cheek. Not everyone knew it, but he had walked me to and from school from first to third grade.

"The school is going to give you a bus pass," my dad said.

"What for?" We only lived seven blocks from school. I could practically see my school from the front door of our apartment building. My mom said, "It'll just be another option. You can use it on rainy days."

I rolled my eyes. I hadn't been that worried until now, but it seemed like everyone was trying to tell me I should be.

When we got to gym class the next day, all the boys were sitting on the bleachers, a sea of colored shirts. Principal Conrad was standing next to a police officer. "This is Officer Lucas," our principal started. "He's here to talk to us about safety."

The policeman nodded, standing with his arms crossed against his chest. A long black stick dangled from one side of his belt, while his gun hung on the other side.

Officer Lucas gave us a list of "safety rules." Walk home with a friend. Don't walk like a tourist. Be aware of your surroundings. Stay on the main streets. Stay visible—don't take shortcuts through alleys. If you're worried someone is following you, get to a store or ask an adult for help. "You can't always control what's going to happen," he told us. "But you can give yourself better odds."

I wasn't sure what he meant by *odds*. It suddenly seemed as if it wasn't a matter of if I would get mugged, but when.

He told us assailants—he never called them "muggers" as we did—typically went after people they believed they could overpower. "If it comes down to an altercation, start shouting as loud as you can. Draw as much attention as possible. If you need to defend yourself, go for the vulnerable areas." He raised his hand to Principal Conrad's face. "The eyes. The nose," he said. Then he pointed at our principal's pants. "And the groin region," he added. There was a lot of giggling around the room. "Use your foot, your knee, even your fist. Whatever it takes."

Everyone immediately started talking. "Next time we play Mugger," Max said to me, "I'm going for your groin region."

"Not if I get yours first," I said with a weak laugh.

"Quiet!" Principal Conrad shouted, his voice echoing through the gym.

"In most cases," the officer continued, unfazed by the commotion, "it's best to give them what they want. Things can be replaced. You cannot."

The room fell silent. Officer Lucas turned to our principal. The policeman was clearly done, but Principal Conrad looked unsure about what to say or do next, as if he was also stunned by the officer's words. Finally, Mr. Regan shouted, "Okay, break it up! Red versus blue! Green versus maroon! Let's go! Let's go!" We played dodgeball for the next half hour, the green team efficiently picking off my teammates until there were none of us left.

After gym, Max went to talk to his mom to get the latest. Something had to have happened for the school to bring in a cop. Meeting us outside of public speaking class, Max had a knowing smile on his face. "High schooler," he said.

That was serious. The muggers were going after the big fish. "Who was it?" Dave asked.

"You'll never guess," he said, and we both leaned forward, as if what he was going to tell us would change everything.

"The Knish," Max said. My stomach sank. The Knish was huge, a boy in a man's body. I tried to imagine who could possibly bring him down. What chance did the rest of us have?

"No way," Dave said, and turned to me. "Isn't that the kid who walked you to school?"

I nodded.

"Happened just a block away. And get this," Max continued. "He's in the hospital."

"What?" I said. No one had gotten hurt so far, just some things stolen.

"What happened?" Dave said.

"I don't know." Max's eyes searched the room. We grabbed

seats in the corner, out of Mr. James's view. Max leaned forward, his voice a whisper. "One person said he was shot. Another person said he was stabbed. Maybe both."

There were two presentations in Public Speaking. Micah Bandon solved a Rubik's Cube twice, once in under a minute with both hands and then in the same time using one hand. "You need to concentrate to do it with one hand," he said, which made everyone in the class crack up. After him, Brad Yost tied a black cape around his neck and did magic tricks, separating a pair of large metal rings, pulling a long scarf out of his sleeve. Kid stuff, really. He finished by reaching behind Mr. James's ear, revealing a quarter, and saying, "Thanks for the tip, Mr. J."

I watched, but my eyes kept wandering to the windows, trying to see outside, to where the Knish was mugged. I couldn't see a thing. The windows, a long row of unshatterable panes at the top of the wall, were too high. Mr. James had told us once that the building had been constructed as a fallout shelter, but that just seemed like one of those teacher facts, like the birthdate of a president or the number of feet in a mile. Not anything I really needed to know. Staring out the windows, all I could see was a tiny sliver of the building across the street and a patch of gray, overcast sky.

That night I sat in my room, practicing with my safe. My presentation was in two days and I wanted to be ready. I took one of the neckties we sometimes used for Mugger and blindfolded myself, opening and closing the safe over and over again. The whole process was usually very satisfying, the locks slipping into place with a decisive click, but at that moment, I was dogged by a sense of uncertainty, the same way I felt playing dodgeball, never knowing whether I should throw or duck.

I heard someone shuffle into the room and pulled off the blindfold. There was my mom, standing at the foot of my bed, holding a basket of laundry.

"What are you doing?" she said, looking at me as if I was insane.

"Practicing," I said.

She nodded, her expression still suspicious, and then sat down on the edge of the bed. "I heard about Richie."

"The Knish?" I said. "You heard?"

"I ran into his mother on the elevator."

I nodded. In our building the elevator was the center of the world. If someone sneezed, it was news in the elevator. "He's in the hospital," she said. "He'll be okay."

I tried to picture it—the Knish, lying in a hospital bed, like something out of some television show. I worried she was going to tell me I had to go visit him, but instead she said, "Are you sure you're okay?"

I didn't quite know how to explain how I felt. I picked up the safe, the bullet rattling inside. "I'm fine," I said.

Dave and I got a ride to school the next day. It was his day to present in Public Speaking, and he was going to make his legendary toaster oven pizza. Between all the ingredients and the toaster oven, he had too much to carry so his dad drove us, offering to pick me up. I didn't mind the ride. It was raining and windy that morning, which meant the walk to school was going to be brutal, the rain slapping you in the face the whole way. Sitting in the safe and warm confines of the back seat was something I could get used to.

Max was supposed to present at Public Speaking as well. He was going to juggle, first two and three balls, then finally four balls for his big finish. Both Dave and I had seen him practice at home, and it was such a strange sight—this stocky, pear-shaped kid, uncoordinated most of the time, who could shuffle balls in the air with ease. We looked around for him when we got to class, anxious for the latest mugging update.

That's when we heard the news.

"They got him after Hebrew school," a boy who went to Rodeph Sholom with Max told us. "Rabbi Lebowitz called my parents last night. He called everyone. They're going to send the Jew Van to take us home from now on."

Dave and I didn't speak. I didn't know if Max was home or in the hospital or dead. I wanted to ask Mr. James, but I figured he would tell us if something bad had happened. He didn't. He sat in the back of the class as I helped Dave set up. Dave's presentation went all right, but the news about Max had clearly thrown him. The proportions on his first batch of toaster oven pizza were off, way too much sauce to cheese. I wasn't presenting, but I felt out of sorts as well, as if moving forward through our normal day like nothing had happened wasn't right.

When Dave finished, Mr. James told us to take out a piece of paper and write down, step-by-step, how to make a peanut butter and jelly sandwich. "Don't skip any steps," he said. He didn't say anything about Max or the muggings.

Dave left his pizza-making equipment at school until he could get a ride home with his dad on another day. We walked instead, headed to my house. The rain had stopped, but large puddles flooded across the streets. In many places the water was so deep, you couldn't tell where the sidewalk ended and the street began. Dave and I had to wander out into the street and around parked cars just to make our way downtown. He kept talking about Max getting mugged, but I was distracted, looking down alleys, expecting someone to jump out and attack us. On Eighty-Ninth Street, we passed a parent patrol, the first I'd ever seen. This older man wearing a fluorescent yellow vest over a shirt and tie was leaning against a car, eating a cinnamon roll from one of the food trucks. He didn't look like he could protect us from much. "Straight home, boys, okay?" he said, and bit into his roll.

On the elevator up to my apartment, Dave said, "Should we play Mugger?"

"I don't know," I said. "It's kind of weird without Max."

When we got to my apartment, though, my mom told us Max was waiting for us. He was sitting on my bed, rolling my old Magic 8 Ball between his hands, looking at his fortune. He wasn't bruised or beaten up. Nothing was in a cast. No missing limbs. He looked fine.

"You're alive," Dave said.

"Of course I am," he said.

I said, "Are you all right?"

He shrugged. "I guess."

Max clearly didn't want to talk about the mugging, but Dave and I pressed him. Where did it happen? Who was it? Was it one mugger or a gang? Were they black? White? What did they take? Did they have a weapon? We wanted details.

He told us he was walking to a store near the synagogue to

buy some chips when two kids came up to him. They were a little older than us, maybe seventh or eighth graders.

"One of them asked me if I had any money," he said.

"How'd they ask?" I said. "Like 'Gimme your money'? Like
we do in Mugger?"

"No," Max said. "They talked to me for a while. Asked me
how I was doing. What grade I was in. Where I went to school."
He paused, shaking his head. "Then one of them asked me if I
had any money. But not in a mean way. Like he wanted to bor-
row some and maybe give it back. It was so weird."

I didn't get it. I couldn't imagine someone being nice about
stealing your money. It didn't make any sense.

"What did you say?" Dave asked.

"I told them I didn't have any," he said, hesitating before
adding, "Although I did. I just didn't want to give it to them. It
was my money."

I thought of what the policeman said: It's best to just give them
what they want. Things can be replaced. You cannot.

"One kid said 'Let me check' and started to go through my
pockets," Max said. "I tried to push him off, but the other kid
held my arms."

"Couldn't you get them to stop?" I said.

"How?" Max said, his voice suddenly agitated. "What was I
supposed to do? Ask them to stop? 'Could you please not do
that?'" He shot me a look. "There's no 'base' in real life, Marty.
There's no 'time-out.'" He took a breath, sighing before adding,
"They found the money just as some woman came around the
corner. She could tell something was up. She called out and they
ran." Dave and I looked at each other. There was something a
little disappointing about how uneventful it was.

Dave said, "So they took your money and left?"

Max shook his head. "No," he said, raising his hand to his left cheek. "One of them punched me before he ran." He dragged his fingers along his lip and I could see it—the swollen corner of his mouth. Max pulled down his lip, exposing a dark red cut on the inside. "Cut by my own teeth," he said. "Bled something crazy."

"Did it hurt?" I said. I'd never been hit by anyone. The closest I'd been to a fight was Mugger.

Max shook his head. "Not really. It's still a little sore." He dropped his hand, looking around the room. "Whatever. We going to play or what?"

Dave and I shared a surprised look, and then nodded. I volunteered to be the victim. Max didn't seem up to it. Dave was on me in an instant, using his usual tactic of taking all the little things he could get—my jacket, my tie, my shoes, even my socks. Max went for the safe, as he always did, but he was more intense than ever, digging his nails into my wrists, his face turning bright red. At one point he actually grabbed my ear. "Nothing above the neck!" I shouted. "It's against the rules!"

"We're mugging you, Marty," Max said. "There are no rules."

Our eyes met for a second and his eyes glowed, like a crazy person, not like Max at all. He started pinching my arms, trying to get the safe loose. "No pinching!" I shouted, but he didn't stop. He was determined to get the safe away from me this time, as if it wasn't about the game any longer, but simply something he had to do. At one point he pulled on my hand so hard the safe actually fell to the ground, but I wasn't going to let him get it. I did the only thing I could think of: I raised my knee as quickly and as hard as I could, catching him right between the legs. The groin region. Max dropped to the floor with a thud.

Dave looked at me, as stunned, I suspected, as I was at how effective the knee move was.

"I'm sorry," I said, reaching out to help Max. He rolled away, moaning in pain. I didn't know what to do. I wondered if I should get my mom, but I didn't want to get her involved and have to explain what we had been doing.

"My fucking balls," Max said, rising slowly. "I can't believe you kneed me in the balls." He looked at me and I could see a smear of blood appear on his lips. His cut must have reopened. "It was an accident," I said, although we all knew it wasn't.

For a second, I thought he was going to cry. His eyes welled with tears, his face trembling with unease. "I gotta go," he said, grabbing his coat, walking toward the door. "Max!" I called, but he ran out, the front door slamming behind him.

The next day, Max was back at school. We didn't talk about what had happened at my house. I avoided it. For a moment, we shared an awkward look, and then he told us about the latest mugging, two fourth graders. Nothing special.

It was my day to present in Public Speaking, but Little Peter Chin was up first. I wasn't particularly tall, just over five foot, but Peter was tiny, one of the smallest boys in the middle school. He had supposedly skipped two grades already. He was on the maroon team with me. Most of his time outside of class was spent getting stuffed into garbage cans or lockers by high schoolers. "Hello, classmates," he said, standing in the front of the room. He adjusted his glasses. "A lot of people have been getting mugged, so I thought I'd bring some things I've learned to use for defense." He was carrying a rolled-up cloth, which he spun open on the table. Inside were a series of pockets, each containing some kind of strange-looking tool.

Peter picked one up, a small black star, no bigger than his hand. "This is a *shuriken*," he said. "Also known as a throwing star."

The room went silent. Mr. James cleared his throat and said, "Peter, I don't know if you can have those on school property."

"Don't worry, Mr. J.," Peter said, his expression placid. "These are all training tools. They're not sharp." He pressed the tip of the star into his palm. "A real one would easily tear through flesh." Mr. James nodded, although he looked as surprised as we were. "Some refer to the *shuriken* as a hidden dagger, because you can stab with it," he added, jabbing his hand out in a series of quick punches.

He put away the star and pulled out several other tools: This thing called a *kama*, which looked like two pickaxes tied together. A foam-covered stick called a *tonfa* that reminded me of the stick that hung from Officer Lucas's belt. He demonstrated how they worked, manipulating each one in his hands with ease. Everyone was transfixed. All of a sudden, Little Peter Chin was a ninja.

"Last, but certainly not least," Peter said, pulling out two long rods, "these are *nunchaku*. Also known as nunchucks. I'm sure you've seen these." We all had. Anyone who had seen any martial arts film had seen them. But never in real life. Never in a classroom at school.

Peter took a step back from the table so we could see him better. He closed his eyes for a moment and took a deep breath, his little body rising and falling. Then he opened his eyes again and started to windmill the nunchucks, slowly at first, swinging them in front of him, then by his side, every so often switching hands. Soon, he picked up speed, flipping the nunchucks behind his shoulder, under his arm, around his back. The pair of black rods became a blur, like the wings of a hummingbird. After a minute he came to a stop in one deft motion, catching both rods in one hand. We all cheered.

He turned to face us again. "But my sensei says there is one weapon even more powerful than any of these," he said, putting the nunchucks away. We sat, eagerly waiting to hear what it was. I thought of broadswords and spears, that cool spiked-ball-and-pole thing. Peter Chin pointed at his head. "Your mind," he said. "Sometimes the best strategy is knowing when not to fight. Force must only be applied in the most dire of circumstances."

And that was it. Peter Chin had lost us. For a few moments, he was a heroic warrior, but in a flash he was Little Peter Chin again, the small Asian boy who never spoke to anyone and who was terrorized by older kids. "Thank you," he said, and walked back to his seat without a word.

"Thank you, Peter," Mr. James said.

It was my turn next. I walked up to the front of the class, my safe cradled under my arm. I gave the history of the safe, telling them how it had been my grandfather's and how I'd found it in his attic when we were cleaning out his house. I told the class that when I had found it I didn't know the combination, but that I had figured out how to open it by feel. Then Dave came up and wrapped the necktie around my eyes. The room was silent. I couldn't see a thing, but I could feel everyone's eyes on me. They all wanted me to open it, to see what was inside. I started turning the dial, feeling for the click of the lock. The click was subtle, this little bump in the turn, and you could easily miss it if you weren't paying attention. Sometimes it took me a few spins to feel the mechanism catch. I went through the process, two, three, then four times. I kept spinning and spinning, but couldn't feel a thing. There were no clicks. It was as if this were a different safe.

Kids in the class started chattering about how I'd never get it open. "Wait a second," I said, pulling the tie off my head. I started to work on the safe again, holding it up to my ear, listening for the sound of things slipping into place.

Still nothing.

"It's okay, Marty," Mr. James said. "The point is to talk about the process, not the outcome."

"Lame!" someone shouted.

"I bet he can't even open it!"

"What's inside?"

"Wait," I said. "I can do this."

I worked at the safe for another minute, trying to force it open. I wondered if it had gotten damaged in our last game of Mugger when it fell to the floor. Maybe I wasn't doing it right. Dave looked at me, raising his hands in confusion. Max shook his head. Everyone else looked bored, ready to move on. Even Mr. James stood up, collecting his papers, his eyes shifting between me and the clock on the wall. Class was almost done. Only Peter Chin looked at me seriously. He leaned forward, a big smile on his face, as if he was convinced the safe would open at any moment and all would be revealed.

"Okay," Mr. James said, walking toward the front of the room.

"Really! I can open it," I insisted. I shook the safe, the contents shuffling around. "There's a bullet inside!"

"Why don't you take your seat, Marty," Mr. James finally said, this time not a question but an order.

———

"We know you can open it," Dave said, as we left school. I was still holding my safe in my arms.

"Yeah, we've seen you do it," Max said, and then he turned to Dave. "I think we have, right?"

Truth was, they hadn't. None of my friends had seen me open it.

"You want to come over?" I said. They both gave me a look. "Watch TV or something?"

"Sure," Max said.

We walked to the corner and I was about to turn down the stretch of streets that led home, when Max stopped. "I don't know," he said, his eyes switching between the streets ahead and the sky above. "Looks like it might rain."

The sky was gray, but it was overcast, not the kind of gray that meant rain. Dave and I shared a look. "Yeah, it does," I said.

We ran to the bus stop, as a bus was about to pull away. I figured the driver would keep going, making us wait for the next, but he saw us and stopped.

"Step to the back, boys," he called out as the door opened.

The bus was packed. Kids from my school were everywhere: gathered around seats in the front, jammed into the middle aisle, hanging on straps all the way to the back. I could see everyone— lower schoolers, middle schoolers, even some high schoolers, kids we often saw on our walk home now armed with bus passes, taking the free ride. Dave and Max waved their bus passes at the driver and moved in, but I was having trouble getting out my pass and holding on to the safe at the same time. "It's okay," the driver said, waving me on.

"I know I have it," I said, still searching.

"Just move to the back," he ordered.

I threaded through the crowds, trying to catch up to Dave and Max. They were moving quickly. The bus began to move, so I tried to find something to hold on to, but nothing was within reach. The only thing keeping me balanced was the crush of bodies against my own. The bus picked up speed, everyone pressed together, bouncing and swaying in sync.

Finally, a space opened up. I was about to slip through to grab on to a pole, when I saw him: The Knish. He was in a seat by the window, staring out at the passing streets. From the knee down, his leg was in a cast. A set of crutches lay beneath the seat. I wanted to get away, but then he turned and saw me as well. His eyes were surrounded by a deep black and blue, his face covered in scrapes and cuts. He didn't look like himself. He looked much older, as if the mugger had not only hurt him but beaten the baby-faced kid out of him as well.

I took a step back, anxious to get away, when someone stuck out their foot and tripped me. I didn't see who it was. I went down quickly, tumbling to the ground, dropping the safe as I fell. The safe hit the ground with a thud, the door swinging open. Everything spilled out—baseball cards, pictures, the moon rock—all of it scattering across the floor. I thought I even saw the bullet go flying toward the back of the bus. People turned around and moved to help, which only made it more difficult to see where everything had gone.

A group of hands pulled me up. "Marty!" Max said, rushing over. "Are you all right?"

"Someone tripped me," I said.

"Who did it?" Max asked, looking around.

"I don't know," I said.

The bus began to slow down and the driver announced our stop. "My safe," I mumbled. People handed me things from the floor, anything they could find. Someone passed me my safe and I stuffed everything I could back inside. I tried to shut the door to the safe, but it kept swinging open, as if the lock was broken for good.

The bus pulled to a stop.

"This is us," Max said, stepping toward the exit with Dave. Crowds of people filed out, including the Knish, hobbling on his crutches, hopping down the steps. Max held the door open. "Marty! C'mon!" he said, as I continued to pick up what I could.

"What do you want to do?" Dave said, standing in the door. People were backing up behind him.

"Do not block the exit in the rear, please!" the driver shouted.

I looked around at the mess of photos and baseball cards still scattered on the floor. There was no way I was getting everything back, not now. I could stay on the bus and try to collect it all, but who knew how long that would take or where I would be when I finished? Only further from home.

I took a step toward the exit, looking back one last time. My heart raced. I didn't want to let it all go. For a second, I thought I saw the bullet wedged under someone's foot, but when I moved toward it I realized it was just a piece of gum. "Release the doors in the rear!" the driver called out.

I stepped off the bus, clutching my safe in my arms. Behind me the bus door hissed, closing. A few people stared at me through the window, their expressions concerned, although I couldn't tell if they were sorry for me or mad that I'd held up the bus.

"Are we going or what?" Max said.

We started walking. The Knish was ahead of us, struggling at the curb and then making his way carefully across the street. Physically, he was so much larger and sturdier than any of us, but at that moment, bent over his crutches, his eyes fixed on the ground ahead of him, measuring his steps, it seemed as if a strong breeze could have blown him over. My friends and I followed slowly behind him, letting the distance between us and the Knish grow. He was bad luck, a reminder of how dangerous the world was. None of us said a word. The Knish made it to my apartment building long before we got there. We didn't want to ride the elevator with him. We didn't want to be anywhere near him. My hands were still wrapped around the safe, holding it against my chest, just as I did when we played Mugger, although now I was trying to keep the door closed, but it kept bouncing open, refusing to stay shut any longer.

birthday season

FOR MY FRIEND KEVIN Johnson's thirteenth birthday his father ordered pizzas and a case of Coke, and then handed out *Playboy* magazines. I got the Halloween issue. On the cover, a woman in nothing but a tall, black, pointed hat straddled a broom, her body twisted and arched so that you couldn't see anything except the side of her breast fading into an inky black background. A few of my friends opened their magazines, casually paging through as if they were reading *Highlights*. I froze. My few experiences with dirty magazines had been private and quiet, in the bathroom, or hiding inside the closet, turning pages by flashlight. Never a public event.

"Check this out," Max said, holding the centerfold of his "Girls of the Big Ten" issue for everyone to see. A woman stood in an end zone, stretching to catch a ball suspended above her. Other than thick strokes of black glare guard under each eye and a pair of cleats, she was naked, and apparently thrilled to be so. "Touchdown," Max said. Everyone laughed. Everyone except Kevin, the birthday boy, who stared at his dad.

"What?" Mr. Johnson said. "I thought you'd like it."

Mr. Johnson owned some kind of trucking company, and he

normally resembled a truck himself—large and sturdy, wide eyes like headlights—but that day, he seemed defeated. Kevin looked at the cover of his *Playboy*. A woman wearing a red fur vest sat in Santa Claus's lap as he read from the "naughty list." Kevin tossed the magazine across the floor before walking out of the room. His dad followed. It took about two seconds before everyone was flipping frantically.

Kevin's parents had separated earlier that month and his dad had moved out. "They keep saying it's not my fault," Kevin told me. The week before, his mom had taken Max, Dave, me, and Kevin out for his birthday to see *Friday the 13th Part III* in 3-D, an R-rated movie my parents would never have let me see. Mrs. Johnson bought the tickets, loaded us with popcorn, soda, and candy, and then made us wait while she smoked cigarettes before the movie began. When the movie started, she took a seat behind us. When I turned to look back I could see tears trailing under her cardboard 3-D glasses. "It's like they've freaking lost it," Kevin said. "Happy fucking birthday to me."

"That sucks," I said, although part of me was a little jealous. I knew divorce wasn't a good thing, but so many kids' parents were splitting up at my school that it began to seem normal, almost cool. I couldn't help but see an upside: two of everything—Christmases, birthdays, vacations. It sounded like a sweet deal.

"I can't believe my dad handed out *Playboy*s," Kevin said. "What a joke."

"I don't know," I said. "*Playboy*s beat a loot bag any day of the week."

The fall was birthday season at my school, one party after the other from early September through November, everyone turning thirteen. Up to that year, the parties had been similar—tickets to a baseball game, touch football in the park, playing Atari at someone's house if they were lucky enough to own one, maybe a movie if there was something worth seeing. You ate pizza and ice cream cake until you felt sick and then got a bag of toys or candy to take home when the party was done.

That year, the parties had changed. Many of the birthdays had been organized around trips to museums, fancy dinners, or Broadway shows, as if parents were trying to tell us we weren't little boys anymore. The results were disastrous. In September, Brian Slosher's father took a large group of us to the Japanese steakhouse Benihana. Within fifteen minutes, one table had started a drooling contest to see whose spit sizzled the longest on the grill. Josh Fox's mom had brought a bunch of boys to see *Joseph and the Amazing Technicolor Dreamcoat* and someone started chucking M&M's from the balcony onto people in the orchestra.

My birthday was at the end of October. I'd always done the same thing: bowling. I loved the rituals of bowling—rubbing chalk between my palms, letting my hand hover above the air blower, slipping my feet into shoes often still warm from the person before me, even the etiquette of letting the bowler in the lane next to me go first, although I was often too excited to wait. I wasn't a particularly artful bowler; I threw the ball straight, without seductive spin or curve, and I still hadn't mastered the graceful leg swing at the end of the throw. I had graduated from six- and eight-pound balls—"ladies' balls," my dad would say with a smirk—to the coal-black ten-pounder. There was something thrilling about the sound of the ball rolling down the lane, fading away from me. Once I threw it, I would always stand at the edge of the lane, twisting and gyrating, urging the ball in a particular direction with my body, as if my movement might help it catch another pin. I envied those people that could just send the ball soaring down the lane and then walk away, confident of a strike. I needed to watch until everything settled, because I was never sure I knew what was going to happen.

My parents just assumed I wanted another bowling party. "Should I reserve the lanes?" my dad said to me a few days after Kevin's party.

"I don't think I want to bowl this year," I said, which wasn't the truth. I did want to bowl, but bowling was clearly out. I was supposed to think bigger. My mother and father looked at each other in disbelief.

"What do you want to do?"

I shrugged.

"We could go to a game," my dad suggested, which in late October meant hockey or preseason basketball, basically birthday suicide. I might as well have taken my friends to the ballet.

"Maybe a nice dinner?" my mom said with a tone that made it sound like something done at around four thirty in the afternoon when you're eighty years old.

"I need to think about it," I said, but I was dogged by thoughts of bowling, the quiet roar of a ball heading down the lanes echoing in my ears like approaching thunder.

My friend Dave's birthday was the week after Kevin's party. Dave, a geeky string bean of a kid, had arranged a day of video games, ice cream cake, and pizza at his house, until his mom stepped in at the last minute and changed the plans. She had recently remarried and insisted they throw a joint birthday party with her new husband's daughter, Libby, who was turning thirteen as well. "I know it was Brian's idea," Dave told me. Brian was Dave's new stepdad, who rumor had it had been his mother's psychiatrist. "He's got this thing about togetherness and sharing." Brian even scheduled "safe talk time" every Sunday, when the whole family was supposed to sit down and talk about whatever was bothering them without fear of someone getting defensive. "Most of the time it's just him bitching about us not putting our dishes in the dishwasher or leaving lights on around the house," Dave said.

At Dave's party, we were substantially outnumbered. He had only invited the three of us, while Libby, who went to Chaplin, an all-girls school on the Upper East Side, had apparently invited every girl in her grade. The party was catered; waiters in pressed white shirts and bow ties circulated, carrying trays of tiny triangular-shaped sandwiches that tasted like buttered grass. The four of us huddled around a bowl of Doritos, the only recognizable food, until stepdad Brian came over, shaking his head.

"Come on, guys," he said. "Mingle. Socialize."

Max looked at me, his mouth rimmed with orange dust from the Doritos, and rolled his eyes. Dave turned away. Kevin wiped his hand on his corduroys, picked up a can of Sunkist, and then said, to our surprise, "Okay."

Whether or not we acknowledged it, my friends and I took our cues from Kevin. He had moved to New York City last year from California because his dad's business had expanded to the East Coast. He looked like the television version of a California kid: sun-bleached hair, a string of white beads tight around his neck at all times, a dirty rope bracelet on his wrist.

He often told us stories about his life in California, learning how to surf, going to beach parties, kissing girls around bonfires, and swimming in the ocean at Christmas. It sounded magical. My friends and I had latched on to him quickly, sensing that he understood something about the world we were still just starting to grasp. At Dave's party, he circled the room and we followed obediently.

"Hey," he said to two girls by the window.

"Hey yourself," one of them said. She was tall, with straight brown hair that lay flat on her head and reflected the light outside like sun off a batting helmet.

Kevin asked, "You friends with Libby?"

"Friends?" she said, her expression suspicious. "I think we played together once when we were in second grade. She invited the whole class."

"I knew it," Dave said.

Across the room, Brian and Dave's mom were organizing a game of Jeopardy. "Remember to answer in the form of a question," Brian shouted.

"What is," Max said, patting Dave on the back, "really, really embarrassing?"

"You're her brother?" the brown-haired girl asked Dave.

"*Step*brother."

The other girl, who had red hair sculpted into a wave over her forehead, perked up. "Is it true that Libby's dad was your mom's shrink?"

Dave nodded.

"That's so sick," she said. She wore a frilly skirt and a tight pink tee shirt that showed off her substantial chest and drew all our gazes like an eclipse we weren't supposed to stare at.

"At least she knew him well," the straight-haired girl said. "My dad left my mom for a salesgirl he met at Barneys."

Kevin introduced us. The brown-haired girl's name was Jenny. The busty girl was Abby. A lengthy silence followed, during which time Jenny stared out the window and Abby crossed her arms, hiding the goods. I figured this was a sign that our conversation had ended and that we could reestablish our position around the Doritos, but Kevin reached into his pockets and pulled out a pack of Pall Mall cigarettes. His mother's brand. "Anybody want to smoke?"

The six of us huddled on the slate-gray steps of the stairwell, clouds of smoke hanging in the air around us. Kevin and I had smoked cigarettes a few times behind the school and in the park, but we didn't really know what we were doing. This Jenny girl was a pro. She tried to teach us how to blow smoke rings. "You've got to make your mouth into an O," she said, "and then push out with your tongue. Like this."

She curled her lips into a small circle, twitched her mouth, and a luminous white ring emerged, holding its shape briefly before dissolving into the air.

"What'd you do? I don't get it," Max said, looking at us and then trying again himself. Kevin bobbed his head, but nothing came out. I tried and ended up doubled over coughing. Jenny blew another perfect ring.

"I bet I know who taught you that," Abby said, raising her eyebrows. Jenny ignored her. Kevin finished his cigarette and butted it out on the side of the stairs, sending a stream of tiny embers down the airshaft.

"Dude!" Dave said. "You're going to burn down my building!"

"Relax," Kevin said. "It's out."

Abby shifted on her step as if she couldn't get quite comfortable. "Who has a birthday party like this anymore? I thought someone was going to suggest we play Pin the Tail on the Donkey."

"Don't get me started," Dave said.

"I like your necklace," Jenny said to Kevin, who was lighting another cigarette.

I was focused on blowing a ring, but all I could produce were shapeless clouds of smoke. Finally, on the edge of coughing, I jutted out my jaw and a weak, tiny circle emerged, the ghost of a ring. "Check it out! Look!" I said, pointing to where it was, but the door to the stairwell swung open and blew away my smoke ring. It was Brian. "What's going on out here?" He waved his hand in front of his face. "Are you smoking?"

Kevin confessed to bringing the cigarettes. Brian called all of our parents and then sent us home before the party was even over. I got a lecture from my mom and dad about smoking, which was tough to sell, given that they had both smoked for years. They grounded me for a week.

When my grounding ended, Kevin and I went shopping for Max's birthday present. Max was the only one of my friends having a bar mitzvah, which didn't mean much to me except that I had to bring a bigger gift and wear a suit and uncomfortable shoes. The party was still a few weeks away, but Kevin and I hadn't hung out much since he started going back and forth between his parents' apartments. We got on a bus headed downtown and sat in the back.

"What are we going to do for your birthday?" Kevin asked.

"I don't know."

"Let me guess—bowling."

I didn't know if he was making fun of me or could just see through me. He dropped it and we rode in silence until we got into midtown. "I've got to go talk to a lawyer tomorrow," he said, staring out the window. Outside, people in midtown were spilling out the front doors of office buildings. Rush hour. "I think he's going to ask me who I want to live with."

"*You* have to choose?"

Kevin shrugged and closed his eyes, letting his head lean against the back of the bus. I tried to think of who I would pick if I had to decide between my mother and father. My father and I were interested in more of the same things, like baseball and bowling, but my mother took care of me when I was sick and she could cook, which seemed critical on a day-to-day basis. I'd only seen my dad flip burgers on a grill in the summer, which might mean tough times in winter. Either choice seemed unsatisfactory, a kind of trick question, like deciding if you'd rather be deaf or blind, but knowing that giving up either one meant losing too much.

We got off the bus at Thirty-Fourth Street and went to Cosby's, a sporting goods store in Madison Square Garden. My mom gave me ten dollars to spend, so I bought Max, who was a huge Yankees fan, a pair of pinstripe sweatbands and a yo-yo with Yankee announcer Phil Rizzuto shouting "Holy Cow!" whenever it went up and down. At the bus stop on our way home, Kevin asked me if I wanted to go to the movies with Jenny and Abby, the girls from Dave's party. I was surprised to hear that he had talked to them.

"What movie are you going to see?" I asked.

"Seriously?" he said.

A bus arrived, crowded with people. We got on and squeezed our way through until we were jammed in the middle. Kevin held on to a bar and I held on to Kevin. "You want to come along or what?" he asked, and then added, "I think Abby likes you." I knew he was making it up, but I was highly susceptible. I had never kissed a girl. I couldn't argue with opportunity.

"Yes," I said, as the bus lurched forward.

—

We met the girls at his dad's apartment on Sunday. Abby was cuter than I remembered, her hair tied in a ponytail, freckles covering her cheeks, and a giant Bonne Bell lip gloss dangling around her neck, but I couldn't stop staring at Jenny. She had her hair loose and was wearing a zip-up pink sweater over a *Star Wars* tee shirt with Chewbacca on it. We couldn't pick a movie, so we decided just to hang out, which made me that much more nervous. At least at a movie I wouldn't have had to make conversation. The four of us played *Pac-Man* on Kevin's Atari for a while, girls against boys, in couples, and so on. When that got old, Jenny suggested we play suck and blow. I looked at Kevin, confused.

"You guys know suck and blow, right?" Jenny said. We went into Kevin's room to play and sat on the floor in a circle. She explained that the object of the game was to pass a playing card around with your lips, sucking hard to keep it on your mouth until you passed it to the next person. It wasn't kissing, but you couldn't get much closer.

"What happens if it falls?" I asked.

"Then you have to tell us a secret," Jenny said, a sly smile on her face. "I'll start." To my surprise, Jenny turned to me, raising the nine of diamonds to her lips, drawing air in quickly. She tilted her head and cupped my face with one hand. Up close, I could smell the shampoo in her hair. Strawberry. She opened her eyes wide, signaling that she was going to let go, and then put her hand on my knee, bracing herself. Her warm touch shocked me and I immediately pulled back, the card drifting to the floor.

"Secret!" Abby shouted in delight.

I didn't have many secrets, and certainly not the kind I wanted to share, but I'd heard a few stories about what my cousin Evie had done that had gotten her in trouble. "I sometimes drink stuff out of my parents' liquor cabinet and replace it with water."

"You never told me that," Kevin said.

"Then it wouldn't be a secret," I said. The girls smiled, seemingly impressed.

It was my turn. I brought the card to my lips and started to suck, which sounded like a basketball with a slow leak. Abby grabbed me and pushed her face toward mine so fast our heads knocked. When I pulled back, I was surprised to see the card fastened to her lips, her eyes wide with delight. She waved Kevin over quickly. Kevin pressed his mouth against the card and they shifted back and forth as Kevin tried to position himself. Abby grunted some kind of instructions but Kevin couldn't figure out what to do and started to laugh. The card popped out of Abby's mouth.

"All right," Jenny said eagerly. "What's your secret?"

Kevin didn't say anything at first. He turned the card in his fingers as if holding it one particular way would make all the difference. "I'm moving back to California."

"That's a secret?" Abby said. It was news to me. I wondered if moving was part of his discussion with the lawyer.

"Nobody knows," he said.

"What do you mean?" I said.

"I just decided. I'm not telling anyone. I'm just going."

"You can't just go," I said.

"Why not?"

I could think of a number of reasons why not. Getting there, for starters. He looked at me in a way that told me this wasn't the time to argue.

"I want to go to California," Jenny said.

"Come along," Kevin said, and smiled. He put the card to his mouth and turned to Jenny. She moved closer to him and put her lips against the card. Pretty soon, the card fell, but the two of them stayed on the floor, their mouths fixed together, their eyes closed. It looked like they were trying to devour each other. Abby and I got up and went into the living room.

"Her last boyfriend was in high school," she said. I didn't say anything. I was beginning to doubt that she liked me. We started playing *Pac-Man* again. "I like *Ms. Pac-Man* better," she added.

A few minutes later, the front door opened and Kevin's dad walked in. A woman followed behind him. She wasn't nearly as old as Mr. Johnson. "Marty," he said to me. "I didn't know you guys would be here." He looked at Abby. "Hello, I'm Kevin's dad."

"Hi," Abby said, pulling the cap off her Bonne Bell lip gloss and spreading a thick layer across her mouth.

"Where is Kevin?"

Kevin walked in from his bedroom, Jenny following behind.

"Big man," his dad said.

Kevin looked at the woman behind his dad and said, "Who are you?"

"This is Gina. I've been meaning to introduce you."

"Nice to meet you," Gina said. She dug her hands in her pockets, and then looked at Kevin's dad as if waiting for him to say or do something.

"And who's this?" his dad said, extending his hand to Jenny.

"Just a friend," Kevin said.

"I didn't know you guys were coming over," his father said. "You should have told me. I could order Chinese or something."

"That's okay," Jenny said, looking at Abby and nodding. "We should go."

The girls left. Kevin and I retreated to his room and sat on the floor, flicking suck-and-blow cards into the garbage can until I had to go home.

———

The weeks leading to Max's bar mitzvah were a frenzy of freakish birthday parties. Lunch at the Russian Tea Room. A trip to the New York Stock Exchange. Chamber music at Lincoln Center. A gallery opening in SoHo. One movie, but it was a boring foreign film about homeless children in Brazil. Kevin had been invited to all the parties but hadn't gone to any since Dave's. I barely saw him outside of school because he was hanging out with Jenny and going back and forth between his parents' apartments.

Everyone came to Max's bar mitzvah. Temple Rodeph Sholom was packed with people, a sea of suits, dresses, and yarmulkes. Dave was sitting near the front with his mom, Brian, and Libby. I could see Kevin and his mom sitting on one side of the room; his dad sat on the other side with Gina. Through a sea of heads I saw Jenny and Abby near the front. Max had asked Kevin to invite them because we went to an all-boys school and it looked cooler to have a few girls at your party.

The service went on forever. I spent most of it adjusting the cap on top of my head as the rabbi went on about responsibility and faith and becoming a man. Even from the back I could see the sweat pouring down Max's face as he hacked his way through Hebrew.

After the ceremony, we headed to the reception. Max's parents had rented out part of a ballroom in Tavern on the Green, and it looked like some kind of magical winter palace, with white Christmas lights coiled around arms of bare trees, the glass walls reflecting rows of white candles. Tables with linens were arranged neatly around a dance floor, bars stationed at every corner. When we walked in, the parents headed to get drinks while kids raced to get tables as far away as possible from the adults. Jenny and Abby came to sit with us. Max stole a couple bottles of champagne and we passed them under the table, filling and refilling small paper cups from the bathroom. We all kept watch, making sure no parents snuck up on us.

"Who's that with your dad?" Max asked Kevin.

"Some woman."

"Dude, she's hot," Max said, but Kevin looked away.

The deejay started playing music and people slowly filled the dance floor. I kept my distance from my parents, who were in the middle of the dance floor, my dad pretending to reel in my mom like a fish on a line.

"Do you want to dance?" Jenny asked Kevin.

"I don't dance," he said, his eyes fixed on his dad dancing with Gina. His mom was on the other side of the room, talking to Dave's parents.

"You'll dance with me, Marty," Jenny said, pulling me onto the dance floor. I hated dancing most of the time, but I couldn't say no to Jenny.

We started dancing, or at least something like it. I stepped side to side and balled my hands up in front of me like a boxer in a fight. Jenny bounced, swinging her head around. "Abby likes you, you know," she said.

I nodded, unconvinced. Abby hadn't even acknowledged me at the party. I focused on my moves. I was a weak dancer in general, and the addition of champagne made me feel even more uncertain. The song hit a slow part and I didn't quite know what to do with myself, so I slowed my gestures to a glacial pace, trying to imitate a man walking in space.

Jenny asked, "Has Kevin said anything to you about me?"

He hadn't, but I knew that wasn't what she wanted to hear. "I think he likes you," I said. The song picked up again. Jenny smiled broadly. At that moment I felt like I alone knew how to make her happy.

When the song ended, we went back to our table and kept drinking small cups of champagne. Max, Dave, and I started flicking butter pats onto the glass ceiling. The hostess came around and told us to stop unless we wanted to leave.

"It's my party," Max said. "I'm a man today."

"So act like one," she said, and walked off.

A few minutes later, Kevin's dad walked over with Gina on his arm.

"Hey, fellas. Congratulations, Max," Kevin's father said.

"Kevin," Gina said. "Would you like to dance with me?"

"I don't dance," Kevin said.

Max stood quickly. "I do."

Gina looked at Kevin's father, smiled, and led Max to the dance floor.

"You all right, Kev?" His dad put his hand on Kevin's arm.

Kevin didn't answer. He turned to Abby, his expression determined. "Let's dance," he said, taking her by the hand and leading her from the table. Jenny sunk in her seat. Kevin's dad left. I kept drinking.

When the song ended, Max came back, beaming. "What a woman," he said. Abby and Kevin moved to a window seat by themselves. Jenny glared in their direction. The waiter arrived carrying plates of food.

"I'm starving," Max said. "I almost fainted out there."

Dave poked the food on his plate. Some kind of fish. "I don't think it's cooked."

"It's poached salmon," the waiter said. "It's meant to be served cold."

"Screw that," Max said, and left the table. A few minutes later he came back with a smile on his face. Dave asked, "What's going on?"

"You'll see," Max said. Kevin was still talking to Abby by the window. Jenny turned to me. "Why is your friend being such a jerk?"

I had to say something. "They're probably talking about you," I said, but she looked distressed, her eyes welling with tears. I looked over at Kevin and Abby. They were kissing. Jenny ran for the bathroom. Abby must have seen her, because she followed her into the bathroom.

"Dude," Max said when Kevin returned to the table. "What are you doing?"

"I thought you were with Jenny," Dave added.

"Yeah," I said, trying to sound angry.

"Whatever," Kevin said, slouching in his seat. "I guess we're divorced." Everyone laughed, even me.

Fifteen minutes later, Jenny and Abby hadn't emerged from the bathroom, but a pizza guy had arrived with four pizzas for Max. Across the room, I could hear a woman shouting and I figured it was the hostess complaining to Max's dad, but it was Kevin's mom. She was yelling at his father, pointing toward Gina. She was gesturing wildly, out of control. My parents stood between them like referees at a boxing match.

"Look at them," Kevin said. "They can't even be in the same room together." He stood up. "I'm out of here."

Just then the music stopped and the waiters rolled out a giant birthday cake. "Is it an ice cream cake?" Dave asked Max.

"No, it's some Black Forest thing my mom picked out," Max said. "I don't have a clue what it is. Maybe it's made of trees."

I turned back to Kevin, but he was already gone.

"I cannot believe he brought that woman," my mom said in the taxi on the way home.

"Well, they are getting divorced," my dad said, and my mother's mouth hung open. She said, "And that makes it all right?"

"I'm just saying..." my father started, and then my mother cut in, saying, "It was totally inappropriate." My dad raised his hands in surrender. There was a long quiet as the car stopped and started along the avenue. I asked, "Are you guys getting divorced?"

"Why would you say that?" my mom said.

"I don't know," I said, my champagne buzz turning into spins.

"We're not," my dad said.

"Just checking," I said.

Outside, the sun was starting to set. Thick doughy clouds hung low in the sky. Our taxi sped up Central Park West, weaving between cars, making me nauseous. I was wedged between my parents, slumped so low down in my seat I couldn't even see over the divider. The whole world seemed to be pushing down on me.

"We'd better decide what you want to do for your birthday," my dad said.

"Maybe nothing," I said.

"What do you mean?" he said.

"If he doesn't want to do anything, don't press him," my mom said, putting her hand protectively on my shoulder. That was all it took. I threw up all over the cab divider, all over my pants, all over my uncomfortable shoes.

"Oh my god!" my mother shouted. "Oh my god!"

"It's okay, it's okay," my dad repeated, and told the driver to pull over. He let us off by the park and I leaned over the wall, heaving repeatedly, emptying myself of what felt like the whole fall's worth of birthday dinners and lunches and cakes, as my parents debated whether it was the salmon or the pizza that had done me in.

That night, Kevin's mom called our house. Kevin hadn't come home and he didn't go to his dad's either. "Do you know where he is?" my mom asked me. I thought of California, sunny skies, bonfires, and beaches. I shook my head.

The phone rang again about an hour later. This time I picked it up.

"Don't tell them it's me," Kevin said.

My dad walked in the kitchen. "Hey, Dave," I said into the receiver.

My dad looked at me suspiciously and then left. "Dude, your mom's been calling. Where are you?"

"I'm downstairs," he said.

"What are you doing here?"

"I'm leaving. For California."

"Are you kidding me?"

"I'm going. I thought you could come."

"Don't be an idiot. I can't go."

"C'mon, Marty. Don't you ditch out on me."

"I'm not," I said, and then added, "You're not going to California. You'll never make it."

"Sure I will," he said, but I could hear the doubt in his voice.

"You're not going anywhere," I said, but Kevin didn't say anything. All I could hear was the whirr of street noise for a second, and then he hung up.

The next day, I didn't see Kevin until lunch. Dave, Max, and I were sitting talking about the party, about how drunk we all were, how I threw up. Evidently one of Max's cousins got caught in a broom closet with a waitress. At least that was the story.

"What are we doing for your birthday?" Max asked me.

"That's right," Dave said. "It's next weekend."

"Nothing," I said. "I don't want to do anything."

"Don't be lame," Kevin said, as he squeezed in next to me. Everyone knew Kevin had tried to run away. All our parents had gotten calls. Still, no one said a word. "It's your birthday. We all know what you want to do."

"Yeah," Max said. "But please. No cold poached salmon."

The four of us went to East End Lanes the next Saturday with my mom and dad. The alley was crowded with birthday parties. We had to wait for a lane to open up because I hadn't made up my mind until the last minute and my parents hadn't reserved a lane in advance. We ate pizza and ice cream cake while we waited. I opened presents. A set of pens in the shape of baseball bats. A New York Mets garbage can. A book on classic baseball blunders. My parents bought me my own bowling ball, a twelve-pounder called the Wizard that looked like a murky crystal ball, and a pair of two-tone suede bowling shoes.

"Now you can finally turn pro," Kevin joked.

After nearly an hour, a lane opened. The Wizard was heavier and more difficult to control than any ball I had ever used before. The first few times, I sent it straight into the gutter. Soon, though, I started to get a feel for it, how to hold the ball in my palm, when to release it on my follow-through, how to even create a little spin, turning the ball down the lane. By the second game, I had even gotten a few strikes. My friends and I cheered, shouting "Turkey!" as we had done in previous years when one of us was on the verge of getting three strikes in a row. When I threw the third strike, we howled with delight, and then looked at each other, uncertain, as if we didn't know what to get excited about next.

On my last throw, I waited for the kid in the next lane to go. He was younger than me, maybe nine or ten. He hugged the ball against his chest, not even using the finger holes, and then bounced it down the lane. The ball careened off the bumpers and he called after it, yelling "Strike! Strike!" The ball reached its destination, carving out eight pins. His family and friends exploded with cheers. "Nice shot," I said, as he walked back. It was my turn. I positioned myself along the arrows in the floorboards and went into my motion. The ball eased out of my hand, gliding down the lane, but I knew instantly the throw was off, no chance of a strike. When it reached halfway, I turned and walked away, knowing I couldn't change what was going to happen.

a rifle is not a gun

A WEEK INTO MY first trip to summer camp, everyone started to call me the Assassin.

It all began at riflery class one afternoon. I was stretched out on a ratty old mattress, listening to Wilson, the riflery teacher and groundskeeper, shout out instructions. Gnats buzzed around my head, the air thick with humidity. "Don't pull the trigger," he said. "You're not Dirty Harry. Treat it like your dick. Squeeze it gently, for Christ's sake."

I looked over at Carter, my cabin mate and only friend. He rolled his eyes. We'd spent the first week of camp off on our own, drifting around the windless lake on a Sunfish in the mornings, playing soccer in the afternoon. That morning we decided to try something new. From the expression on Carter's face, I could tell he regretted the decision as much as I did. We were deep in the woods, surrounded by bugs and poison ivy and boys we didn't know at all, shooting bullets at tiny scraps of paper propped on the side of a hill. Carter fired three shots in rapid succession and then squinted through his sight. "Crap," he said.

I tried to line up the crosshairs with the target in the distance. It seemed miles away. I took a breath as Wilson had instructed and held it, squeezed the trigger. The sound was a high-pitched snap, a firecracker going off, and my body shook from the rifle's kickback. When I looked through my sight, though, there it was—a small hole in the target near the edge of the outer ring. "I think I hit it," I said.

"No way," Carter said. "I think I'm firing blanks."

I lined up another shot as carefully as I could, took a deep breath, and fired again. This time, the rifle's kickback shuddered through me, my body snapping like a whipped towel. Through the sight, though, I could see it clearly—a round tear in the target, this one even closer to the center.

"What do we have here?" a voice said behind me. It was Wilson. He was standing next to an older boy who was looking through binoculars and jotting down notes on a clipboard. The kid was weird-looking—his head too small for his tall lanky body, his skin a mess of acne. He was probably from Sycamore, the area of camp where the older boys lived in tents. We were in Maple, for thirteen-year-olds. The Sycamore boy looked up from his clipboard and said, "Two and Seven." Wilson lowered his head to me, his expression almost amused. "Ever shoot before?"

"Never," I said, which was the truth. Fact was, I'd never even held a gun that wasn't filled with water.

"What's your name?"

"Martin Kelso."

"Okay, Mr. Kelso," he said. He kneeled down next to me, so close I could smell the bug spray rising off his body. "I want you to shut your eyes. I want you to breathe slowly. I want you to imagine hitting the target." I followed his advice, closing my eyes, listening to all the sounds—bugs spinning by my ear, leaves rustling on the trees, the platform creaking under the weight of our bodies. I tried to imagine a bullet flying through the air, and all I could think of were those slow-motion videos of a bullet smashing through lined-up phone books. Wilson said, "Open your eyes and fire."

I did. Wilson didn't budge, listening for the Sycamore boy's report. For a moment he was quiet, so I figured I'd missed it. "Bull," he said.

Wilson let out an enormous laugh that echoed inside the canopy of trees. He slapped my back. "Look out for this one. He'll take you out at half a klick." He continued down the row, taking his time with each boy, but I just kept firing, peppering the target with holes. The world around me faded away, the space between the platform and the target collapsing as if it were within hand's reach. I picked a spot on the target and then I would fire, hitting it exactly. It was like nothing I'd ever experienced in my life.

On the walk home, Carter and I each held our target in our hands, his nicked randomly in a few places, while mine was in shreds. "That was lame," he said.

"Yeah," I said. "Lame."

Word of my shooting made it to camp before we returned for dinner.

"Where'd you learn to shoot like that?" Brian, one of my cabin mates, said when we sat down at a dining hall table.

"You're from New York City, right?" his brother Matt said. Brian and Matt were twins from Michigan, two gangly thirteen-year-olds who'd been coming to the camp for years and lived to play pranks. There were six of us total in our cabin: Carter and me; Brian and Matt; Albert, a boy who ran a candy black market out of his trunk; and Jimmy, whose birthday fell just after the cutoff but still looked small enough to be in Beech, the section of camp for the youngest kids.

"You should hang out with us," Albert said, gesturing to Brian and Matt. The three of them did everything together. Activities. Meals. Their beds were gathered on one side of the cabin while Carter, Jimmy, and I slept on the other. "Maybe at the Hawthorn dance," he added. Hawthorn was our sister camp across the lake. Sometimes at night, on the walk home from dinner or lying in my bed, I could hear the voices of girls, high-pitched and bright, drifting across the water. "And if you need anything," Albert whispered, leaning forward, "M&M's, Neccos, Whatchamacallits, you let me know."

I looked at Carter, who raised his eyebrows in surprise. Albert had never spoken to either of us before that moment. "You're like some kind of assassin," Brian said, loud enough for everyone to hear. Matt laughed and then started to chant "Assassin! Assassin!" Soon, several other tables joined in. And that was it. At that moment, in the middle of the Tamarack dining hall, Martin Kelso disappeared. I became the Assassin.

After that day on the riflery range, Carter and I settled back into our original routine: In the morning, we floated around the lake in a Sunfish, talking about our families and friends and life back home. Carter could sail, but there was hardly any wind. In the afternoons, we played soccer or softball, whichever let us play on the same team. The routine was comfortable and familiar. In many ways, that predictability was what had drawn us together on the first day: We were the two new kids in the cabin, both of us from big East Coast cities, me from New York, Carter from Boston. We liked a lot of the same things—baseball, candy, video games. We ate all our meals together and sat side by side at assemblies. We made plans, signing up for an overnighter the last week of camp, a canoe trip to a nearby chain of lakes. We figured we would get a two-man tent, a bunch of candy, and stay up all night. We made plans to hang out after the summer ended, as if the life we were leading at camp would somehow continue and we would know each other forever.

Still, it wasn't difficult to see that something had shifted that day at the riflery range. A week after, people were still coming up to me, calling me the Assassin, asking how I'd done it. Everyone wanted to know the story. I'd played it down at first, particularly around Carter, but when he wasn't around, I sometimes got into telling it, making it far more dramatic than it had ever been. "I could hit it even when I closed my eyes," I told someone. I'd never had so many people want to talk to me. Riflery became the most popular activity. I sometimes thought about going back. I could still feel it—that sense of control and power, of willing something to happen and then doing it—but I also knew Carter had no interest, and part of me was afraid I wouldn't be able to do it again. I'd be going back to being just Marty. The Assassin would be gone.

The night before the dance with Hawthorn, Carter and I were walking up the hill toward our cabin when Brian, Albert, and Matt caught up to us. They told us they were thinking about pulling a prank. Brian, Matt, and Albert had already pranked one of the cabins across from ours, sneaking in and filling their sneakers with sand when they were in the showers. Another cabin had pranked us, taping clear plastic wrap across the frame of our front door in the middle of the night so that we walked into it on our way to breakfast. Brian and Matt had pranked each other several times—Brian putting Matt's hand in warm water in the middle of the night so that he would pee in his bed, Matt knotting the ends of all Brian's socks. They'd gotten Albert as well, nailing his shower flip-flops to the floor. Silly stuff. But they had never included me or Carter.

Carter asked, "Who are we going to get?"

"Jimmy," Matt whispered. Carter and I looked at each other. Jimmy's first week had been rough—crying a lot, holed up in the infirmary and counselors' offices because he was so homesick. You'd see these kinds of kids every few days, pulled out of one of the activities, folding into the arms of a counselor in tears. Then you'd come to your cabin one night and all their stuff would be packed up or gone, as if they had never been there at all. Jimmy looked like the obvious candidate from our cabin.

"Serious?" Carter said. Jimmy was ahead of us, walking with one of his old friends from Beech. "That's just mean."

Albert turned to me. "What do you think?"

The truth was that Carter was right. Pranking Jimmy was easy, like taking out the weakest prey. Natural selection at work. He didn't stand a chance. Still, with everyone's eyes on me, I could feel that this was one of those moments where a line was drawn and you had to stand on one side or the other.

I turned to Carter. "It's just a stupid prank," I said.

"See?" Albert said. "The Assassin thinks it's no big deal."

Carter shook his head, raising his hands in defeat.

The prank began perfectly. Matt had stolen a packet of blue Kool-Aid from the cafeteria and poured it into a showerhead. We were all in our stalls, waiting for Jimmy to arrive. The rigged shower was the only one available. Carter had his back to the whole thing, washing soap out of his hair, as if he had no interest in what was going to happen.

Jimmy finally walked in. He looked down the row of showers, and then turned to walk into the rigged shower. "I'm done," Carter said. "Take mine."

"I'll just go—"

"Nah," Carter said, grabbing his towel. "That one is busted."

Jimmy paused, as if he wasn't sure whether to believe him, but then he looked at Carter and smiled. I could see the trust in Jimmy's eyes. He went into Carter's stall and turned on the shower. Brian and Matt raised their hands in disappointment. Albert shook his head in disbelief. Carter dried himself off, not looking at anyone, and headed out the door.

"What's going on?" Jimmy said.

I turned off the water, grabbed my towel, and ran out of the showers, soap still on my hands. Carter was already halfway up the hill. I twisted the towel around my waist and jogged to catch up to him, my flip-flops slapping against the dirt path. "Wait up!" I shouted.

"Don't you want to wait for your friends?" Carter said, not slowing down.

"Shut up," I said, struggling to walk and keep my towel on.

Albert approached us on the dinner line. Crowds of boys and counselors were holding trays, waiting on the long line, the noise of their voices echoing off the high ceilings of the barn, but he walked right up to us, stopping the line, wedging himself in. "What the hell, Carter?" Albert said. Matt and Brian stood behind him like sentries. "We had it all planned."

Carter looked scared, as if he hadn't thought through the consequences of what he had done. I surprised myself by moving between them. "It's no big deal," I said. "We can get someone else."

Albert stayed still, staring at Carter, until he said, "Yeah, we will."

"Gentlemen," a voice said behind us. It was Wilson, the riflery teacher. "Let's keep the line moving. The masses are hungry."

Albert, Matt, and Brian went ahead of us and we started to move again. I was at the end, next to Wilson. I grabbed a burger and a boat of fries, keeping my back to him as best I could.

"Haven't seen you back at the range," he said behind me.

I turned. "What?" I said, even though I'd heard him.

He smiled. "Skills like that you don't want to waste."

I didn't know what to say. I didn't want to have to explain that I was scared that I wouldn't be able to do it again. "You should be thinking about joining Club," he added. Riflery Club was by invitation only. Serious camp royalty. They had private practices that weren't listed on the sign-up boards. A secret handshake. Their end-of-camp overnight was legendary. Rumor was they made blood oaths and had target practice with live animals. The only person I knew in the club was Albert. "Think about it," he said, and I nodded, walking quickly to our table.

Carter was quiet throughout dinner. Boys around us were

talking about the dance the next night, how someone would inevitably try to spike the punch and how a Hawthorn girl always went missing with a Sycamore boy. After dinner, on our walk up the hill to our cabin, I could hear Albert, Matt, and Brian behind us, talking about a boy in Birch who had gone home that afternoon.

"I saw them pack him into a car," Matt said.

"He was bawling like a baby," Brian added, and they all burst into laughter.

Carter kicked a stone, which went shooting off into the woods. "Those guys are dicks," he said.

"They're not so bad," I said, although I wasn't sure why I was defending them.

Behind us, someone started a chant of "Assassin! Assassin!" I knew it was Matt and Brian, maybe Albert. Carter stayed silent, his hands in his pockets, his eyes focused on the ground. Soon, the whole group of boys on the path was chanting along, smiling and laughing, although I couldn't tell if they were cheering or mocking me.

The dance itself was like every other one I had ever been to—boys and girls divided into packs on opposite sides of the room. Carter and I stood at the side, watching from a distance. No one dared step foot on the dance floor. Finally, Carl Whipple, a husky Sycamore boy who everyone called the Cannonball because of the wake he left when he jumped in the lake, walked over and asked one of the girls to dance. She agreed. Within a minute, the dance floor was filled.

Carter and I were headed to the snack table when Matt and Albert ran over to us. "Assassin," Matt said. "Check this out." He pointed across the dance floor to Brian, who was making his way to a group of girls standing in a corner of the dance floor. He said something to a girl with squiggly blond hair, and she shook her head decisively. Brian turned and walked back, his expression defeated. Matt howled and Albert made the sound of something blowing up. "Crashed and burned," he said, as Brian returned.

"Why don't *you* try?" Brian said to Albert.

Albert smirked, apparently taken aback by Brian's challenge. "Okay," he said. He thought about it for a second, before adding, "How about I ask the same girl?"

Brian and Matt looked at each other. This wasn't about the girl anymore.

The music changed to a terrible slow song, and the dance floor cleared. Albert didn't seem fazed at all, walking slowly across the empty floor to the circle of girls. He started talking to the blond girl. The conversation went on longer than Brian's had, and it was clear that Albert was doing most of the talking. Eventually, she nodded and smiled, and then he took her hand, leading her onto the dance floor. "You've got to be kidding me!" Brian shouted. Albert and the girl swayed back and forth, alone on the dance floor, his hands on her hips, her hands on his shoulders. Everyone was watching them. When the song finished, he took off toward us, leaving her stranded alone in the middle of the dance floor. He raised his arms in victory. "How'd you do that?" Matt said.

"Charm," Albert said, turning to Brian as if he was taking aim. "Some people have it and some don't."

"Let someone else get a shot," Matt said.

Albert looked at me and Carter and said, "What about one of you?"

"No thanks," Carter said.

Albert nodded, as if that was the answer he had expected. I heard someone, Brian or Matt, whisper "Pussy" under his breath, and then the two of them burst into laughter. "Assassin?" Albert said, looking at me.

I didn't really want to dance, but then again, there wasn't a way to say no without looking like a complete wimp. I wouldn't have even considered it back home, but here, at camp, hundreds of miles from my real life, I felt like a different person. "Okay," I said.

I looked around the room. My experience asking girls to dance was slim to nonexistent. Breaking into one of these packs of girls seemed impossible. The easiest move would be to go for one of the really ugly girls who never expected to be asked, but getting turned down by one of them might have been worse. There were a few girls sitting alone or in pairs on the benches lining the walls, which seemed like better odds. I saw one girl standing near the punch bowl, watching people dance. She had straight blond hair and a Rubik's Cube key chain hanging off her jeans. I took a deep breath and walked over.

"Hi," I said.

"Hi," she said, making a face as if I wasn't speaking English.

"Do you want to dance?" I could almost feel the eyes of my cabin mates on me. *Say no*, I thought. *Say no*.

"No," she said, and I felt a wave of relief, until she added, "not to this song. Can you wait for the next one?"

"Sure," I said.

We stood next to one another, not talking. I started to stretch, as if I was prepping to run out onto the soccer field. "I requested a song," she said, finally breaking the silence. "It's supposed to be next. That's what the deejay told me. I couldn't decide if I wanted to hear the Beatles or Supertramp. I love Supertramp. Do you know them?" She kept going, telling me about the decision process of picking the song, reciting lyrics. I listened, staring at her hair, which stayed perfectly still despite how much she moved. When she finally stopped talking, I looked at Matt and Brian and Carter, standing a few feet away, staring at me. I shrugged, shaking my head. The song changed and she took my hand, pulling me onto the dance floor. Her palms were warm with sweat. Some boys started shouting, "Assassin! Assassin!"

"What are they saying?" the girl asked.

"Nothing," I said.

We danced through that song and then the next one. She told me her name was Robyn ("with a *y*") and that she was from Salem. "You know, where they burned witches to death." As we danced, she twisted side to side, the Rubik's Cube on her hip swinging and hitting me in the leg over and over again, but I didn't mind. It was all going well until an older kid from Sycamore bumped into me, by accident or on purpose—I couldn't tell. All I knew was that he pushed me forward onto Robyn, one of my hands bracing myself on her shoulder, the other landing squarely on her chest and sinking in. I pulled my hand away quickly, but her face turned bright red. "Are you okay?" I asked. She didn't say anything, just stared at me. It was dark on the dance floor, but I could see her eyes were filling with tears. I thought about running, sprinting for the door and not stopping until I got to my cabin and my bed. It would have been so easy. But at that moment, I stopped thinking about who else was on the dance floor and what people were thinking. All I knew was that I didn't want to leave Robyn. "Why don't we go to the bonfire," I said, taking her hand. She looked at her hand in mine, smiled, and then wiped away her tears. "Okay," she said, and I led her across the dance floor and outside.

We sat at the edge of the bonfire, close enough to feel the heat rolling off in waves. Sycamore boys kept bringing in long beams, dumping them in, making the flames reach higher into the sky. Wood crackled around us. At one point she told me she was cold, which I couldn't understand, given the heat coming off the bonfire, but I took off my sweatshirt and draped it over her shoulders. I hadn't had much experience with girls, but I knew that I should probably ask her questions. In the past, I wouldn't have said anything, but sitting near the fire, Robyn sitting so close our arms touched, it occurred to me that I had nothing to lose. "What's Hawthorn like?" I said, asking about the camp, her friends. I told her jokes about my friends, and she laughed. I couldn't stop. I felt completely comfortable. I asked her what she liked to do at camp. "Crafts class," she said, pulling something out of her pocket. "I made this the other day." It was a ceramic frog painted with a green glaze that made it glow. "That's amazing," I said, and Robyn smiled.

Pretty soon the counselors from Hawthorn called for the girls to get on the buses to leave. "Wait a second," she said, as we walked to her bus. She ran over to one of her counselors. "Here," Robyn said, running back and handing me a piece of paper with her address on it. She took my hand and put something in it. I looked down to see the green frog. "So you won't forget."

"Thanks," I said, and without thinking about the crowd of boys watching the bus leave or the stares from Hawthorn girls leaning out the windows, without thinking about what I was doing or why, I leaned in and kissed her. It was quick and soft and burned at my lips until the moment I pulled away. Robyn looked at me, her eyes wide in a way I hadn't seen all night. "I hope I see you again, Marty," she said, and then turned to get on the bus. Girls howled from the windows. Boys started shouting, calling out "Assassin!" but all I could hear was Robyn's voice saying my name. I replayed it over and over in my head, trying to make the moment last as long as I could.

We all had to clean after the dance, picking up pieces of broken Styrofoam that looked like snow scattered around the grass. At one point, I saw Carter but avoided him, not letting our eyes meet. I was still soaring after my encounter with Robyn, and I worried something he would say might take that feeling away.

When it came time to walk back to the cabin, Carter was gone, so I walked up the hill with Matt, Brian, and Albert. The twins were wild, attacking each other on the road, laughing uncontrollably. I didn't know if it was something in the punch or the presence of girls that had made them so crazy.

"Let's do a prank," Brian said, halfway up the hill.

"Yes!!" Matt said. "Who should we get?"

They all turned to Albert. "Let the Assassin decide," he said.

I knew what they were doing. I knew what they wanted me to say. "What about Jimmy?" I said.

"No," Albert said, shaking his head. "You were right. That's too easy."

I looked down the path, where all the boys were coming up

the hill. It was getting so dark I could barely make out their faces. I could just hear their voices, the march of their feet in unison on the path. I said, "How about Carter?"

The fact that I said it didn't surprise me. I knew what they wanted to hear. What surprised me was how easy it was to say. The words came out without even a hesitation on my part. I knew it was wrong and that it would probably change things between Carter and me and everyone else, and yet I still managed to convince myself that it was what I had to do. Maybe not the right thing to do, but what I wanted to do.

In the end, what we did wasn't that bad. We moved Carter's cot, trunk, table, and lamp out in front of the cabin, in full view of all the other cabins. We didn't mess with any of his stuff, just shifted it outside. It wasn't like it was going to rain. Carter finally appeared over the hill and I could tell, the moment he saw the cabin and his stuff, that he understood what was going on. His whole body slumped, as if he had been kicked in the stomach. He wandered over to his bed and lay down, not even coming in to see us. If he had come in, we probably would have joked about it, maybe helped him carry his stuff back inside. It might have resolved any bad blood between all of us, and let him know we didn't mean anything by it. In his mind, I knew, it had become us against him. He stayed on the bed, not moving, like he was going to sleep. I stood in the window, watching him. I could hear Matt, Brian, and Albert trying to stay quiet, but laughing all the same. When one of the counselors appeared, he walked over to Carter and said something to him. Carter sat up and shook his head. His back was to me, his shoulders rising and falling, his body shaking with sobs. The counselor kept talking and Carter nodded, standing up and starting down the hill again, presumably to the infirmary. I wanted to tell him I was sorry, that it was all a joke, but instead I stood there, watching him, until he disappeared into the shadows on the trail.

The next morning, I woke up wondering if all of Carter's stuff would be gone. Part of me wanted that to happen—his clothes, trunk, shoes, his bed, any trace of him, disappeared as if he'd never been there. Instead, everything was back in its place. Someone had put it all back without even waking me up. Everything, at least, except Carter himself. He wasn't around, and his bed looked like it hadn't been slept in. He wasn't at breakfast either. During announcements, the camp director told all the campers that pranking was finished. "Anyone caught will be sent home immediately," he said.

I went to look for Carter on the lake after breakfast. The sky was gray and it looked like it might rain, but I knew that wouldn't stop him. He was an experienced sailor, a natural, although we'd hardly done much sailing at camp. On some level, though, I knew the water was where he felt most comfortable. So it wasn't a surprise when I saw him standing at the edge of the lake, untying a Sunfish. "Wait up!" I shouted, running over. Carter didn't respond, not even raising his head. I said, "I'll get my life vest."

"Don't bother," he said. He climbed into the boat, pushing off with his oar.

"Hey!" I said.

A gap of inky dark water opened between us. Carter's back was still to me, but he turned, his face in profile. "Did you even try?"

"Try what?" I said.

"To stop them," he said.

I could have lied. I could have told him that I had nothing to do with it. I could have told him that it was all their idea. But it seemed worse at that moment to try to run further away from what I had done, rather than just come clean. "Don't be such a pussy," I said.

My words stung the air like a gunshot. Carter turned away again and paddled the boat out, stopping every few strokes to feel for some kind of wind to help him take off.

I walked back to the dining hall, to the activities board, unsure what to do with myself. Crafts, hiking, ropes. It all sounded silly, like stuff for little kids in Beech. I didn't want to do anything.

Riflery wasn't even listed on the board. I didn't know why. That didn't stop me from heading out on the woods trail. Rain had started to fall, drumming on the leaves above me, but the canopy of trees kept me dry. For some reason, the walk seemed longer than last time, and a few times I wondered if I was lost, until I saw the painted trail marker hanging on the side of a tree and heard the pop of rifles firing.

A group of boys were already stretched out on the platform, shooting at targets. A low cloud of smoke hung above them, not moving. I watched them reload and fire again, their shots going off in unison.

"Look who finally made it back," Wilson said.

"I didn't sign up," I said.

"There is no sign-up today," Wilson said. "It's only for Club."

"Sorry," I said. "I can leave."

"Hang on a second," Wilson said, walking over and taking me by the shoulder. "Tell you what. We're almost done here. But why don't you come with us on our overnight tomorrow?" Several boys on the line stopped shooting and nodded. "Out in the deep woods, away from the camp," Wilson continued. "It's a different world. Easier to clear your head. Easier to find your center."

The riflery overnight was the same night as all the overnights, including the one I'd planned to take with Carter, but then again, that was probably off. I looked beyond Wilson, at the other boys, now standing, waiting for my answer. "C'mon, Assassin," someone said.

"You in?" Albert said.

I thought of Carter, floating around the lake by himself, waiting for wind that would never come to take him. I thought of how much time the two of us had spent drifting in the weak current. "Yes," I said.

We set out at dawn the next morning, meeting at the riflery range, loaded down with our sleeping bags and overnight packs. Wilson led the way, walking us further down the path, away from camp, deeper into the woods. The path grew thinner and thinner until it was a stretch of matted-down grass and weeds. The only way to know where to go was to follow the person ahead of you, trusting they knew where they were headed.

After hiking for two hours, stopping only for water and handfuls of trail mix, we reached a dirt road lined by a long fence. Signs with the words "Private Property" and "Keep Out" and "No Trespassing" hung on long stretches of barbwire winding around the top rail of the fence. Wilson eventually led us to a break in the fence and, despite all the warning signs, walked us through. "This way," he said, pointing to a small trail that led deeper into the thick forest on the other side of the fence. I wanted to ask where we were and where we were going, but I knew I wasn't supposed to question anything. We marched on, the path turning downhill, then up again, winding and twisting so much it felt as if we were walking in circles.

Finally, after another hour, we arrived at a clearing. There was a platform like the one we used back at camp, although it was beat up—warped and bleached, grass and weeds sprouting between the slats so much that it looked like the whole thing had grown out of the landscape. "All right, gentlemen," Wilson said, jumping up on the platform. "Let's make camp, have some lunch, and then shoot."

Wilson put Albert and me in a two-man tent, while most of the older boys shared larger four- and five-man tents. I was relieved to be with someone I knew. After a lunch of peanut butter sandwiches, we took our positions on the platform. Unlike back at camp, we weren't shooting at paper targets but at wooden and metal sculptures shaped like animals—deer and birds and rabbits, even a moose—propped on the side of the hill in the distance. With the naked eye they looked almost real, like animals rising out of the brush. Then you looked through your sight and you could see the damage—dents in the metal, hunks of wood dug out of the shapes like deep wounds.

"Concentrate," Wilson said, walking behind us. "Try to clear your mind."

I tried to think of nothing, but the more I did, the more I thought of everything—how things had been left with Carter, whether or not I would ever see Robyn again, the end of camp, which I realized was only a few days away. Rifles exploded around me. I looked at the dome of blue sky, the green hills rising around us like walls. My heart pounded in my chest. I fired and fired and fired, but couldn't hit a thing. From the sound of Albert wrestling with his rifle, he wasn't having the best day either.

"What's the problem?" Wilson said, appearing behind us. I stayed quiet.

"It's the gun," he said. "My shot keeps drifting to the right."

For a moment, Wilson didn't say a thing. He just bent down and took the rifle from Albert's hands. He examined it, looking at the barrel, running his fingers along the stock as if it could speak to him. Everyone had stopped shooting and was watching us. He raised the gun and fired from a standing position, hitting one of the targets with a distinct clang of metal.

"First of all, a rifle is not a gun," he said. "A rifle is a tool. A gun is a weapon. If you don't understand the difference, you don't belong in Club."

"I know," Albert said. "But—"

"Second," Wilson continued, "never blame the rifle. Take responsibility. You decide where the shot will go. You pull the trigger. You are in control."

Albert opened his mouth to say something, but didn't. He sat back down. Wilson handed him back the rifle and walked over to me. "How are we doing?"

I lowered my head, afraid to look him in the eyes. "I can't hit a thing," I said.

"If you don't think you'll hit it, you won't," he said, kneeling down. He took my rifle, held it up so that his eye was right in front of the barrel. Insane. One little pull of the trigger and he was dead. It suddenly occurred to me that I was deep in the woods with complete strangers. If I didn't follow this man's advice, I might never make it back. He handed the rifle back to me. "Start believing you'll hit it, and maybe you will."

We went back to shooting, but it didn't go much better. I hit a few targets, but it was luck as much as anything else. In the end, I might as well have closed my eyes.

That night at dinner, I was starving, as if I hadn't eaten in weeks. We devoured hot dogs and beans and potatoes Wilson made for us over the fire. They tasted amazing. The older boys started telling jokes and talking about girls, teasing this one kid from Sycamore who had supposedly been found in a canoe with a girl they called "Town Bicycle." I looked at Albert, confused. "Everybody gets a ride," he told me with a sly smile. I laughed as if I knew exactly what he meant.

Eventually, Wilson told us to pack it in. We drifted to our tents and got ready to go to sleep. The sun was barely down, but I was exhausted. Albert had brought a stash of candy and we silently made our way through packs of peanut butter cups and chocolate bars. "Carter must have been pissed you came here," Albert said.

"Maybe. I don't know," I said. "Probably."

"That guy," he said. "What's his problem anyway?"

"I know, right?" I tried to imagine what Carter was doing right then. Probably sitting in his bed, maybe getting ready to go to sleep. "Can I ask you a question?"

"What?" Albert said, stuffing another peanut butter cup in his mouth.

"What'd you say to that girl at the dance? I mean, why'd she say yes to you and not Brian?"

Albert shrugged. "I don't know," he said. "I just asked and she said yes."

It didn't make sense. I thought he had bribed her. It occurred to me that some people just had that power. I didn't know if I was one of them.

I heard the sound of footsteps around us, and then Wilson said, "Lights out, gentlemen. No more chatter. Time for sleep." Albert rolled his eyes, but still leaned back in his sleeping bag, following orders. I stretched out as well, the darkness of the tent so complete that I fell asleep almost instantly.

We were awakened the next morning by one of the older boys, leaning his head into our tent. "It's time," he said.

I popped up, unsure where I even was. "Time for what?"

"Get dressed," Albert said, sliding out of his sleeping bag. "You'll see."

Outside, a gauzy mist hung in the air. Thick clouds draped over the side of the hill. Soon the sun would rise and burn it all away, but right then the world was damp, caught between the night's chill and morning heat.

All the boys were gathered on the platform again, but they were assembled on the opposite side, taking turns shooting into the nearby hillside. I hadn't noticed any targets that way, so I had no idea what they were shooting at. I was too far back to see anything clearly. Every time someone fired off a few shots, they would cheer and then pass the rifle on to the next person. I waited until I got close, the acrid smell of gunpowder hanging dully in the air. Ahead of me, Albert took the rifle and lay down to shoot. That's when I saw it, across a short swath of woods— a wooden pen, maybe ten by ten feet, busy and filled with rabbits, packed like a crowded subway car. The rabbits scattered about, jumping from side to side. I could see that many were hopping over the bodies of other rabbits, gutted and bloodied from the rifle shots. Albert fired twice, sending one of the rabbits flying out of the pen from the force of the shot. The boys behind me shouted in delight. "Your turn," Albert said, handing me the rifle.

My stomach twisted, my mouth going dry. "That's okay," I said, begging off.

Albert laughed as if I was joking, and then looked at the other boys. "I knew he'd pussy out," he said.

"None of that talk," a voice said behind me. It was Wilson.

He walked over to us, taking the rifle from Albert. "It's a Riflery Club tradition," he told me. "A little initiation," he said, holding up the rifle and firing off two quick shots. "It's about remembering why people used to shoot. To survive. To protect themselves. To feed themselves. It wasn't a sport. It wasn't *camp*," he said, holding the rifle out to me. "It was life."

I could hear the murmur of a threat in his voice, as if not taking the rifle wasn't an option. I took it. "I've never shot anything alive."

"Everyone has to start sometime," Wilson said. The light around us was dim, but I could see Wilson's expression, serious and focused, as if he wasn't asking me if I wanted to do this or not.

"Isn't it illegal?" I said.

"Those are my rabbits," he said, his voice turning stern. "I can do with them what I damn well please." I realized this place—all of it—was probably his land. He walked up to the edge of the platform and stared out at the pen, before turning back to me. "And you know what those rabbits will do to one another? You think they just eat carrots and hop around like the Easter bunny? Not quite. They're vicious. They'll nip and bite at each other until they bleed and die a slow death. It's a fucking tragedy," he said, and some of the boys behind me laughed. I looked out at the pen again, at the rabbits packed together, and thought, *Of course, they'll kill each other*. Trap them like that, practically on top of each other, and it's inevitable. "We're doing them a favor, saving them from themselves." He walked over to me, holding out the rifle. "But hey, if you don't want to do it, don't," he said, before adding, "*Assassin*."

At that moment, Wilson seemed no better than Albert or his pals pranking people at camp. I took the rifle, which felt heavier than it had before. I lay down and looked through the sight. The rabbits looked enormous, as if they were close enough to reach out and touch. I found one in a corner of the pen, sitting still. For a second I thought he was dead, but then his head turned as if he was actually looking at me.

I closed my eyes and fired.

The boys cheered and began chanting "Assassin" over and over again, until I stepped aside and made way for the next boy to step up and take his shot.

We got back to camp before dinner. Carter was gone. His bed was stripped, his trunk nowhere in sight.

"He left this morning," Jimmy told me. "I came back from dinner and..." His voice trailed off.

"Figures," Albert said, walking into the cabin behind me and falling into his bed. Matt and Brian jumped in next to him.

I sat on my bed, dropping my pack on the floor with a thud. "Why do you think he left?" Jimmy asked me. I didn't want to tell him the truth—that you made choices, picked sides, and lived with the consequences. "Maybe he wasn't feeling well," I said, and Jimmy nodded. Then Albert called out, "Jimbo. Come join us." Jimmy looked at me, his eyes wary, and then turned to join the boys across the room. I watched him climb up on the bed, squeezing between Matt and Brian. I climbed into my bed, turning my back to everyone. In exactly twenty-four hours, I would be back in New York, back home, riding in a cab with my parents through the transverse that cuts through the lush green of Central Park dividing the East Side from the West Side. My mother would look at me and say, "You're being awfully quiet," and then touch my chin gently. "Everything okay?" She wouldn't wait for an answer, instead turning to my father and saying, "He looks older, doesn't he?"

"He is," my dad would say. "Four weeks older."

But for now, I was still deep in the woods, the cool night air bleeding around us. The boys in my cabin got up, making their way out toward dinner. "C'mon, Marty," Jimmy said.

"You go," I said. "I'm not hungry."

Outside, I could hear the rest of the boys in Maple heading down for one of their last meals, talking cheerfully, making jokes, as if they either weren't thinking about going home tomorrow or didn't want this time to end.

change of light

I was sitting on the floor of a ratty old hotel room outside DC, just five hours into a road trip down south, when my cousin Evie asked me to kiss her.

"I'm not kissing you," I said, taking a swig of the beer we were splitting. Evie had gotten it from the hotel bar, persuading the guy working there to sell it to her despite the fact that she was eighteen, four years older than me. That was Evie's gift—getting people to do things they weren't supposed to do. When she started laughing at his jokes, I knew he didn't stand a chance.

"I'm offering you a little help, Marty," she said to me in our room.

I didn't want to be on this trip at all. Evie and Aunt Beth were originally supposed to go by themselves, delivering my cousin to North Carolina for college, where she was starting in the fall. But then Evie broke up with her boyfriend. And then Aunt Beth got nervous about making the drive since Evie had only just gotten her license. My mom, always the fixer, offered to help out.

"We'll make a vacation out of it," my mom had told me, and I could see the desperation in her eyes, the wish for the kid who, in the past, would have followed her anywhere. She opened a map, asking me to pick a place along the way I wanted to visit. I closed my eyes and pointed my finger randomly on the map. It landed in the middle of the Atlantic Ocean. "You're going and you'll like it," my mom said.

I never suspected kissing my cousin would be part of the trip. "Think of it as training," Evie said to me that night in the hotel. "It doesn't *mean* anything. It's like a scrimmage before the real game."

We were sitting at the foot of the bed, in the direct line of the air conditioner, the only spot in the room that got cool. Evie had turned to face me, so close I could practically feel the heat off her body. I took another sip of my beer. I'd never really liked the taste, and this one was no better, but I'd already learned that it wasn't about liking it or not. The buzz was starting to make my head spin. I looked at Evie, who smiled and pursed her lips. I couldn't tell if she was drunk or just crazy. Her long, dark brown hair slipped in front of her face, her tank top draping open, her tits practically falling out. I looked away again. "Isn't kissing your cousin against the law or something?"

"You've never kissed a girl, have you?"

"I've kissed tons of girls," I said. Truth was, my kissing experience was extremely limited. Kissed once unexpectedly on the cheek by Colleen Shayle under the monkey bars of the playground in third grade. Kissed once by my grandmother, who'd gone for my cheek but caught me flush on the mouth. I had kissed a girl named Robyn at camp last summer, but it was so long ago it felt like it was someone else's life.

"Go ahead then. Kiss me," Evie said, almost an order. I wanted to believe she was actually trying to help, but this seemed like it wasn't about me at all. My mom told me that Evie had broken up with her boyfriend just before we'd left and that she might be a little off, but I had no idea that things were going to get this strange. "It's not like we're having sex," she added.

"Gross," I said, taking another swig, although I nearly choked on it and started coughing.

"Relax," she said, reaching out and lifting my chin. "Close your eyes." I did what she said. I could still hear the television, some documentary about space travel. A man with an earnest voice went on about how unlikely it was that we were alone in the universe. In the next room, behind a door only a few feet away, our mothers laughed. "Nice and gentle," Evie added, taking the beer out of my hands and placing it next to her.

And then I felt her kiss, the brush of skin on skin, the give of her lips against mine, her tongue slipping between my teeth. There was an electricity to it, a friction igniting around my mouth and making its way down my spine, outward through my chest to the tips of my fingers and toes. I was on fire. I pulled back, instinctively crossing my hands over my lap. It was as if I had been shocked awake from a dream and just realized where I was: sitting in a hotel room, kissing my cousin, getting a hard-on. I looked up to see tears rolling down Evie's cheeks.

"What?" I asked her.

"Nothing," she said. I closed my eyes again, moving toward her once more, my mouth ready, but she put her hand on my shoulder, stopping me. I opened my eyes and could see that her expression had changed, turning serious. I said, "Was I that bad?"

She straightened up, wiping her face with her arm. "You did great," she said. She stood, pulling her hand through her hair and smiling, although it looked like she was going to cry again. This was the Evie I remembered—an emotional spinning top. I never knew quite where she would come to rest. She walked into the bathroom and I climbed into one of the two double beds, crawling under the blankets. I heard the bath start to run, old pipes hissing and rattling in the wall. When she finally shut the door, the room went dark, the only light the blue glow of the television flickering all around me.

The morning after the kiss, I steered clear of Evie as much as possible, sneaking out of the hotel room as soon as I woke up, and then eating breakfast with the moms at the hotel café. "Everything okay?" my mom asked.

"Just tired," I said, filling my mouth with limp scrambled eggs. Truth was, I couldn't get it out of my mind—the warmth of Evie's lips, the way my mind raced after she left, the way I sat in bed, wanting to see what might happen when she came back and yet equally afraid of it. When it became clear she wasn't coming back any time soon, I jerked off silently and quietly and quickly into the pages of the King James Bible, unable to get to the box of tissues in the bathroom.

By late morning, we were back in the car, ready to head out. I pretended to be asleep until I realized Evie was sitting up front. In the driver's seat. Driving.

"Are you sure this is a good idea?" I said.

"She needs the practice," Aunt Beth said. Her voice was bright with enthusiasm, but I could hear the doubt in it as well. She crossed her arms as if she were cold. This was the Aunt Beth I knew well—trying to be positive and supportive, but stressed by an awareness of all the ways everything could go wrong. The woman had lost her husband to cancer, and as far as I could see, her daughter was crazy. She had good reason to be nervous. Evie pulled onto the road that led away from our hotel, eyeing me in the rearview mirror.

"Eyes on the road," I said. She gave me the finger.

"She's doing fine," my mom said, sitting right next to me, her hand braced against the seat in front of her, as if that was going to help. "You'll understand when you learn to drive," she added, trying to make me feel better. I couldn't wait to drive, to dictate where we were going instead of being just a passenger stuck in the back seat, but that seemed like a lifetime away.

I tried to distract myself from Evie's driving, grabbing a book from my backpack. The book was *The Martian Chronicles* by Ray Bradbury, my summer reading for ninth grade. I'd been given a list of books to choose from and picked it, not because I knew it, and not because I had any interest in science fiction, but because when I looked down at the list I thought it said "*The* Martin *Chronicles*." That was a book I wanted to read. Maybe it was the story of the life I was going to live. It didn't hurt that my mom had ticked off the ones she thought I would like and that wasn't one of her choices.

"Reading in the car is going to make you sick," my mom said.

"I'll puke on Evie," I said.

I cracked open the book, reading the opening line, which I'd read at least twenty times already. "*One minute it was Ohio winter…*" It took only half a page for my stomach to start to churn. I looked away, out the window, at the lush green trees and deep blue sky running along the highway. The heat outside the car, thick and heavy, made everything quiver as if we were underwater.

Somehow we survived an hour of Evie working the radio as she drove, occasionally slipping into the next lane or tailgating a car right in front of us, before my mom took over. Evie moved to the back seat. I tried not to make eye contact with her, but I stole looks at her long, tanned legs in jean shorts, the same tank top she wore last night. She put on her sunglasses, enormous dark lenses that swallowed her eyes. I couldn't tell if she was staring directly at me or sleeping. For years she'd worn her long brown hair in a ponytail, this long rope that lay on her back like a plumb line. Now, though, her hair was undone, gathering around her shoulders. She looked a bit like her mom around the eyes and mouth, and I could see the outline of the adult she was becoming, traced into everything about her.

Eventually, we turned off the highway and then down a dirt road, slowly rising along the side of a mountain. We pulled up in front of a massive inn that looked like something out of a horror movie. Aunt Beth told us it had been built by a famous architect who had designed it to feel like a tree house.

"It's like we're floating in the trees," Aunt Beth said, although I had no idea what she was talking about. It looked just like a normal hotel parked deep in the woods.

We got our keys and headed to our rooms. Evie and I were roommates. Again. This time, though, there was only one queen-sized bed in our room. "I think we got the wrong room," I said, turning to my mom.

"That's all they have," my mom said.

"Serious?" I said.

"Aren't you going to carry me over the threshold?" Evie said, pushing me out of the way.

I dropped my bag. "I'll take the couch."

"What a gentleman."

Evie wasted no time, going through the drawers and cabinets in our room. She lay on the floor, pulling back the sham and peering underneath the bed. This was her typical routine when she got to a hotel—looking for things left by previous guests. She'd done the exact same thing in the DC hotel, digging through every space in the room until she'd found a single earring. Nothing cool. I knew where she'd gotten the habit: Before he died, her dad had been a salesman, always traveling and staying in hotels all around the country. Every time he got home from a trip, he would tell Evie stories about what he'd discovered in his room. Usually it was boring stuff like keys and socks and change, but there were unexpected things as well: A diamond ring. A tooth. A kitten. Once even a gun. I never quite got why she felt like she had to do the same thing. It was as if she were trying to find something he might have left behind, which freaked me out completely. He was gone and had been for years. She walked over to the couch and started flipping pillows.

"Hey, that's my bed!" I shouted.

"Aha!" she said, and a shiver went up my spine. She turned around wearing a pair of eyeglasses, the lenses so thick you had to wonder how the person who owned them was able to leave the room without them. She started to walk toward me, stretching out her arms to hug me. "Don't I look hot in these?"

"Stay away from me," I said.

She laughed, walking to the window. She stood there, staring out at the trees as if she could actually see anything with those glasses. Sometimes she went into these states, like a trance, where she was no longer aware of anything around her, and I wondered if she was still in the same room with me. I said, "What are you looking at?"

"What?" she said, startled. She pulled off the glasses. "We used to come here every year."

"Fascinating," I said, and began putting my couch back together.

"I can't believe my mom wanted to come back." She reached out, resting her hand against the window. When she pulled it away, her handprint lingered on the glass. "Then again," she said, turning to me, "the restaurant used to have these bear burgers and chocolate shakes that were so fucking good."

I asked, "Are there bears here?"

"Relax, city boy," she said. She climbed up on the radiator, standing in the window, her body framed by the green of the trees like some kind of forest animal. "I wish I had some weed," she added. "We could get high and gorge ourselves."

"I'm sure the moms would like that."

"We could go hiking in the woods and—"

She spun around, nearly falling off her perch. Her eyes were as wide as when she was wearing the glasses.

"What?" I said, suddenly nervous. She scanned the room, before settling on the bedside table. She grabbed the binder with all the hotel amenities and services and started flipping through it. "I wonder if it's still here," she said. She stopped on a specific page. "Yes!"

"What?!" I insisted.

"Come with me," she said, grabbing my hand. She knocked on the adjoining door to the moms' room and opened it. Inside, my mom and Aunt Beth were still unpacking, their suitcases open on the bed, clothes arranged in neat piles beside them.

"We're going for a walk!" Evie proclaimed, and then shut the door again before they had a chance to say anything, before even I could protest, as if I would have had any say in the decision.

———

The ropes course was high up in the trees. There was nothing about it I liked—the idea of heights or trying to walk like some kind of circus act across a wire. Evie, much more of a thrill seeker than me, enjoyed this kind of thing. Looking up into the trees, what seemed at least five stories up, I could just make out the network of different ropes and connections, rows of wooded slats and wires suspended in the air, net meshing running up the sides. They looked like flimsy cobwebs trembling in the wind, zigzagging between the treetops. I figured the whole course finished somewhere, but I couldn't see where that was.

"I'm really not interested," I said.

"It's so much fun," she said, nudging me forward. "I promise."

We approached a picnic table where a young girl was sitting, selling tickets. "Hi, guys," she said. She was cute, with short brown hair and freckles. She didn't look much older than me. "Two tickets," Evie said.

The girl sized up Evie and me, and then frowned. "I'm sorry," she said. "You need to be fifteen for the high ropes. You could try the junior course," she added, pointing to a series of logs planted firmly on the ground, cargo netting on either side, making it nearly impossible to hurt yourself.

I should have been relieved to get out of it, but I hated hearing I was too young for anything. My body was starting to look like a teenager's—hair sprouting in unexpected places, my legs and arms long and lanky—but the skin on my face wasn't covered in acne like so many people I knew. It made me look even younger than I was. "It's okay," I said, starting to move away. Evie grabbed me.

"I think he looks fifteen, don't you?" she said to the girl. Evie smiled, and I could see it happening again: The girl blushed, pushing her hair behind her ear. She looked around and then handed me a ticket. "I guess he does," she said.

"Thanks," Evie said.

On the stairs up, I said, "How do you do that?"

"Do what?" Evie said, as if she had no idea what I was talking about. It occurred to me that she really didn't know. She had no clue about her power—this innate force, a kind of gravity that she could draw on without thinking about it. She took my hand, pulling me up the rickety stairs. I wasn't exactly thrilled to risk my life, but even I couldn't fight her powers sometimes.

A platform had been built high up in a tree, a circle of wood around the trunk like a doughnut. A skinny guy in nothing but shorts, boots, and a tie-dyed shirt sat balanced on a thin rail. He was rubbing his arms and neck, spreading some kind of lotion that reeked of coconut. He looked Evie's age, maybe a little older. "Welcome to the top of the world!" he shouted, extending his arms.

Evie cheered, dancing on the platform, making it shake. I moved closer to the tree, my hands grasping for a hold on the rough bark, as if that might help me when the whole thing came down.

He asked us who was going first, and Evie jumped ahead. "All right, pretty lady," Coconut Man said. I watched as he helped her step into the harness, holding it open for her legs. She held on to his shoulders for balance, the two of them smiling at each other in a way I could see wasn't about the ropes course anymore.

He told us his name was Bruce and showed us how everything worked. The harness was attached to a trolley that ran along a safety wire above you as you walked across the bridge. If you actually fell, it would catch you. "Totally safe," he told us. "My dad will meet you on the other end of the course," he added, adjusting the clips on Evie's harness. "If you slip, just sit back, relax, and enjoy the view. I'll come get you."

"You mean like this?" Evie said, leaning back into his body.

Bruce laughed. "Yeah," he said. "You know what you're doing."

Evie walked to the edge of the platform where the course began and Bruce clipped her safety line to the trolley. "See you on the other side!" she said, taking her first steps onto the bridge. She began to move quickly, without hesitation, the bridge swaying beneath her in rhythm with her step. I could hear the wooden slats creak under her feet, the ropes stretch and bristle, but she didn't seem to notice. She glided, not slowing down for a moment, the trolley clicking like a bike coasting downhill. "It's so beautiful up here!" she shouted.

"You got it!" Bruce called out, before coming over to me. "Older sister?" he said, tightening the straps across my thighs.

"Cousin."

He tugged on the harness. "She's something," he said.

"I guess," I said, looking at the lattice of cords around my waist. "You sure this is safe?"

He nodded. "Totally. Just take your time."

I walked to the edge of the platform, extending my hands toward the guide ropes on either side of a bridge. Ahead, I could still make out Evie crossing the bridges with ease, disappearing behind leaves, out of sight. My heart was racing. I told myself I didn't have to do this. There was absolutely nothing making me go. I could turn around and climb down the stairs and go back and eat a burger and drink a shake and watch television and live my life and everything would be okay.

Then I heard Evie's voice out in the trees. It was an eerie sound, distant and yet close, somewhere between a laugh and a cry. I don't know why, but I moved toward it, stepping off the edge, taking my first few steps onto the bridge. My feet shimmied beneath me, swaying side to side on the first slat. I tensed up, pulling the rope railing toward me as if that would help. I only seemed to rock more. "Relax, little man," Bruce said behind me. I turned and watched him take a pretend can of oil, squirt his knees. "Nice and loose."

I took a deep breath, bent my knees, and started forward again. I counted my steps, not looking down. I noticed, though, that Bruce's advice worked: I swayed less now that I was bent at the knees. I was able to stretch out my arms, relaxing my grip. I soon found a decent pace, the trolley clicking along in step as I made it to the next platform. I walked across two more bridges without a problem, my body settling in. The next rope bridge was longer, dipping in the middle and passing through a tunnel of leaves in the treetops. I stopped midway, the trolley going quiet, and looked around. It was so peaceful up here: the wind rustling in the leaves, flashes of sunlight flickering like bright stars through the canopy of trees. It was a part of the world I'd never seen before and never considered, this strange space caught between the treetops and the ground below. I knew I was standing on a bridge, but I had this sensation that I was flying, some kind of bird soaring beneath the cover of the trees. I looked down and could see the dirt path that we had taken to get here, but surprisingly it didn't scare me, as if my being suspended between the sky and the earth was the most natural thing in the world. For the first time this whole trip, I stopped thinking about everything and everyone—Evie, Bruce, the girl at the ticket table, my mom, my friends—and surrendered to the calm of it all.

Eventually I crossed three more bridges, slowly making my way through the maze of ropes, the course heading down. I was actually enjoying myself. On the last platform, I could see Evie in the distance, standing on a platform with an older man. Probably Bruce's dad. She waved and called out, "C'mon, slowpoke!"

I started across the bridge, a wide, long one that didn't have netting on the sides, just rope railings that should have been enough to protect you. We were only about twenty feet above the ground. I tried not to think about it. The wind picked up, the tree branches around me rustling, the bridge swaying. The trolley clicked above me. I was about halfway across when my safety line went taut. I looked up and saw the problem: a loose branch, hanging on the line, had gotten snagged in the trolley and locked it up. I pulled on it trying to set it free, but nothing happened. "I'm stuck!" I called out.

"Give it a good tug," Bruce's dad, standing on the edge of the platform, called out. I pulled it as hard as I could but only wedged the branch in deeper. In a flash my heart began to race again as I realized I was going nowhere. All around me there was noise—the sound of Bruce's dad telling me not to move, Evie shouting not to worry—but I couldn't speak. I adjusted my grip on the rope rail, and my ticket to the ropes course, inexplicably still in my hand, slipped out of my grasp and drifted down into the thicket of bushes and rocks where I was convinced my body was headed. I couldn't believe this was how I was going die— falling from a stupid rope bridge in Virginia I never wanted to get on. All because of Evie.

"Hang on tight," another voice called out. I turned to see Bruce moving quickly across the bridge, his body as silent and quick as a cat.

"Well, that's a bummer," he said, walking up next to me. He fastened a cord from his harness to mine, securing me in. "This is no good," he said, looking at my trolley. "Bearings are busted."

"What?" I said, my heart racing still. "What's wrong?"

"No worries, little man," he said, attaching my safety line to his trolley. "We'll just go mama-bear style."

"What?" I said. He attached another line from his waist to mine, locking us together. We walked the rest of the way in step, my body swallowed in a fog of coconut lotion. Evie stood waiting for us at the platform, shaking her head as we arrived and then said, "Maybe we should stick to the junior course."

Evie and I went back to our room. She lay on the bed, going on about how awesome it felt to be up in the trees, how it was like the time she took acid, how it was better than sex. I stretched out on the couch, staring out the window at the treetops and clear blue sky. I just wanted to forget that it had ever happened. The smell of Bruce's coconut lotion was all over me.

"I've got to tell Ted," Evie said, picking up the phone and dialing. In the next room my mom and Aunt Beth were cackling about something.

"Hey," Evie said into the phone, her voice a soft whisper. "Yeah, it's me, baby."

Great, I thought.

"I'm in Virginia. At some kind of inn with my family."

I couldn't hear the voice on the other side, but I could see Evie squirming to get comfortable. "I don't know," Evie said. "Just missed you."

She was silent for a moment, before adding, "I know that's what we said."

She turned away from me, her shoulders slumping forward. I thought about shutting off the television and going into the bathroom, maybe leaving the room completely. "I just thought—" She started to nod, as if whoever was on the other side on the phone could see her. "Okay," she said. "Okay. Bye." She turned to me for a second, her eyes full of tears. *Great*, I thought. "Bye," she said again, and hung up the phone.

I knew better than to say anything.

"Knock, knock," Aunt Beth said, opening the door to our room. "How was 'cousin time'!?"

Neither of us said a word.

"Sarah and I are going for a walk," she told us, calling my mom by her first name, which always threw me. "Who wants to come?"

"We just got back, Mom," Evie said, rolling over and burying her face in her pillow. Aunt Beth smiled. I didn't give Aunt Beth a lot of credit—she often seemed clueless, like someone in a boat adrift, trying desperately to find their bearings—but she knew her daughter well enough to know something was up. She asked, "Is everything all right?"

Evie could have said nothing and let it go, but that wasn't her way. When doors opened up, she walked through them, for better or worse. She flipped back, staring at her mother with a kind of venom I hadn't seen from her on this trip. There was always a quiet storm of emotions brewing under the surface with Evie, and sometimes it had to break through. It was hard to imagine that only a moment ago she'd been glowing about walking the ropes course. "Sure, Mom. Everything is great. Why wouldn't it be great?"

Aunt Beth crossed her arms over her chest. "Evie," Aunt Beth said. "What's going on?"

"Nothing, Mom," she said, sitting up. "How are you?"

Aunt Beth looked startled by the question. "I'm fine."

Evie smiled, shaking her head, her eyes gleaming. "Are you? Are you really? Because I don't know what kind of person is fine who takes her family back to the place she used to come with her husband." She paused before adding, "Her *dead* husband."

Aunt Beth's head drooped in defeat.

"Maybe," Evie continued, "we can find which room you guys stayed in and have a séance or something."

"That's enough," Aunt Beth whispered.

I looked at the open door connecting our two rooms. "Mom," I called out.

Evie ignored me, saying, "Maybe you can get in the bed and you guys can reenact your honeymoon—"

"Mom!" I shouted.

"Evie!" Aunt Beth pleaded.

"Unbelievable," Evie said, shaking her head.

"Mom!"

Evie said, "This is fucking bullshit."

"Watch your goddamn mouth, Evelyn!" Aunt Beth snapped, and the room fell silent. I didn't know what to do.

My mom appeared in the doorway. "What is it?" she said. "What's wrong?"

Evie looked at my mom and then at me, her eyes narrowed.

"Nothing," Aunt Beth said, trying to collect herself. "Everything is fine."

"You think so?" Evie said, bounding out of bed and pushing her way past her mom. She grabbed her purse and ran out. The door slammed behind her, the whole room shaking before it settled down again.

The moms decided to go on their walk, but I stayed in our room. *The Martian Chronicles* sat next to me. "*One minute it was Ohio winter*," I read—again—before I drifted into a fitful sleep.

Evie didn't come back, not after they got back from their walk, not even at dinner. Instead, Aunt Beth and my mom and I ate on the deck, watching the sun dip behind the trees, igniting the skies a bright orange. "Do you think we should be worried about Evie?" my mom asked.

Aunt Beth shook her head. "She just needs a little time. Let the storm pass." She looked up at the sky, smiling. "Red skies at night, sailor's delight. Tomorrow will be a good day."

After dinner, the three of us walked back to our rooms. When I tried my key, I discovered that the inner security chain had been latched on. I squeezed my face in the space, calling out, "Hello?"

Bedsheets rustled inside and then Evie appeared, her hair a tangled mess, dressed in an oversized tie-dyed shirt I'd seen before. "Hey, cuz," she said. She smiled, guilt blazed across her face. "Favor time."

"Serious?" I said.

"C'mon, Marty," she said. "Do this for me and I won't tell them how you defiled the Bible at the last hotel."

I couldn't believe she knew.

"What do you want?" I said.

"Just give us an hour," she said. She looked back and we could both see his two big feet stretched out at the end of the bed. There were bottles of beer lined up on top of the television. "Please," she said, turning her lip up in a pouty face like she used to do as a kid.

"At least get me my book," I said.

Evie ran back in the room, and the door creaked open, but I didn't want to look anymore. "Here," she said, handing me my book. "You should actually try reading it."

"Thanks," I said, as the door shut behind me.

—

The hotel was pretty quiet, just a few people gathered in the restaurant, some watching a baseball game on television, others sitting by themselves, drinking. I sat at a stool, figuring I'd watch the game, even though it was the Braves against the Cardinals, two teams I couldn't have cared less about. The bartender walked over, an older man with a belly sagging over his belt.

"Good evening, sir," he said, laying a napkin down in front of me. He looked down at *The Martian Chronicles*. "Great book," he added.

"It is," I said, as if I knew.

"What are we drinking tonight?"

I thought of what Evie would do in this situation. "I'll have a beer," I said.

The bartender nodded and I did my best to keep a straight face. "Excellent choice," he said, and reached down into the cooler in front of him. He pulled out a brown bottle and flipped the top. "One root beer," he said, smiling. "Cheers."

I took a sip, slumping down in my seat.

I finished my root beer and went to the game room, where I played *Asteroids* for over an hour, my fingers sore from hammering on the fire button so hard. When I got back to our room, Bruce was gone and the room was dark, except for a thin swath of light coming through the blinds from outside. The smell of coconut oil lingered in the air. Evie lay under the covers, her back turned to me. "I made your bed," she said. I stretched out on the couch, not bothering to take off my clothes. "You're the best," she said, her voice a sleepy whisper.

"Right," I said.

Above me, I could see between the blinds, the night sky glazed white with stars. I thought how busy the sky looked, how almost crowded it seemed, how there was bound to be someone or something out there, and still how far away it all felt.

We headed toward the coast the next morning, passing from the winding and rolling green hills of Virginia to the flat exposed straightaways of North Carolina. Evie's grandma lived on the Outer Banks in one of those beach communities that boomed during the summer months and then turned into a ghost town the rest of the year. The closer we got, cutting across marsh and wetlands, the smaller the roads became. Pretty soon, we were on a single-lane road, the air damp with saltwater, heat baking everything brown. Cars with boat trailers and roof racks piled high with suitcases lined the road. We had supposedly come down a few times when Evie's dad was still alive, and everything felt vaguely familiar, although I didn't remember Evie's grandma's house or her grandma that well. All the same, it was a strange sense of déjà vu, like visiting a place I'd seen on a television show or in a movie but couldn't remember its name.

Evie's grandma, though, seemed to remember me. "Look at you," she said, when I emerged from the air-conditioned car into the syrupy North Carolina humidity. She turned to my mom. "I remember when you were carrying him in a backpack."

"Not anymore," my mom said, pulling suitcases out of the trunk.

"He looks just like you," she said, taking my face in her hand.

My mom didn't say anything but looked up and smiled at me, her expression almost sad. I grabbed my bag and darted into the house before I could hear any more.

⟵

The ocean was freezing. The best thing to do would have been to just dive in, but the water was rough, waves almost as tall as I was, crashing down with a roar and a spray of foam. I looked down the shore and there was barely anyone swimming. Mostly it was little kids, running from the surf as it rolled up the beach, playing a game of cat and mouse with the water. I stood knee-deep, the dumbest place to be, neither in all the way nor out. Waves crashed into me, knocking me off balance.

"Don't be such a wimp," Evie shouted, sprinting by me. She hurdled over the first line of waves, screaming at the top of her lungs from the cold. Once she was out deep enough, she dove in, her body slipping into the wave and disappearing. I remembered from our time on the beaches at the Cape how she liked to do it: swimming underwater, out past the breakers for as long as she could hold her breath. I could remember that sense of unease I felt as a kid as I watched her get swallowed by the surf, waiting to see when she would emerge further out. It was always longer than I expected.

A few seconds later, though, there she was, a tiny head coming out of the water, bobbing up and down in the dark calmer water. She let out a cry of joy and then said, "C'mon! It's awesome out here!"

I ran in, refusing to let her get the better of me. I put the frigid water out of my mind. A large wave rose up ahead, and I sprinted as fast as I could, diving under the crest just as it broke over me. The world went quiet, this magical silence, both unexpected and familiar. I knew I should have stayed under as Evie always did, but I panicked, rising up, coming out too soon. Another wave broke over me, a wall of water crashing down hard. I turned my back to it, trying to stand firm, but another wave followed, this one even bigger, knocking me back, pushing me to the ground. I flipped over, my shoulder dragging against the sand. The ocean's power was something I'd forgotten, the way it could toss you around so easily. Pushed to shallow water again, I stood, my head still spinning from the fall.

"Nice wipeout!" Evie yelled. Her head was a black silhouette in the distance.

Shaking off the fall, I dove back into the water and finally made it out to where Evie was floating on her back. "Have you forgotten everything I taught you?" she said.

I tried not to stare at her body, slick with seawater, but she had squeezed herself into an old bikini and she was practically falling out of it. "Shut up," I shouted, turning to look at the shore. My feet kicked beneath me, searching out the sea floor, but it was too deep. A line of houses stood buried in the dunes, like a row of faces staring back at us. "I can't believe you don't come here all the time," I said.

"I hate this place," she said, looking up.

"Why?" I asked, regretting the question the moment I asked it. I didn't want to get her riled up.

"Too many memories," she said, staying surprisingly calm. Her body bobbed in the water, in rhythm with the waves. "Too much history. It's like there's a memory under every fucking rock. My mom lives for this shit, but I just want to put it all behind me."

I was going to say I understood, but my memories of this place were nonexistent. Evie shouted, "Look out below!" raising her arms straight up, the fastest way to send you to the bottom, if that's what you wanted to do.

After swimming, Aunt Beth and Evie and Grandma Ellen went to the graveyard where Evie's dad was buried. It was Grandma Ellen's idea, I could tell. Evie didn't want to go. She sat by the door chewing on her fingers, like a child afraid to go to the doctor. The way Aunt Beth skittered nervously around the porch before they left, I was pretty sure she wasn't interested in going either, but it didn't seem like there was a choice.

The plan was to meet them at the pizza place down the road, so my mom and I hung out at the house for a while before walking the mile to the restaurant. We ordered a pizza and a Greek salad, but I wasn't hungry and just picked at my food. "Do you remember this place?" she asked.

"This place?" I said, looking around at all the generic pizza parlor touches—the red-and-white tablecloths, drawings on the wall of fat men with mustaches and white coats throwing pizzas. We could have been anywhere. I shook my head.

"You and Evie used to make us come here on rainy days," she said, smiling. "Here and the bowling alley."

"I guess," I said.

"Evie always ate her pizza backwards, starting with the crust. You followed her exactly."

"I don't remember," I said, but of course I did. It was one of the only things that stuck with me from that time.

"You did everything she did back then," she said, and started laughing. "Once, after a day at the beach, you both wore your bathing suits on your head the whole night because she told you it was the new style."

My mom cackled, and people in the restaurant turned toward us. "Mom," I said, giving her a look.

"Okay, okay," she said. "It never happened."

They got there fifteen minutes later. Evie devoured several slices of pizza, not talking to anyone. Eventually, my mom paid the check and we headed toward the car. "This is the perfect time of day," Aunt Beth said. She was right. The sun was still out, but the edge was off the heat. A thick wall of gray clouds had gathered along the shoreline, but above us was clear blue sky, as if the world was split in two.

"We should take a walk," Aunt Beth said.

"It is going to rain," Grandma Ellen said with certainty in her voice, pointing at clouds. "Within the hour."

Aunt Beth looked at my mom, unsure what to do. "Well, that gives us plenty of time," my mom said. Grandma Ellen shrugged and shook her head as if we were all idiots.

"Why don't you let me and Marty drive home?" Evie said. "I'll take him to DQ."

Aunt Beth and my mom shared a look, and I knew it had to do with whether or not they trusted Evie. Evie sighed. "C'mon," she said. "I have a legal driver's license, people. And it's just down the road."

"Let her drive," my mom said, and Aunt Beth agreed.

The DQ was a glass-front walk-up stand sitting in the middle of a massive parking lot. Barely a shop at all. I could imagine it would get crowded at times, the parking lot jammed with cars, but now the whole thing looked silly, like a tiny boat floating in an empty lake.

Evie and I ate dipped cones and sat on the trunk of the car, watching the wall of clouds creep toward the shore. She had stayed quiet on the drive over, and I wondered if it was because of the visit to the graveyard.

"What grade are you going into?" she finally asked.

"Ninth."

"High school," she said. "Big leagues. That's where the fun begins."

"Really?" I said, turning to look at her.

"No," she said, shaking her head. "It sucks. Maybe you'll have more fun than I did."

I thought about what I expected next year. More of the same. Homework. Pressure about college. Fights with my parents. Not much upside.

"Girlfriend?" she asked.

"No," I said. Our school had been all boys through eighth grade, but then went coed in high school. I figured the presence of girls around us would only make things more complicated. As if we needed one more thing to worry about. "At least you're off on your own," I said.

"Amen to that," she said, throwing her cone toward a group of gulls gathered by the garbage. One of them pounced on it and soared off over our heads.

"You can drive," I said. "That's so cool."

"It's not like I'll have a car," she said, which I hadn't thought of. She leaned back, resting her head on the roof.

"I can't wait until I can drive," I said. You could feel the temperature changing, the breeze picking up. It was definitely going to rain.

"What kind of car would you get?" she asked.

I thought about it for a second, before saying, "A two-seater. Something with no back seat in it so that's never an option."

Evie laughed. "Good call."

"What about you?" I asked.

Evie closed her eyes. "I don't know. I don't really care," she said. "Something fast. Or maybe a jeep so I can drive over anything in my way," she added. "I have an idea," she said, bolting up, and wearing the same look as when we ended up on the ropes course back in Virginia.

"What?" I said.

"Let's teach you to drive," she said.

"When?"

"Like now."

"Now? Here?"

"It's perfect," she said. "This is what empty parking lots are for. Shit, my dad used to take me here all the time to drive. And I was younger than you." I guessed that Aunt Beth had no idea. "You up for it?" I looked around. The parking lot was huge and empty. The only people around were the two teenage girls working the DQ, leaning on the counter because they had no customers. Every fiber in my body told me that it was the wrong thing to do. "Totally," I said.

The dashboard was much more elaborate than I had imagined. I'd sat in the front seat of my parents' car before, but only when I was younger, when the only thing I could really do was hang on the steering wheel or flip the blinkers. Now there were pedals I had to think about, and mirrors, not to mention how far up I had to move the seat.

"Just turn the ignition and start the car," Evie said.

"What do I do with my feet?" I asked.

"You only need the right one," she said. "Keep it on the brake for now. The big pedal in the middle."

I followed her instructions and felt the car rumble to life around us, vibrating beneath me. I was plenty tall enough to see, but the hood suddenly seemed enormous, this vast stretch of car ahead of me. Evie told me to shift into drive and press on the gas. "Ease up gently," she said, and I did. We started to roll.

"We're moving," I said.

"That's what happens," she said. "Give it a little more."

I pressed harder on the gas. We lurched forward until she shouted "Brake!" and I slammed my foot down on the big pedal. "Jesus," she said. I looked over at the two girls in DQ watching us, their expressions unimpressed.

"Don't push too hard. Nice and gentle," she said. "Okay?"

I nodded and shifted out of park. We started rolling again as I squeezed softly on the gas pedal. The car picked up speed, heading straight. I turned the wheel a little and the car began to veer around the DQ. "That's it," Evie said.

I straightened out and drove across the parking lot until we reached the other side. Evie cheered. "This is amazing," I said.

"You think this is good…" she said, raising her eyebrows. "Open her up a little."

"What?"

"More gas!" she called out.

I put the car in drive and pushed harder on the gas than I had before. The car took off. Evie hooted as we sped toward the DQ. "Don't run into it!"

I turned slightly and we swept around the DQ, doing a full circle. I looked up from the wheel for a second and saw the girls inside the DQ still watching us. "Yeah, girls!" I shouted out the open window. "Coming through!" I did a full circle and headed back toward the other side of the parking lot. Evie was laughing as I pulled around. Pretty soon, I had one arm leaning out the window as I turned around the DQ, waving to the girls. The clouds, thick and gray, had moved over us, cooling off the early evening, but my whole body was tingling, as if I was on fire.

She let me drive for the next ten minutes, circling the DQ, doing figure eights in the open lot. On the last spin, I made the turn at the back of the lot and spotted another car pulling in. A police car. "Shit," Evie said.

"Oh my god," I said, sinking in my seat.

"Put it in park and turn it off," Evie said.

I turned the key the wrong way, the engine rattling and grinding until I turned it the right way and it went quiet. The police car made its way slowly toward us.

"Get over here," Evie said, trying to pull me over to her side, but it was too late. The police car pulled next to us. I couldn't see the policeman in the front seat, just his silhouette. For a while he just sat in his car, talking to someone over a CB radio, not getting out. The two girls in the DQ opened a back door and looked out at us.

"What do we do?" I said to Evie.

"Nothing," she said, and sighed. "Let me handle it."

After about two minutes, he got out of the car and walked around to my window. He was probably my mom's age, maybe a little older. He wore dark sunglasses, his eyes hidden behind them. "Afternoon," he said, leaning down to our window. "License and registration, please."

I looked at Evie. She went into the glove compartment and shuffled through the papers until she found the registration. Then she pulled out her wallet and got her license. She passed them to me and I handed them to the officer. He stood up, studying the papers. He was so close to the car that I could smell his cologne, this flowery smell like the bathroom of our hotel.

"I'll need the license of the *driver*," he said.

My heart started to race and I looked over at my cousin.

"I'm the driver, officer," she said. "I was just letting him try. We weren't leaving the parking lot."

The officer pulled down his glasses, an expression of exasperation behind them I recognized all too well. He turned to me. "How old are you?" the officer said.

"Fourteen," I said.

The officer sighed, like a man who had seen this kind of thing before. I could see the rain starting to fall, dotting the gray pavement of the parking lot. The two DQ girls ran back inside.

"Officer," Evie said. She told him we were staying down the road with her grandma. When she said Ellen's name, he nodded as if he knew her. Then Evie said, "Can't we just forget about this?"

I watched for a sign that he was giving in, as everyone else did with Evie, but when he looked up, his expression turned stern. "No, ma'am," he said. "We cannot."

Evie looked stunned, as if the world didn't make sense. He told her to get out of the car and into the front seat of his squad car with him. The skies opened up, the rain coming down slowly at first but then in heavy waves until I could barely see them through the windshield. Eventually, the officer got out of his car and walked slowly to my window, unfazed by the rain. He told me to get in the back of his car.

"Am I going to jail?" I asked.

"Not today," he said.

He drove us to the house and told us to stay in the car while he spoke to Grandma Ellen and Aunt Beth and my mom. Finally, he came out with Grandma Ellen and Aunt Beth. "What about my license?" Evie said, as he opened the doors of the car, letting us out. Grandma Ellen wouldn't even look at us as she got in the car, presumably to go pick up Aunt Beth's car.

He smiled, nodding at Aunt Beth, and said, "Good afternoon, ma'am."

"Upstairs," Aunt Beth said to Evie, and they marched up.

I walked into the kitchen, where my mom was waiting. "What were you thinking?" she said.

"I don't know," I said. "Evie said it would be fine."

"Jesus, it's like you're five again."

I sat down at the table. "Nothing happened, Mom. We're okay."

"Nothing happened?" my mom said, her expression incredulous. "Nothing happened? Evie's license is suspended. She's not getting it back for at least a year. If that."

I nodded. It wasn't like she was going to use it.

"And you," she said, searching for words. "You..."

"What?"

"Let's start with the fact that you're grounded when we get back. For a month."

"A month?!" I shouted. That was all my time with my friends when we were supposed to hang out. That was the plan.

"Yes, a month," she said. I'd never seen her this angry and I couldn't understand it. "Your father and I will decide what other punishment you get."

"Other punishment?" I said. "I drove the car. No one was hurt. It's not fair."

My mother looked at me again like she didn't know who I was. "Fair? Fair? Did you even think about what could have happened? You could have killed yourself. Or Evie. Or someone else!"

She was right, I knew it, but it still seemed excessive. "I can't believe how much you hate me."

I didn't think she could get any more upset, but she covered her mouth with her hand, her face turning red. "Hate you? I'm doing this because I *love* you."

"This is fucking bullshit," I said. My mom went silent and just stared at me, her expression pure disbelief. Finally, she said, "What did you say?"

"Nothing," I said.

She slapped her hands together as if she was trying to snap me out of some trance. "It's like...It's like I don't know you," she said. "Just, just...Go to your room."

"I don't have a room," I said. I didn't even know where I was sleeping.

"Then find one," she said. "Plan on staying there for the rest of the evening."

I walked upstairs, passing the room where Aunt Beth and Evie were talking, the door open. Evie was at the edge of a bed, while her mom leaned against the dresser. If they were having a fight, I couldn't tell who was winning.

I moved on until I found a small room with a single bed on one side and a dresser on the other. I lay down on the bed. A window faced onto the water, although I couldn't see the ocean from my spot. All I could see were clouds and patches of sky peeking through, growing darker as night drew near.

⌒

The next morning, everyone was in the kitchen, drinking coffee, dressed and ready to go. Everyone except Evie. My mother came over and wrapped her arms around me, which was a complete surprise. "You okay?" she said. I nodded. "You're getting too big," she added, squeezing me tightly.

I felt this inexplicable sadness bubbling up from the pit of my stomach and I pushed myself away, saying, "Where's Evie?"

My mom didn't say a word.

"On the beach," Aunt Beth said.

I walked out on the porch, looking out toward the water, as rough as it had been the day before. Evie was nowhere in sight. "Down here, Sport," a voice said from beneath me.

Evie was under the deck, in jean shorts and a tee shirt, sitting between these tall wooden stanchions that held up the whole deck. "Your mom pissed off?" Evie said, as I came down the stairs.

"Very," I said. "Yours?"

"My mom doesn't get pissed," she said. "She gets sad. It's way worse."

I looked down the beach, the tide so high half the shore was gone. There was no one on the beach except for a few morning walkers and fishermen surf casting, sending their long lines as far as they could over the waves. Evie said, "You know why they fish in the morning?"

I shook my head. I figured it was because there were fewer people around, splashing in the water, scaring off the fish. "It's called a 'change of light' time," she said. "For some reason the fish eat more now."

"Why?"

"I don't know," she said. "It's like the light is some kind of lunch bell for them. A signal." She paused. "My dad told me."

She laughed and the distance between our ages suddenly seemed gone. She said, "You ready to swim?"

I looked at what she was wearing, and then at my own tee shirt and shorts. I knew our moms would be angry. I also knew she wasn't kidding. "Yep," I said.

We sprang up from the sand, running full tilt toward the water, side by side. Evie stripped off her shirt, throwing it to the sand. She wasn't wearing anything underneath, and her breasts glowed white in the sun and surf. I followed, pushing my way against the tide, diving when she did, under the first wave, consumed by the silence of the water, swimming forward, and then coming up again when I knew I'd reached the other side. There was Evie next to me. "That's how it's done!" she shouted. I looked back and I could see our moms staring out at us, raising their hands in disbelief. I cried out, a long howl of triumph, as if I'd finally made it to some kind of finish line.

We got Evie to campus by lunchtime and unpacked the car. The whole place was teeming with parents and students, people carrying boxes and suitcases, unloading trucks and vans. I felt younger than I had the whole trip. By early afternoon we were done, ready to leave.

Aunt Beth and Evie cried loudly, wrapped in each other's arms. It surprised me to see how close they were, even after everything that had happened. Then Evie wrapped her arms around me and kissed my head. "No more driving without a license," she whispered.

"Got it," I said. I hadn't wanted to be on this trip at all, and now I felt sad to see her go.

"Nice and gentle," she said.

"Right," I said.

⟶

We were back in the car that afternoon, headed up 95. It was a more direct route than the one we'd taken down, the road wide and straight and dull, packed with cars and trucks moving quickly north. We'd drive straight through, stopping once, and be home by tomorrow. "I'm sure Dad misses us," my mom said from the front seat.

The back seat of the car felt vast and empty. We drove for long stretches, stopping for dinner at a roadside diner and then in Maryland at a motel. Aunt Beth and my mom took one room and no one argued when I insisted on my own. Maybe they wanted time alone together, maybe they thought I needed space. Maybe they were just sick of me. I didn't know. There were two double beds inside and I couldn't decide which one to sleep in. I settled on the one further away from the window, closer to the door, as if I might need to make a quick escape. I stretched out, turning on the television, but couldn't find anything to watch. The comforter felt like sandpaper against my skin, so I threw it to the ground and lay on the blanket beneath. I opened *The Martian Chronicles* again, trying to get into it, but kept reading the same line over and over again. *"One minute it was Ohio winter…"* Finally, I put the book down and looked around the room. There was nothing much in it besides the beds, a worn armchair, and a dresser with a television on top. On the walls were two photos of a forest, like fake windows out onto the world. In the next room, I could hear my mom and Aunt Beth, their voices low murmurs, like listening to a conversation underwater.

I started opening drawers. I lifted pillows off the beds, pushing the mattresses from the box springs. I looked behind the paintings, on the undersides of drawers. I flipped cushions on the chair, flipped through pages of the Bible, blocks of words a blur to me. I got down on all fours in the closet, searching the corners, and then looked up on the shelves, trying to find something, anything, that might have been left behind.

nueve

THE DAY THE ELEVATOR men went on strike, tenants swarmed into my parents' apartment for an emergency building association meeting, eager for answers and free Chinese food. "How am I supposed to get to work every morning?!" a woman cried as she piled lo mein on a paper plate. A man spearing a dumpling with a chopstick shouted, "My dog needs to be walked twice a day. I live on the seventeenth floor!" Everyone was worried about something, whether it was getting to doctors' appointments or the supermarket or making plans for the Fourth of July, which was a little over a week away.

My dad sat in a folding chair, nodding and taking notes, his dress shirt soaked with sweat stains under his arms. He was president of the building association, in charge of communication between the management company and the tenants, which basically meant delivering a monthly list of complaints about issues like poor water pressure or the lack of storage in the basement. "I'm having a party," Mrs. Hartstone said to everyone in the room. She was this white-haired lady who lived below us on the eighth floor. For years, she had complained that her chandelier danced when my friends and I ran around our apartment. "How am I going to get deliveries? You don't expect my guests to walk up eight floors?"

My dad dabbed his forehead with a wad of napkins from the China Dragon. We were deep in the first summer heat wave, the temperature stalled around one hundred degrees during the day and ninety at night. I gathered a couple of egg rolls and retreated to my room. An hour later, I heard the front door of our apartment opening and closing over and over again. My dad appeared at my door. "I have a job for you," he said.

I needed a job. My parents had been on me all spring to get some kind of work for the summer, because it was time, they said, that I got some "real world" skills. It wasn't the real world that I was worried about. It was the fact that they had cut off my allowance when school ended, and without a job I either had to mooch off my friends or stay home all the time. To make matters worse, I had dragged my feet and all the decent jobs—stock boy, office guy—were taken. I needed something, although I hadn't thought of running an elevator as an option. "Is there a dental plan?" I asked.

He told me the job would pay six dollars an hour, not bad considering my friends made around five. I had to sort the mail every day, but I didn't have to wear the polyester uniform that made the elevator men look like they worked on *The Love Boat*. The hours were long—eight in the morning until six at night— but as jobs went, it sounded easy. In theory, I never had to leave the building. "How many weeks of vacation do I get?"

"The strike won't last that long."

"What about child labor?" I was fifteen, after all.

My dad smirked. "You start tomorrow. Bright and early."

I had never given elevators much thought prior to that summer. For most of my life we had lived on 108th Street in a building where the elevator was automatic and thoroughly forgettable, a large metal coffin with a porthole window through which you could watch floors rush by in flashes. Its only remarkable quality was its unpredictability, sometimes stopping on random floors or breaking down, trapping those inside. I could often hear riders ringing the alarm for help all the way in my bedroom, but like most people in the building, I assumed someone else would do something about it.

The summer before I turned ten years old, we moved to the Leonard, an apartment building on West End Avenue, in a better part of the neighborhood. The Leonard was much grander than our old place, dressed up with a wide, gilded canopy with the name of the building scripted across the front. The lobby was equally impressive, with marble floors, leather couches, and indoor trees. Still, the elevator was the centerpiece. A soft, leather-cushioned bench folded down at the back. Air-conditioning kept the elevator a comfortable temperature in all seasons. It wasn't particularly large, but no one ever got trapped inside, because it was one of those manually driven, gated boxes, which meant the driver could always open the door to get out. The men who drove the elevator were gracious and kind, mostly Dominican and Puerto Rican guys who spent their time delivering people to the lobby and their floor, carrying groceries, and polishing the wood and brass until you could see your own reflection.

All different kinds of people lived in the Leonard, although the tenants were divided into two groups: renters and owners.

The ones who owned were people who had moved to the Leonard in the last few years, paying tons of money when the neighborhood became chic and management started selling off apartments. The renters were people like my parents who had been there longer and were happy not to own. I didn't think about the difference much, but I had heard my mother once complain that the non-renters walked around the building like "they owned the place," to which my father said, "They do."

My dad offered to let me practice running the elevator before I started working, but I figured years of watching the elevator men was all the training I needed. The next morning, I stumbled onto the elevator a little after eight, still half asleep, wearing baggy shorts, a white tee shirt, and flip-flops. The call panel was lit up, a constellation of lights from nearly every floor. I shut the door and closed the gate, ready to get to it, figuring I just had to find my rhythm and it would be okay. The only control, after all, was a short, stubby black lever, about the size of a suitcase handle, which slid along a channel in the panel. To go up, you pushed it to the right. To go down, you pulled it to the left. How hard could it be?

I found out. The control was much more sensitive than I had imagined, and I overshot nearly all of my landings. I often had to jog the lever back and forth, jerking riders up and down to get close to the floor. Most people were encouraging and thanked me for helping, although I could see a lot of worried and queasy looks in the reflection of the brass call panel. A few times I heard people saying they hoped the strike would end soon, although I wasn't sure if they were concerned about the welfare of the elevator men or their own safety with me driving.

Not everyone was so supportive. Around eight thirty, with

the elevator packed, I stopped to pick up Mrs. Hartstone on the eighth floor. "Please proceed to the lobby," she said, squeezing into the crowd.

"What about the people on other floors?" I said. There were at least another half-dozen floors lit up on the call panel.

"This elevator is not a clown car," she said. "I don't think we need to break a world record today."

I was about to protest, when a voice behind me said, "It's okay, Marty." It was Mr. Sexton, one of my parents' closest friends in the building and my relief at the end of the workday. He was pressed against the wall, hugging his briefcase up around his chin. I headed to the lobby but still couldn't nail the landing, leaving a good half-foot climb. "Watch your step, please," I said, repeating what the elevator men said every day as a courtesy, although in this case it was a real warning.

I figured the flood of people would slow down after rush hour, but a whole new wave started around ten o'clock. Nannies with strollers headed for the park. Cleaning ladies, hoisting baskets of dirty clothes on their hips, riding to the laundry room in the basement. An endless stream of deliveries and dog walkers. I had no idea so many people worked for tenants in the building. You could pay someone to do just about anything. My parents didn't have anyone like that working for them. I wondered why. They never seemed particularly happy to do chores, and I would have gladly let someone else clean my room or wash dishes.

Then there were the people who didn't seem to have any jobs or responsibilities. Joggers heading for a run in the park in the middle of the day. The midday rush of people leaving for lunch and then returning an hour or two later. A few people who just went in and out of the building all day, running errands, which made me wonder why they couldn't just plan one big trip for everything. And there was this one old woman, about a hundred years old, who told whoever was on the elevator with her that she was going out for her "constitutional," only to sit down on the lobby couch and fall asleep.

Sue Foreman got on around noon. Sue was a senior at my school, the kind of girl I imagined had no idea I existed. As we drove down, the buzzer rang for five, but I ignored it, instead staring at Sue in the reflection of the brass panel. She was wearing an oversized bright yellow tee shirt from Busy Bee Day Camp. It was so long you couldn't see her shorts, just long, tanned legs stretching down to spotless white sneakers. "You go to my school," she said, catching me mid-stare. I nodded. "Is this your summer job?"

"Until the strike is over," I said.

"I can't believe they're striking. What do they expect us to do, take the stairs?"

I shrugged. I hadn't given the actual strike much thought. Sue's eyes searched the elevator, taking it all in, as if she had never been in one before. "I couldn't do it," she added. "Stand all day."

I didn't know what to say, but I remembered my dad once telling me the best way to deal with women was to agree with them. "It sucks," I said.

She smiled and my heart swelled. We were having a moment. My mind raced into our future. Hanging out at lunch. Hand in hand through the school hallways. Movies on the weekend. A vast introduction to sex, maybe right there on the elevator. Despite heading down toward the lobby, my body seemed to rise up, buoyed with possibility. My thoughts swirled, so much so that I missed the fact that we had passed the lobby, still moving at full speed. The elevator's automatic shutdown mechanism kicked in, the engine screeching and jerking us to a stop. Sue braced herself on the wall. I hung on to the control lever, nearly buckling at the knees.

"Are you okay?" I said, turning to Sue.

"Yeah," she said, her voice shaking. I drove the elevator back to the first floor, missing the landing by a foot. Sue jumped out, never looking back. I spent the next few hours replaying the event in my head, deciding it might have been better had we both been killed right there.

Around two, just as the lunchtime traffic slowed, the mail arrived. I sat in the lobby and made my way through a large canvas bag, sometimes lingering over a bill or letter, trying to see what was inside by holding it to the light. I flipped through magazines and catalogues on everything from stuffed birds to sportswear to antique weapons.

The moment I finished the mail, people started coming home from work. I didn't get a moment's break until six o'clock, when Mr. Sexton arrived to work the evening shift. "How's she ride?" he said with a smile.

"Up and down," I said.

———

"How was your first day?" my dad asked as I sat down for dinner.

"I don't think I'll be making it a career."

"Now you know why they're striking," my mother said.

I said, "Why are they striking?"

"Better pension. Better wages," my dad said.

I poked at my plate of leftover Chinese food. "Give them whatever they want. That job is terrible."

———

Later that night I met Max and Dave on the steps of the Natural History Museum. Dave was working at his mom's office, filing papers, stuffing envelopes, and running errands. "If one more person calls me the 'gal Friday' I'm going to stick them in the shredder," he said.

"At least you don't have to deal with customers," Max said. He was working at Steve's Ice Cream, famous for letting you mix in anything you wanted, like crushed Oreos or peanuts. He had brought us a pint of chocolate loaded with gummy bears. The three of us sat on the steps of the museum, smoking a joint Max had stolen from his cousin, while Dave and I made our way through the tub of ice cream.

"Don't you want any?" I asked Max.

"If I never eat ice cream again it will be a good thing," he said.

"You wouldn't believe what they ask me to do," Dave continued. "This one guy had me take his dog to the groomer. Said the heat was getting to little Coco. I had to sit in this weird office, surrounded by blue-hairs and their shih tzus, while some girl shaved his poodle. When I left, the dog looked like a goat."

Max took a hit of the joint, passed it along, and then said, "Try smelling like Mocha fucking Fudge all day."

Nearby, some kids were skateboarding off the steps, attempting flips and tricks, but they kept falling and then getting up and doing it again. It was depressing to watch. "Any cute girls at the store?" I asked Max.

"Sure. Maybe. I don't know," he said. Dave passed the joint to me and said, "The girl who shaved the dog was kind of sexy."

I took a long drag and exhaled. The smoke hung in the air. "What about you?" Max said. "How's the elevator?"

I had called them the night my dad hired me to run the elevator. They both thought it sounded like the easiest job in the world. "It's okay," I said. "Harder than I thought."

"Yeah, right," Dave said.

One of the skateboarders did a kick flip off a bench, but as he landed, his skateboard cracked, splitting in two, splinters flying everywhere. He picked up one piece, looked at it, and then threw it on the sidewalk in disgust.

Stepping onto the elevator the next morning, I had the strange sensation I had never left. The morning rush started on schedule, people pouring in, smiling, and taking their positions. Many of them turned to read a posting on the back wall, advising tenants to expect power surges because of the heat wave. Below the advisory was a list of ways to conserve energy. Do not leave your air conditioner running when you're not home. Run your dishwasher at night, if you must run it at all. Unplug all appliances not in use. Every day, the newspapers warned of possible blackouts. As far as I was concerned, a blackout would be great. No electricity, no elevator.

Around two o'clock, Carlos walked into the building. He was

a short, stocky Dominican who normally worked the day shift. I had known him ever since we moved to the building, but only on the elevator. Only in his uniform. That afternoon he was wearing shorts and a tee shirt with cutoff sleeves. I didn't recognize him at first.

"*Nueve*," he said, calling me by the number of my floor. "*Que pasa?*"

"Nothing," I said, even though I knew the Spanish word was *nada*. I would have felt stupid saying it, as if I didn't have a right to.

"What are you doing here?"

"Working."

"You? You running the elevator?" He slapped his hands together and laughed.

"What's so funny?" I looked at myself in the lobby mirror—a mop of thick brown hair, a concert tee shirt for the Police I was starting to outgrow, some cutoffs. I didn't look the part. We walked through the lobby, passing the hundred-year-old lady asleep on the couch. "I see Mrs. Keller is taking her walk," he said, smiling.

When we got to the elevator, I didn't know if I should let him drive, but then he stepped to the back and lowered the bench to sit down. "Basement, please." I eased the lever to the left and we glided down. "You know what? I'm glad it's you," he said. "Anybody else, I might be pissed. But you, your family, you're good people." The elevator guys loved my mom because she spoke Spanish with them, and my dad, a lawyer, sometimes did pro bono work for them if they were in a jam. He had only taken the job as building association president because other tenants had pushed him into it, fearing that it might land in the hands of someone like Mrs. Hartstone and that she might make life in the building miserable for the renters.

When we got to the basement, Carlos walked toward the locker room, where the elevator men changed into their uniforms. He probably wasn't supposed to be there, given the strike, but I wasn't going to make a big deal of it. I stepped off the elevator, asking, "You want me to wait?"

"I'll be right back," he said.

There was no air-conditioning down in the basement, just a few fans circulating hot air. I could hear washing machines humming and cleaning ladies talking in Spanish. I turned and saw that I had overshot the landing as usual, leaving a foot-high gap between the top of the elevator and the doorway, and for the first time, I could see the mechanics of the machinery sitting on top of the elevator itself, dimly lit by the light streaming down the air shaft. I had always imagined the inner workings of the elevator as sterile space, as pristine as the inside of a watch, and yet here it was, layered with grime, these large metal wheels and pulleys connected by long, thick threads of wire and steel cable stretching up the air shaft. Thick black grease and dirt covered everything. There was something unexpected, almost frightening about it. It was hard to believe I was looking at anything that was part of the Leonard. Carlos came back moments later carrying some clothes balled under his arm. "Don't know how long I'll be away," he said.

I drove him back to the lobby. My landing was good, as if I actually knew what I was doing. "Look at you," he said, laying his hand on my shoulder. "Maybe you want to take my job?" His expression turned serious. My stomach sank. We were close enough so that I could feel the heat radiating off his body. I didn't know what to say so I turned and opened the door. From behind me, I heard him break into a big laugh. "You should have seen your face!"

"Very funny."

"Relax," he said. "How you like driving the elevator?"

I didn't want to sound too enthusiastic, but I also didn't want to make it sound awful. After all, it was his job. "It's okay," I said.

"Don't let it get in your head. Up. Down. Up. Down. It can mess with you. Just remember: You're like the captain of the ship. The boat don't sail without you."

In the lobby, a large sack of mail leaned against a wall. "Shit," I said.

Carlos laughed again. "Now you sound like one of us, Nueve."

By Friday, the strike was going strong and I was busier than ever. Crowds of people were leaving for the long weekend. They poured out of apartments wielding suitcases, bags of food, and baskets of beach toys. Everyone needed help loading cars. I got a few tips, a couple of crumpled dollars passing discreetly in a handshake as if it were some kind of a drug deal. Even when I got nothing, I smiled and helped out any way I could. By the end of my shift, I was exhausted. I had never needed a weekend so badly.

Returning to work on Monday was as depressing as going back to school any September. Even though it felt as if the whole building had left on vacation that weekend, there was still a morning rush of people headed to work. My driving had improved and people no longer acknowledged my presence, seeming to have accepted me as another fixture in the building like one of the trees in the lobby. The heat didn't let up, the temperature hovering in the high nineties. A new posting was up, announcing management's plan to limit nonessential power in the building, which included restricting use of the laundry room to the mornings and limiting air-conditioning in the lobby and elevator to rush hour. In other words, the only people the restrictions really affected were me and the cleaning ladies.

At noon, I was sitting in front of a fan in the basement when twelve—Sue's floor—rang in, along with fifteen and eight. Before the weekend, I might have ignored the other calls and gone to her floor first, but I was too hot for another round of humiliation. At fifteen, Mrs. Keller, the hundred-year-old woman, stepped on. "Time for my constitutional," she said, as if she might leave the building for once. On twelve, Sue got on. I stared forward, silent, telling myself not to acknowledge her. "Hey," Sue said.

"Yo yo!" I said, like an idiot.

The buzzer rang again. Eight lit up for the second time.

Mrs. Hartstone got on. "What the devil took so long?"

I shrugged.

She turned to Sue. "I'll be expecting you and your parents at the party, dear." Sue smiled. "Clara," Mrs. Hartstone said to Mrs. Keller, "will you be able to make it?"

"Wouldn't miss it, Eleanor."

We rode in silence to the lobby. I nailed my landing.

As everyone walked out, Mrs. Hartstone turned and said, "A moment, please."

"Me?"

"Is there anyone else here, young man?"

I looked back inside the empty elevator.

"I have an important question for you," she said.

What had I done wrong? I wondered if she knew I had borrowed her fashion magazines to jerk off. "As you may know, I'm having an event tomorrow evening for the Fourth," she said. I nodded, although I only knew because she had her party every year and never invited my family. Ever since my dad became building association president, she had stopped even saying hello to him in the elevator. I couldn't imagine she was having a change of heart.

"I understand no one is scheduled to work the elevator that evening," she said, which was true. My dad and Mr. Sexton had been taking turns, each working every other evening, but no one was working after I finished the day shift on the Fourth. Tenants were supposed to fend for themselves. "As it is too late to secure help, I would like to pay you to work that evening, from six o'clock until it is finished. In the past, that has been around midnight."

If I took the job, I would be working from eight in the morning until twelve at night. A full-day shift. She couldn't pay me enough.

"I will pay you twenty-five dollars an hour for your services," she said. "That's one hundred and fifty dollars, if all goes as planned."

One hundred and fifty dollars. Half a week's paycheck for six hours. School was only eight weeks away. Even if the strike ended the day after the Fourth, I could probably get through the summer with that and what I had already earned. "Okay," I said.

"There is one condition," she added. "The party is no small

occasion. It's a business event. It is crucial to maintain an air of propriety and professionalism."

I nodded, although I had no idea what she was talking about.

"This," she said, pointing at my tee shirt and shorts, "will not do. I understand the dress code has been relaxed. Very well. However, for the party I would like you to wear the proper attire of the elevator personnel."

The uniform. She wanted me to wear the *Love Boat* suit. I thought about arguing for more money, but she had a fierce look in her eye.

"No hat," I said.

"What?"

"I won't wear the hat."

She rolled her eyes. "Fine. No hat." Then she looked around the elevator, sizing the place up. "But we'll tidy this up, yes?"

I had seen the polish and cleaning materials in the basement, but thought about playing dumb. Mrs. Hartstone's eyes narrowed, a signal she was done negotiating.

"Deal," I said.

The day of the Fourth, a quiet settled around the building. There was no mail. The only deliveries were for Mrs. Hartstone—trays of food, flowers and liquor, enough ice to make the whole city a drink. A few people came and went, but the flow of traffic was slow, with stretches of time when I wasn't sure what to do with myself. If the frenetic pace of working the elevator wore me down, the boredom of standing around doing nothing was worse. It made no sense, like wishing for homework on a snow day.

About a half hour before the party, I went to the basement to get the cleaning stuff and grab a uniform from the locker room. Twenty-five dollars an hour, I kept telling myself.

I was shocked to find Carlos stretched out on the bench by the lockers. I hadn't seen him come in. Then again, I had no clue how long he had been there.

"*Hola*, Nueve!" he shouted. "*Que pasa?*"

"What are you doing here?" I asked.

He rocked back and forth, his eyes half open. An empty bottle sat next to him. "Where else am I going to go?" he said. "This is my home." He stood, raising his arms as if in celebration, and then sat back down, steadying himself on the bench. "I'm home."

I walked over to the rack of uniforms and pulled off one that looked about my size. "Now you going to wear the uniform too?" Carlos said. "You do want my job."

"I have to work a party," I said, trying on the jacket.

Carlos's eyes widened. "Oh, I get it."

"What?" I said. A wave of guilt washed over me.

"Hartstone," he said, nodding. "She called around yesterday, trying to get one of the regular guys to work. No one took it. My wife told me I'd better take it. I didn't and…" He slapped the bench. "Anyway, I wondered who it was."

"It's only tonight," I said.

"We all got to do what we got to do."

"It's just tonight," I repeated.

"It's okay, Marty," he said, using my real name, something he never did.

I felt a little sick to my stomach, like I had been on solid ground and just stepped onto a boat. "It's none of your business anyway," I added, although I regretted the words the moment I said them.

Carlos looked confused, as if he didn't recognize me. "You're right." He stood, rocking on his heels. "I gotta go anyway. I got this thing…" His voice trailed off. He walked out the door and I followed. Inside the elevator, he leaned against the back wall and said, "Lobby, please."

———

I got to the elevator around six, and for the next two hours I delivered carloads of people to the party. Dave and Max stopped by, headed to some Fourth of July bash that Dave's sister Libby knew about. I really wanted to go, but the buzzer didn't stop ringing. Sue got on around eight with her parents, laughing when she saw me in uniform. The hundred-year-old lady smiled, but didn't seem to recognize me. Most people simply ignored me, acting as if I wasn't even there. "I hope she doesn't make one of her endless toasts," one woman said to another woman as they rode up. I turned and smiled, but they turned away, not interested in sharing a moment with the elevator man.

Around nine thirty, the eighth floor rang. When I opened the door, Sue Foreman was standing in the hallway, her arms around some guy who looked about ten years older than her. "Have you seen my mom and dad?"

I shook my head.

"Good," she said, walking into the elevator.

"Maybe they walked," the guy said.

"My parents don't take the stairs," she said.

I tried not to look at them as I drove to her floor, but I couldn't stop myself. In the clear reflection of the panel, I watched Sue lean into the guy's body, as if she were melting into him. I had an urge to lean full tilt on the control and just pass their floor, zooming up toward the penthouse and then blasting through the roof.

I let them off on twelve and drove to the lobby.

Outside, night had settled in, the city finally starting to cool. I heard the first fireworks, a slow rumble in the distance. The elevator buzzer rang, but I ignored it. I needed some air, some time to breathe. Soon, the sound of fireworks was everywhere, deep thunder all around me, although I couldn't see anything except flashes of light reflecting off the buildings and clouds. The buzzer rang again, four short bursts, the sound of it eating away at me. In the past, I'd been able to ignore just about anything—homework, teachers, my parents—but this, the stupid buzzer, I couldn't shut out.

I walked in and drove up to eight. There was Mrs. Keller, the hundred-year-old woman, waiting, one hand braced against a wall for support. "I would walk, but my legs aren't what they used to be," she said, stepping on the elevator.

"Don't you want to watch the fireworks with everyone at the party?"

"Not my cup of tea. A lot of noise, if you ask me."

I couldn't argue with her. When I was younger, I hated fireworks. They made me feel as if the world were coming apart. As we rode to her floor, I could hear a series of explosions, drums rumbling in the distance. We passed Sue's floor and I tried not to think about what she was doing. Then, all of a sudden, the lights flickered and the elevator started to slow down. The air-conditioning sputtered and then went dead. Soon, we rolled to a stop mid-floor and the lights went out. I tried to jog the control back and forth to get us moving, but nothing happened. The darkness was complete, the kind of pitch black you rarely got in the city. It was as if we had been swallowed whole by the building.

"Oh dear," Mrs. Keller said.

"Fuck me," I said, and then immediately added, "Sorry."

"What's happening?"

"I think it's a blackout."

I felt my way along the panel in the dark and pushed the alarm button, but no one was going to hear it over the fireworks.

"I suppose this is my punishment for leaving the party early," Mrs. Keller said.

"We'll be going any second," I said, although I knew that wasn't true. The lights often flickered these days, but they hadn't gone completely dead like this before. This was something serious. I could have opened the gate and climbed out myself, maybe even gotten help, but there was no way she could get out of there. *Unbelievable*, I thought. A blackout on the Fourth of July and I was trapped in the elevator with the hundred-year-old lady. I could hear her breathing behind me.

"Would you like to sit down?" I asked.

"Yes, that might be a good idea," she said. I reached out and found her hand, cold and frail, like paper between my fingers. I lowered the fold-down bench and helped her sit. "That's better," she said. "What's your name, dear? I don't think we've met before."

"Marty," I said, and then added, inexplicably, "Martin."

"Martin," she said. "What a lovely name. I'm Clara Keller. Do you know, Martin, I've lived here for forty years and this is the first time I have ever been stuck in the elevator." I nodded, although she couldn't have seen me do so in the dark. "Please sit down next to me. You shouldn't have to stand." I sat on the bench and she moved closer to me, resting her hand on my arm. "That's better," she said. We sat quietly for a while, listening to the fireworks. I imagined my friends hanging out at their party, maybe drinking beers and talking to girls. I thought about my parents, who had gone over to some friends' house on the East Side, their apartment high enough to see the fireworks and the whole city spread out around them. I thought of Sue Foreman humping that guy and how they probably didn't even know there was a blackout. The pace of the fireworks picked up, the slow drone becoming a rapid series of explosions.

"I think it's the finale," I said. "We can get some help after that."

We listened to the finale, the individual explosions becoming one long roll of thunder that shook the walls of the elevator. I had been holding my breath the whole time. "I guess it's over," I said.

Mrs. Keller didn't say a word.

"Mrs. Keller?" I said.

No answer. I reached out and felt her hand. Ice cold. Dead, I worried. *Terrific*, I thought. I'm stuck on the elevator in the middle of a blackout with a dead woman next to me.

Soon, though, I could hear the familiar snore I had heard so often in the lobby. Her head drifted against my shoulder and I sat there, perfectly upright, listening to the sound of stairwell doors opening and closing as people took the only available way in and out of the building.

The power came on about a half hour later. I woke Mrs. Keller and drove her to fifteen. "Thank you for keeping me company, young man," she said, and at that moment I felt that no matter what happened I had at least done something right that night. I had stayed at my post. I had stood at the helm like the captain prepared to go down with his ship. "I want to give you this," she said, taking out her wallet.

"That's really not necessary," I said, although I wasn't going to stop her.

"I insist," she said. She took my hand and I could feel a coin pass from her palm to mine. A quarter.

"Watch your step, please," I said.

I was all set to drive home, ready to put the entire evening behind me, when the buzzer rang. Eight.

"Oh, good," Mrs. Hartstone said, as I opened the elevator. There were only a few people still milling about her apartment. "All the guests took the stairs after the fireworks, and half the staff cleared out, as if the blackout excused them from their jobs. The caterers will get an earful tomorrow." She took me by the arm and led me to the living room. "In the meantime, I need you here. The sink in the kitchen is clogged. There are dishes everywhere. And someone was ill in the master bathroom. People have no sense of decency." She handed me a garbage bag, half full of trash. "There are people cleaning in the kitchen, but I want you to start here, picking up all the trash."

I looked around the living room at all the garbage—balled-up napkins, plates of untouched food, and half-drunk glasses of champagne—scattered everywhere. I said, "Are you serious?"

Mrs. Hartstone cocked her head to the side. "Young man, I hired you until midnight, correct?" She didn't wait for my response, but walked out of the room, already shouting at someone in the kitchen.

I wandered around the living room for a while, not picking up anything, just looking at the mess. Plates under the tables, cups on top of bookshelves, napkins wedged between the cushions of the couch. Someone had actually put a champagne glass in the fish tank, the thing floating on the surface of the water like a dead fish. I found a few full glasses of champagne and drank them down quickly, but the quick buzz didn't relax me. Finally, I got to work. I filled the garbage bag until it was packed and tied it off. Good enough, I figured. It was nearly eleven. I could tell Mrs. Hartstone to pay me for the hours I worked. I was done.

I walked into the master bedroom, where I could hear her barking out instructions at the poor fool who had to clean up somebody's puke. I could already smell the fetid odor coming from the bathroom. "Please try not to get any on the rug," she shouted.

Through the bathroom door, I saw her standing next to Carlos. She was holding her hand over her nose and mouth, shielding the smell. Carlos stood there, mop in hand, not flinching. Our eyes met for a moment. His expression wasn't upset or disturbed, merely resigned, a man prepared to do what he was paid to do. I looked away, not out of shame but out of respect. He hadn't crossed the picket line. He was just doing a job, earning a living.

"Yes?" Mrs. Hartstone said, walking toward me. "What is it?"

I looked up again and Carlos had started mopping, not looking back at me.

"I…" I said. The putrid odor from the bathroom overwhelmed my senses, but I took a breath and said, "I need more bags."

Mrs. Hartstone led me to the kitchen and gave me several more garbage bags. I cleared the rest of the living room and then her library and the bedrooms. On the terrace, I found plates of cake with cigarette stubs pressed in and dozens of glasses perched along the railing. When I finished, I stayed on the terrace for a moment, taking in the view over the park. In the distance, I could see gray smoke hovering above the park, remnants of the fireworks, a thick cloud that would not pass soon.

The moment the clock hit midnight, I went home.

The strike ended the next week.

"Who won?" I asked my dad when I found out.

"Everybody had to give in a little," he said. "The union got their wage increase but not the bump in their pension plan."

"It's all about money," my mom said.

Mrs. Hartstone paid me, but instead of slipping the check under my parents' door or handing it to me, she sent it in the mail. I didn't get it for another week.

Carlos was back at work the next day when I got on the elevator. I was on my way to Steve's Ice Cream because Max had told me there might be a shift opening. I didn't need the money, but just sitting around, doing nothing, seemed like a waste.

"Hey, Nueve."

He shook my hand, as if nothing had happened on the Fourth.

I leaned against the back wall of the elevator, a passenger again. At first, I felt a little lost, unsure of what to do with myself, but looking around, I realized I knew every corner of this elevator.

"*Que pasa?*" he said.

We sailed toward the first floor, the sound of the elevator descending like the familiar and comforting whir of the ocean. "*Nada,*" I said.

ghosts

I was sitting in my grandmother's hospital room when she asked me if I could see my grandfather.

"Where?" I said.

"There." She pointed at the empty chair at the foot of the bed. No one else was in the room. My mom and dad were out getting coffee. I shook my head. She raised her eyebrows at me and then looked away, as if not seeing him was my fault.

My grandfather had died years ago, when I was three years old. I really only knew him through stories and photos. If he had been sitting right next to me I wasn't sure I would have recognized him. My grandma had fallen a few days back, walking from her hair salon on Orchard Street to her apartment on Stanton Street on the Lower East Side. A small stroke. Since then, she had started seeing her dead husband. The doctors told us that stroke victims sometimes hallucinated and it often passed, but we had to wait and see. The whole thing creeped me out.

My grandmother turned to me again and said, "He says you need a haircut."

Hair was her obsession. She was always complaining that my

hair was too long, even when it had just been cut. Every time she saw my dad she told him he needed a shave. "I'm going to get it cut next week," I said. Truth was, I was trying to grow it out, maybe long enough to put it in a ponytail, but my hair wasn't complying. It seemed to only get bushier, like a fern in need of pruning.

My grandma stared at the empty chair. I looked at it as well. The blinds by the window swayed from heat coming through the vents. "He wants to know if you have a girlfriend."

I shifted in my seat. This was complicated. I sort of did and sort of didn't, but it wasn't exactly the kind of thing I wanted to explain to my grandma or my dead grandfather. "Sure," I said.

My grandmother smiled, and then reached over to get a piece of candy out of her purse. She offered me one, but I shook my head. Butterscotch. I couldn't stomach the stuff. "Take!" she insisted.

"I'm okay," I said.

Grandma curled her lips in disgust. Then she said, "So what's her name?"

"Who?"

"Who do you think? Your girlfriend."

"Oh," I said. "Hannah."

She worked the candy wrapper between her fingers and popped the shiny yellow ball into her mouth. "Have you had sex?"

I was silent. I was sixteen. The closest I had come to sex was what I had seen on late-night cable after my parents went to sleep.

"Just don't make a baby," she said. "You're a young man."

We sat quietly in the room, not talking, and I thought she'd fallen asleep, until I heard her laugh, a low, creepy cackle.

"What?" I said.

"It's nothing," she said, still chuckling to herself. She sloshed the butterscotch in her mouth, the candy clicking off her teeth.

"Seriously," I said, sitting up in my seat.

"Your grandfather just knows how to make me laugh."

I looked at the chair. "What'd he say?"

"He wants to know whose hair is longer, yours or your girl-friend's?"

"Ha ha," I said to the empty chair.

My alleged girlfriend, Hannah Murton, went to Hastings, a private girls' school on the East Side. I didn't know she existed until two weeks earlier when I was over at Dave's house and his sister Libby asked if she could use my name for her friend.

"My name?"

"One of her ex-boyfriends keeps asking to get back together. She finally told him she was dating someone else." I still didn't follow. Libby looked at me as if I were dense. "She isn't seeing anyone. Not seriously at least. She just *told* him she was. Anyway, he said he'd stop asking when she told him who she was dating." She paused for a second, before adding, "She knows just about everyone, so we figured it would be better if it was someone no one knew."

"That would be you," Dave said, patting me on the shoulder, but I barely noticed. I was still doing the math on this girlfriend thing in my head. I said, "Wait, so we're dating?" I had never had a girlfriend.

Libby turned to me, her expression exasperated. "You've been going out for two weeks."

Dave smiled. "Way to go, Marty." Then he leaned in and whispered in my ear, "Hannah is super hot."

Libby hit Dave in the arm. "She's a junior. You guys are serious."

"That's a given," I boasted, and Libby rolled her eyes.

———

I pretty much forgot about all of it until Dave stopped me in the hall at school a few days later and said, "I need your track jacket."

I'd gotten the jacket for being on the track team, although it wasn't like I was a star. Anyone willing to pay for it got one. The jacket was big, sitting on me oddly, making my head look small, but I didn't care. It made me feel important. It was warm enough to wear all winter, which was suddenly important now that a December freeze had descended on the city. I asked Dave why he needed it.

"The guy still doesn't believe Hannah," Dave said. "He won't leave her alone. Libby figures the track jacket should scare him off. She used to wear his."

"So she gets my jacket. What do I get?"

Dave put his arm around me, leading me down the hall. The bell rang. Students buzzed around us, heading off to class. "You get a seriously hot fake girlfriend and, according to Libby, quite a little reputation building over at Hastings. She's like the most popular girl in the whole high school. Everyone wants to know who this Marty kid is who is dating Hannah Murton."

I was sold. We walked to my locker and I handed him my track jacket. "I want it back," I said.

"Girls like Hannah run through guys in no time," Dave said, tucking it under his arm. "You'll probably get it back by the end of the week."

———

That weekend, Dave's parents were going away. He invited Max and me to his house on Saturday night. His sister was also having a few people over. "You can meet your girlfriend," he joked.

I had no reason to be nervous—we weren't *really* going out— but I paced around my room for an hour before leaving for Dave's house, uncertain about everything: my hair, my clothes, my shoes, how I smelled. Part of me believed that if I could pretend to go out with a girl like Hannah Murton, then there was some chance in the real world.

I ended up getting to his house a half hour late. The girls were nowhere in sight. As I passed Libby's bedroom, I heard the chatter of voices and the smell of clove cigarettes coming from inside. My friends and I stayed in the living room, flipping through bad Saturday-night television and drinking wine coolers. Right before it was time to leave, I stumbled to the bathroom, seriously buzzed on Bartles & Jaymes.

That's when I saw my jacket walking down the hall.

"Hannah!" I called out. "There's my girl!"

She turned around and looked at me. She had wavy brown hair like a shampoo commercial, doe eyes, and the kind of smile that made you believe she was glad to see you even though she didn't know you, which, in my case, was the truth. I stood still, just staring. She looked confused for a moment and then put it all together with a dazzling smile. "Are you Marty?"

"Righto!" I said in a drunken slur.

"Hey there, boyfriend," she said, reaching to take my hand, lacing her fingers in mine. The touch of her hand was cool, as if she'd just come in from the outside. She laughed to herself and said, "Thanks for the jacket."

"Did it work?"

"I don't know yet," she said, dropping my hand. "I hope so." She started to walk away, but then turned and said, "I owe you one." Then she bent forward and kissed me on the cheek. I could smell her breath, a potent mix of fruity alcohol and cigarettes. She smiled again, letting her hair drift in front of her face, and then slipped away, disappearing behind a cloud of smoke back into Libby's room. She was gone so fast I wondered for a second if it had actually happened. When I got back to the living room, Dave and Max knew something was up. Dave said, "What's so funny?"

"What're you talking about?" I said.

"You're smiling like a fool," Max said.

I put on my best straight face. "No I'm not," I said.

On Sunday my parents and I visited my grandmother in the hospital. The nurses told us they had moved her to another room. She now had a roommate, an older Spanish woman named Mrs. Gonzalez who didn't speak a word of English. This was not good. My grandmother was not exactly the most open-minded person in the world. When we got there, a crowd of people were gathered around Mrs. Gonzalez's bed, talking loudly. My grandma was sitting up in her bed, her purse tucked under her arm.

"It's like the Puerto Rican Day Parade in here!" she called out.

"Mom, please," my dad whispered.

She waved him off, before adding, "You can't hear yourself think!" She looked at the empty chair, which had been dragged closer to her bed. "Charlie thinks I should have a private room."

My dad sighed, not looking at the chair. "There's nothing available," he said.

Grandma looked unconvinced, staring down my father. "You could have at least shaved."

We sat for a while, trying to talk over the noise around us. My grandmother dug through her purse, nervously popping two butterscotch. "You want?" she asked.

I shook my head, but my grandma insisted I take a few for later.

Finally, the doctor came in, a young guy who looked no older than some of the seniors at my school. He had shaggy blond hair down to his shoulders and big sideburns cut squarely at the bottom. Basically the rock star look I was going for but couldn't get. "How are we feeling today, Mrs. Kelso?"

"I feel," she said, "like going home."

Dr. Rock Star smiled, looking over her chart. "I think we need to keep you here a little longer." My parents and the doctor walked outside.

"How can I trust a doctor with hair like that?" my grandmother said.

I wasn't sure how to answer that question.

"What about you? I thought you were going to get a haircut?"

"It's in the works," I said.

Mrs. Gonzalez's family left and she flipped on the television on her side of the room. A Spanish soap opera. On the screen, a man and a woman were slow dancing in a club, their arms wrapped around each other, but the woman was staring at some other guy. Finally, my grandmother said, "Grandpa and I want to know when we get to meet this young lady."

"Who?"

"Your girlfriend."

Evidently a stroke could make her see dead people, but it hadn't put a dent in her memory. I said, "Why?"

She raised her eyebrows at me. "When you're eighty-eight years old you've earned the right not to have to explain everything."

"I'll see what I can do," I said.

On the subway home, my dad told us the doctors didn't know if the hallucinations would pass. Sometimes they did. Sometimes they didn't. "They're going to adjust her medication," he told us.

"She seems pretty normal to me," I said.

"I buried my father a long time ago," my dad said, staring out the train window. We were on an express, the local stations passing by in quick flashes. "I'm not prepared for him to be around again."

My dad leaned forward, his head in his hands. He had always been the steady one in the family, the calm force around us. Still, I could see the wear this was having on him. His whole body was bent over and tired, as if he had just run a marathon and had another one ahead of him. I turned to my mom, who was looking me over suspiciously. "Hey," she said, "where's your jacket?"

I was wearing my gray Members Only jacket, hardly winter wear, but it was the only thing I could find that fit me now that Hannah had my track jacket. I shifted in my seat, crossing my arms for warmth. "At school," I said.

———

The weather warmed at the beginning of the week, but a heavy snow was predicted that weekend. On Wednesday night, my mom and I were sitting in the kitchen when the phone rang. She picked it up and said it was for me. "It's a *girl*," she added, raising her eyebrows.

I rolled my eyes and stretched the cord into the living room, as far as it would go.

"Hello?" I said, almost in a whisper.

"Hey," the voice said. I recognized it immediately.

I started to say "Hey" but tried to change it to "Yo" mid-word and it came out as "Heh-wo!" like I was some kind of disturbed person.

"Marty?" Hannah said. "Is that you?"

"Yeah," I said. "What's up?"

"I have a favor to ask," she said.

"No problem," I said.

"You haven't even heard what I want," she said.

A friend of hers was having a party on Saturday. She wanted me to come. "Okay," I said.

"My ex is going to be there. Maybe if he sees me with you he'll back off."

I knew I was probably getting used, but the idea of waltzing into a party with Hannah on my arm sounded worth it. "Want me to pick you up?" I asked.

She suggested we meet on the corner of Sixty-Fifth and Park Avenue at nine o'clock. She gave me her number in case anything changed. "Thanks, Marty," she added. "I owe you one."

This was the second time she had said that to me. It occurred to me that Hannah might be the kind of person who said that kind of thing all the time, but I didn't care. "See you Saturday night," I said.

Before going to meet Hannah on Saturday, I went with my parents to visit my grandmother in the hospital. My dad had spoken to the doctor, who said that she was doing well. Mrs. Gonzalez had gone home, so she no longer had a roommate.

When we got there, things had indeed changed. Grandma was up, sitting at the end of the bed, facing the empty chair. What's more, she was no longer wearing her hospital gown, but had changed into a long blue dress with large gold flowers blooming across the front. She'd had her hair done, tied up on top of her head in a twist and glistening with this powdery blue frost. Her face was covered in thick makeup, her lips a deep red, almost brown. I barely recognized her. But the biggest surprise was her expression. She was beaming.

"We were just talking about you," she said as we walked in. There was no one else in the room. We all looked at the empty chair.

"Mom," my dad said. "Why are you all dressed up?"

"Can't a woman put on something nice?"

"Of course you can," my mother said, gently slapping my father on the arm. "You look lovely."

"I didn't feel like being in that drab gown any longer. At least not *today*."

"What's today?" I said.

"Jeffrey," my grandma said, smiling at my dad.

I looked at my dad, who nodded, putting something together in his head. "Today," he said, "is my parents' wedding anniversary."

Grandma smiled, setting her hand on the empty chair's armrest. That's when I understood: My grandmother was in love.

The doctor walked in, his amazing hair tied neatly back in a ponytail. "Don't you look lovely, Mrs. Kelso."

"Thank you, doctor," she said, and then looked him over. "You know, if you cut your hair you might actually be handsome."

Dr. Rock Star smirked and nodded. "My mother says the same thing."

"Doctor," my dad said, "may we have a word?"

My parents left the room. It seemed like they were always leaving the room with the doctor. I watched the clock, mindful of the time. I didn't want to be late to meet Hannah. Outside I could see the falling snow, thick flakes drifting by the window. "It's snowing," I said, but my grandmother didn't respond. She continued to stare at the empty chair, smiling and then drawing it closer to her side.

I got to the corner of Sixty-Fifth and Park right at nine o'clock and waited. The storm had picked up, snow falling quickly. In no time my hair was frosted with whiteness. I had worn my Members Only jacket again, and in this ice-cold weather it was definitely not enough. My body began to tremble with cold. Twenty minutes later, Hannah still hadn't showed. I figured the snow was slowing her down, even though she didn't live that far away. Maybe she was just being fashionably late. Snow continued to pile on me, the cold digging into my bones, but I wasn't budging.

She arrived at nine forty-five. For some reason, I had convinced myself that she would come alone. Instead, she arrived in a pack of girls including Libby, Dave's sister, who acted as if she didn't know me. "Hey," Hannah said, dressed not in my jacket but in a stark white parka that came down to her thighs and made her almost vanish in the snowy landscape. She had her arms locked with two girls like flanking soldiers. "You must be freezing," she added.

"I'm fine," I said.

"C'mon," she said, starting to walk, "the place is this way."

The party was on Park Avenue in a giant apartment building. Hannah walked through the lobby, waving to the doorman, who called out "Hannah!" as if they were old friends. She led us up to an apartment on the seventeenth floor and didn't even ring the doorbell, just walked in the front door. Inside, we passed through room after room, the apartment going on forever. Eventually, I heard voices coming from where Hannah was leading us and we found ourselves in the kitchen, which was crowded with people playing drinking games and smoking cigarettes. Hannah said a few hellos and then she and her friends squeezed into the middle of the crowd. I got caught a bit behind them, although my eyes stayed fixed on Hannah. This big kid with shaggy brown hair and a blue hooded sweatshirt started handing the girls beers. "Hey, Hans," he said when he got to her.

She looked up, pushed her hair behind her ears. "Oh, hey," she said, taking the beer. "Where's Marty?" I heard her say.

"Present!" I said, pushing my way through the crowd to get to her.

She hooked arms with me, drawing me closer. The brown-haired kid handed me a beer. I didn't need to be a genius to figure out who he was. "Thanks," I said.

We started to play drinking games on the kitchen counter, rounds of quarters and chase, bouncing coins into glasses over and over again. With my friends I was a decent drinking-game player, but here, in this apartment, where I barely knew anyone, where I didn't recognize myself, I couldn't miss. It didn't matter if I backhanded the quarter, flipped it no-look, or rolled it off my nose, every time it clinked into the glass. "Who is this guy?" one of Hannah's friends said as I passed her a beer. I gave the glasses of beer to different people at first—Hannah's friends, Libby, even Hannah—but soon I targeted her ex, forcing him to drink beer after beer. He wasn't much bigger than me, just older, a man already while I still looked like a boy. Still, I could see the beers starting to take their toll on him, his expression growing weary. "Bring it on, hotshot," he said to me, gesturing for me to get him again. People started to cheer when I sank another quarter or when he drank the beer. It didn't matter. At one point Hannah leaned over to me, hanging on my shoulder. She was completely drunk. "I love your hair," she said, and dragged her fingers through my locks.

I smiled, sipping a beer I had been working on all night. "Thanks," I said.

The game continued, people getting drunker and drunker. Hannah's friends began to target her and she got sloppy drunk, dancing around the kitchen, showing off. She was a sight to see, this gorgeous girl, spinning and gyrating in the kitchen. She seemed at once completely oblivious to the rest of the world and yet very conscious that she was the center of attention. "Hannah's got some moves, huh?" her ex said, his eyes moving between Hannah and me. "You're a lucky guy," he added.

I nodded, quietly drinking my beer.

"I remember some wild times..." he started, his eyes widening at Hannah. A pretty girl with straight brown hair walked over to him, threading her arms around his waist, although he didn't seem to notice.

"Well, she's with me now," I said before he could finish. Everyone looked my way. Her ex took another sip of his beer and smiled at the girl next to him.

Hannah swayed over to the counter, pulling me out into the middle of the kitchen with her. She looped her arms around my neck and started kissing me, her mouth fixed on mine. I was completely sober but in a spin, trying to take in where I was and what I was doing. Hannah's lips were soft and I could taste the bitter flavor of the beer in her mouth. I kept opening my eyes just to make sure I wasn't dreaming. Hannah had her eyes open too, shifting between mine and the rest of the people in the room. I could feel this intense connection between us, as if everything had been leading up to this moment.

A door slammed somewhere behind me in the apartment, interrupting our kiss. Hannah's ex and the girl were gone. Hannah looked around, then pulled her hair behind her head. She brought her hand to her mouth and leaned into her friends. "I think I'm going to be sick," she whispered.

I tried to take her arm, but her friends were around her in an instant. "We'll take it from here, hotshot," Libby told me.

They got her coat and quickly left the party. I followed. Outside, the streets and sidewalks were indistinguishable under a blanket of snow. Hannah leaned against a parked car, her eyes barely open. "Do you want me to take you home?" I asked, extending my hand. My heart was still racing from the kiss. Hannah stood quickly as if to walk away, and then doubled over and threw up. "Fucking hell," she shouted between heaves. Two other girls swept in front of me, gathering around Hannah, pulling back her hair. Libby walked out into the street to hail a taxi.

I said, "You sure you don't need my help?"

"Listen, Marty. Hannah will be fine," Libby said, a hint of caution in her voice. "You don't need to worry about Hannah."

I nodded and stood there until a cab stopped and drove them away. The party was clearly over, everyone headed home, but I decided to walk, refusing to put the night behind me.

———

The next morning, early, my parents got a call from the doctor. My grandmother had suffered another small stroke, sometime in the middle of the night. We rushed to the hospital and the doctor met us in the waiting room. "She's breathing on her own," he said. "That's a good sign."

"Is she awake?" my dad asked.

"She goes in and out," he told us.

My mom said, "Can we see her?"

"You can," Dr. Rock Star said. "Just don't expect too much."

My grandmother was the last in a row of people who barely looked alive. She was back in her hospital gown, but you could still see the traces of what she had on the night before, the fading brush of eye shadow on her eyelids, a thin line of lipstick at the corners of her mouth. We stood at the end of the bed, listening to the whir of machines, the beeps of monitors tracking her vital signs.

"Can she hear us?" my mother said.

"To be honest, we don't know," he said. "But I think talking to her would be a good thing. Sometimes hearing a familiar voice can make all the difference."

We moved alongside of her bed, my dad and mom on one side, me on the other.

"Hey, Ma," my dad said.

"Hi, Clara," my mom said, and then my father burst into tears. My mom put her arms around my dad and started crying herself. I'd seen my mother cry before—at movies, sappy television commercials, even reading a book—but I'd never seen my dad lose it like this before. I sometimes forgot my grandma was his mother, the woman who had raised him, not just the lady who complained about my hair and seemed to hate most people, until recently. Love, it seemed, could make you forgive just about anything.

My grandmother didn't stir.

I didn't know what to say. I wanted to tell her what happened last night, how I'd kissed the most beautiful girl I'd ever seen, how it was a night I would never forget. She would understand.

"Grandma," I said, "I'm going to get my hair cut tomorrow."

I put my hand on hers, her skin as cool as snow beneath my fingers.

___

The next day, I was at track practice after school in Central Park, stretching before our daily jog around the reservoir. I saw some of my teammates talking to someone, pointing in my direction.

Then I saw him walking toward me, wearing his varsity jacket over the same blue sweatshirt I'd seen him in at the party.

"Marty, right?" he said.

"Uh-huh," I said.

"I'm Chris," he said, and then added, "You know, Hannah's ex…"

I nodded. His jacket was a lot like mine except it fit him right, as if he was supposed to be wearing it.

"I want to talk to you."

He seemed bigger than I remembered from the night before, bulkier, taller. Maybe it was just that I felt particularly small and vulnerable in my sweats.

"What's the deal?" he said, his tone harsh. "I mean, between you and Hannah?"

The question was innocent enough, but his stare made me think the answer might be the difference between jogging around the reservoir that day and walking on crutches for weeks. I shrugged, scanning the area for the quickest getaway. Everything was covered in snow, the path indistinguishable from the thick brush around it. I didn't stand a chance. Nearby, some of my teammates waved in my direction before heading out onto the track. Then Chris said, "Are you serious or what?"

In the distance, the sun was setting over the reservoir, the water shimmering this glorious brilliant yellow. "Very serious," I said.

He shook his head, laughing a little. "I can't fucking believe this!" he shouted. Joggers on the track looked over as if they thought, as I did, that he was about to kill me. But he just stood there, taking deep breaths, his lips clenched, staring me down. He kneeled and began dragging his bare hand through the snow. "Fuck!" he yelled, picking up a handful of snow and throwing it at the ground. "How the hell did this happen?"

At that moment, I knew he wasn't going to touch me. He just stared off into space. White clouds of air puffed from his mouth. "I came here to kick your ass," he said, standing up.

"I'd rather you didn't," I said.

"Right," he said, turning and starting to walk away. My coach waved to me, signaling for me to get going. I was about to leave when Chris called, "She's going to fuck with you." His expression wasn't threatening, but genuine. "I'm just telling you, man," he said, before adding, "Be careful." I watched him head toward the park exit and then I started running, eager to catch up to everyone ahead of me.

My dad was on the phone with the doctor for a long time that night. When he got off, he told us that Grandma was stable and awake but that she might have another stroke at any moment. "He told me that people can have many before they…" he said, his voice trailing off. "It might be the beginning of the end, it might not."

I wanted to do something. I thought about going to get my hair cut that night and rushing to the hospital to show her.

Instead, I called Hannah. "Hey, it's Marty," I said when she got on the phone.

"Hey," she said. "Sorry I was such a freak at the party."

"You okay?"

"After I puked, I was fine," she said. "Hung over the next day. No biggie."

"That's good."

"Is that why you called? You're so sweet to check up on me."

"Yeah," I said, before adding, "That's why. I also wanted to ask you a favor."

I explained to her about my grandmother and the stroke. I told her she really wanted to meet my girlfriend. "But I'm not your girlfriend," she said.

"Right…I mean…" I said, stumbling for words. "Sure." My mouth went dry, my body sinking in my chair. "Of course," I said, trying to sound casual. "I'm not your boyfriend either. Check." I wasn't sure if I was telling her or trying to convince myself—the kiss between us still burned in my memory. I wanted to see her again so I could remind her that something had happened that night. "Look, she probably doesn't have much time left. We go, we say hello, we leave."

"I don't know," she said. "It's kind of creepy. Lying to your dying grandmother."

"It'll make her happy," I said, and I realized that, in fact, that was exactly what I was trying to do. And then I said, "Besides, you owe me."

There was silence on the other side of the line, and for a second I thought she had hung up.

"Hello?"

"When?" she said, her tone matter-of-fact. She agreed to meet me after school later that week in front of the hospital.

"By the way," I said, "I saw your boyfriend. I mean your ex."

I wasn't sure why I mentioned it. There was something mean about doing so, but I had something on her. That was rare with Hannah. "What?" she said. "You saw Chris? Where?"

"At track practice."

"What did *he* want?"

"He wanted to know if we were serious or not."

I could hear her breathing over the phone. "What'd you say?"

"I said we were."

Again, there was a pause. Static crackled on the line. "Did he say anything else?"

I thought about telling her how upset he was, but I didn't. "He told me to be careful," I said.

"About what?"

"You, I think."

"What does that mean?"

"I don't know," I said, although it was true: I didn't feel safe around Hannah. I felt like she could crush me at any moment and I might never recover.

"I've got to go," she finally said. "I'll see you later."

My plan was to take Hannah to the hospital, introduce her to my grandmother, and then suggest we take a walk, maybe get a bite to eat. If nothing else, I figured I could walk her home. Even in a winter storm, a walk home sounded romantic.

A car dropped Hannah off in front of the hospital right on time. She wasn't wearing my jacket, but she looked beautiful, dressed in her white winter coat again and a pink wool cap with a pom-pom dangling from the top. "Fifteen minutes," she said.

In the elevator, we stood quietly, listening to some terrible Muzak. "I should tell you something," I said.

"What?"

"My grandma thinks she sees her dead husband."

"Excuse me?"

I explained how she had started seeing him after the first stroke. I told her we played along. "She might talk to him," I added.

Hannah looked frightened. "Great."

In the hospital room, Grandma was lying in bed on her back, staring at the ceiling. She was dressed in her gown and looked worse than ever, her skin a pale gray. Her eyes were red, her face blotchy as if she had been crying.

"Hey, Grandma," I said.

She didn't raise her head, just lowered her eyes, looking at me and then Hannah.

"Who's this?" she said.

"This is Hannah," I said, before adding, "my girlfriend."

"Hi, Mrs. Kelso," Hannah said with a nervous smile.

My grandmother leaned up, looking Hannah over. "She's too skinny," she said. Hannah crossed her arms in front of herself.

"Grandma," I said.

"And pale," she added. "Are you Irish? Watch out for Irish girls. They get pregnant and then you're locked in for life."

My grandmother clenched her mouth shut and then looked at both of us with disgust. She reached over and grabbed the bowl of candy. "Have one," she said.

Hannah took one, unwrapping it slowly. "I love butterscotch," she said. I took one too, unwrapping it and popping it in my mouth. The taste was as foul as I remembered, but I smiled, pretending to like it.

"Why'd you bring her here?" Grandma said.

"I thought you and Grandpa—" I started, and then noticed for the first time how the chair wasn't near the bed anymore but sat off to the side, turned away. I looked up at my grandmother, whose eyes began to tear up. "It's nice to meet you," she added, turning on her side, away from us, away from the chair.

I said, "But I thought—"

"I need to rest," my grandma insisted, although her voice sounded weaker than ever. We walked quickly out of her room and headed toward the elevator.

"She seems like she's doing well," Hannah said as we rode down.

I tried to focus, reminding myself that I was on a mission.

"Do you want to get something to eat?"

"I can't," she said.

"Maybe some other time," I added, refusing to let it end here.

Hannah shrugged. "Maybe," she said.

The elevator stopped on the sixth floor and Dr. Rock Star walked in, chatting with two nurses who were laughing at something he was saying. He saw me and said, "Hey, Marty! Your grandma is doing great. I'm really pleased. She's an amazing woman."

I nodded, although I didn't know how he could say that.

He looked at Hannah and said, "This your girlfriend?"

I turned to Hannah. In her white parka and white scarf, she was a vision, like some kind of winter angel. "Yes," I said, and moved forward to kiss her, catching her by surprise. My lips caught hers, but she pushed her hands between us.

"What are you doing?" she said, raising her fingers to her mouth.

"What do you mean?" I said.

I turned back to the nurses and Dr. Rock Star, who all smiled as if we were having a lovers' quarrel.

The doors slid open and everyone spilled out.

Outside, it was bitter cold. Hannah picked up her pace as she headed toward the curb. "You want to share a cab?" I said. "Or maybe walk?"

"I've got a ride," she said, pointing toward the same car that had dropped her off. The door opened and someone stepped out of the driver's side. Hannah's ex.

"Hey," she said, walking up to him and kissing him as if I weren't even there. She turned and said, "You know Chris, right?"

I looked at her ex, who nodded to me. He didn't smirk or gloat. His expression was grim, almost apologetic. "Hey," he said.

I couldn't move. Crowds of people swarmed around me, trudging down the street, headed into the hospital, but I was frozen in place.

"I'm sorry about your grandma, Marty," Hannah said, and then she jumped in the front seat of the car, escaping the cold.

"You want a ride?" her boyfriend asked, although we both knew I wouldn't go with them. I shook my head. He nodded, opening the back door anyway. "Here," he said, pulling out my track jacket and handing it to me, a peace offering. The jacket was warm from the heat of the car, but in that kind of cold, it wouldn't be for long. He walked around to the driver's side and got in the car. Traffic was slow, cars bumper to bumper, and it wasn't going to be easy for them to get out. I turned back to Hannah, who was in the passenger's seat, fiddling with the radio or the heat. I couldn't tell. The window started to fog up, the glass turning opaque, and soon it was as if she had never been there at all.

i.d.

"TEN DOLLARS," THE DELI guy said when I put the two Budweiser 40s on the counter.

"Excuse me?" I said, prepared for him to ask for my I.D., my fingers already searching my wallet.

"Ten dollars, ten dollars," he repeated, his eyes shifting between me and a set of surveillance televisions scanning the aisles of the store. I handed him several crumpled-up bills and he slipped the tall brown bottles into long, slender paper bags. "Next," he said.

Rob put his two 40s on the counter, the bottles clanking together. The deli guy turned his head from the TVs and looked my friend over. "I.D.," he said.

Rob wasn't fazed. He was used to this. We both were. He opened his wallet and handed the man his fake. The deli guy held it at a distance in front of him and squinted, as if he couldn't quite make it out.

"Is there a problem?" Rob said.

The deli guy looked at Rob and then noticed the growing line of customers. "Ten dollars," he said, his voice urgent, waving the next customer forward.

When we got outside, I slipped my two beers into the deep pockets of my overcoat. The plan was to meet Max and Dave at the movies, but we had a little time to kill, maybe enough to finish off one of our beers. The others we could sneak into the theater. We started walking downtown. Rob threaded through the crowds on the avenue ahead of me. I did my best to keep up with him despite the weight of the heavy glass bottles in my pockets. The avenue was buzzing with people out for Saturday night, the air crisp with a November chill. I caught him at the corner. "Where should we go?"

He nodded down Eighty-Second Street, a quiet residential stretch between avenues. Four-story brownstones, their windows dark, lined the streets like sleeping giants. "Why'd he card you and not me?" I said, although I wished I hadn't. I knew the reason: Rob was black, although it wasn't something I thought about until moments like this when someone drew attention to it.

Rob didn't even look at me, just breathed slowly, clouds of cold white air slipping between his lips, out of his nostrils. He pulled out one of his beers and opened it right in front of everyone walking around. "Fucking Koreans," he said, taking a long swig from the bottle before starting down the block, the noise of the avenue fading behind us.

Rob and I had become friends on the track team the fall of our junior year. I had been on the team since my freshman year because I was fast, a sprinter, but also because it was a vastly better option than gym class. As long as you ran around the reservoir three times a week, you got a varsity letter.

Rob was new to the team. Before then, I knew him as the guy who dated Jessica Minkus, the actress of the high school, the star of every play and musical. Her father was some big investment banker and she was part of the super rich crowd at my school, the kind of kids who took vacations in Switzerland and were headed to Ivy League schools because of legacies or sizeable donations. They rarely acknowledged people like me or my friends. Maybe they thought they were better than us. Maybe they didn't know we existed. It didn't matter. All I knew was that they got out of classes and gym with doctor's notes or because it interfered with their Olympic swimming training or horseback riding tournaments. They got extra time for exams and papers because they had private tutors and therapists who said they needed it. They threw parties on weekends out in the Hamptons filled with drugs and drinking and sex that everyone at school talked about until the next party.

I knew Rob's parents were lawyers and were well off. It was basically understood that Rob was probably headed to Yale, where both his parents had gone, and then on to law school and a career. His future was set. Still, dating Jessica had brought him another level of elite status, which was why it was so strange when he landed on the track team with the rest of us.

We were both sprinters so we were paired as running partners. In theory, we were supposed to run the reservoir in Central Park together three times a week, doing intervals, turning in time cards at the end of the day. We were supposed to compete, making each other better. We did it regularly for a week or so, but soon started changing the routine, getting into our track clothes and then just sitting on the large rocks near the reservoir, out of sight, talking and smoking cigarettes. We learned we shared the same love of horror movies and late-night television. We spent practice debating the greatest slasher film, or going over the plots of the nightly back-to-back reruns of *The Twilight Zone* and *The Outer Limits*. It was hard to imagine I had anything in common with someone who had been part of Jessica Minkus's group, but he reminded me a lot of my other friends. I figured he was glad I didn't want to talk about the breakup. Sometimes I thought about asking him, because I wanted to know what hanging out with that crowd was like, but he never mentioned it so I left it alone.

We should have gotten kicked off the team for skipping practice, but at track meets every Friday, Rob went out and won every race he was in. We had never seen anything like it on our team, perennial losers in an already weak private-school league. Coach Schuler knew we weren't practicing, but it became clear that he was willing to overlook just about anything for a winning season. My times were slipping because I wasn't practicing and I was smoking, but the coach didn't seem to care. A few weeks into the season, after a meet in which he had won every one of his races, Rob went up to Schuler and said, "Marty and me won't be at practice next week."

"You mean Monday?" he said. He looked at me, and I turned to Rob.

"All week," Rob added. Sometimes, it seemed as if he just wanted to see how far he could push things. I looked back up at the coach, who had his lips shut tight. In his eyes, I could see a man debating if this was a fight he wanted to have. Finally, he nodded. "Just be at the meet on Friday," he said, and then walked away.

That next week was amazing: On Monday and Tuesday we hung out at Rob's house during practice, watching television and smoking cigarettes out his window. On Wednesday we took the subway down to the Village after school and went to thrift shops to buy long, beat-up overcoats, thick-heeled boots, and baggy corduroy pants we had to roll at the cuffs.

Finally, on Thursday we went to an arcade in Times Square where we had been told you could get fake I.D.'s. The I.D.'s weren't supposed to be that great, but they worked and that was all that mattered. You could get better ones for a few hundred dollars each, but I didn't have that kind of money and Rob knew it. At the arcade, this guy with a badge that said his name was "Mr. Quarters" stood us each in front of a light blue square of cardboard hanging from the ceiling like a patch of sky and took our photos. Then he shuffled through a pack of driver's licenses, all from Missouri, slid in our pictures, and fed them through a machine. A small string of smoke swirled up as our licenses passed through. "You," he said, pulling out the first freshly sealed driver's license and handing it to me, "are Christopher Bird. Brown eyes."

I flicked the I.D. back and forth between my fingers, the plastic still hot to the touch. "You mean I don't get to pick out my own name?"

Mr. Quarters shook his head. "Twenty bucks." He turned to Rob and said, "You, my friend, you're Brian White." He laughed quietly and handed Rob his I.D. "Sorry."

Rob stared at the card, rubbing his chin. He was working on growing a goatee, but he couldn't really get anything substantial going. It ended up looking like a smudge of dirt. Still, that didn't stop him from playing with the stubble all the time, rubbing his fingertips back and forth across his chin. "Let's get out of here," he said, and I didn't argue.

At Friday's track meet, Rob broke the school record for the 100- and 220-yard dash. I finished a distant but respectable second. Practice, we decided, was for losers.

⟵

We were supposed to meet Dave and Max at the movies at nine. I hadn't seen them much these days because I'd been hanging out so much with Rob. Max didn't seem to care, but the last time I'd seen them and told them I couldn't hang out, Dave's expression dropped, as if I had betrayed him. "Dude," Dave had said, "we never see you anymore."

"Sorry," I said, although I wasn't sure why I was apologizing. Max went out with his friends from synagogue all the time. But Dave didn't have a lot of other friends beyond me and Max.

I decided a horror movie was a good way to bring all of them together. Unfortunately, the only place showing the movie we wanted to see was on the East Side. My stomach had been turning the whole time on the bus ride over, as we got further away from the West Side. There was something I just didn't like about the East Side. I knew it was only across the park from my side of town, but I always felt like it was a world away.

Rob and I made our way down Seventy-Sixth Street, looking for a spot to sit and finish one of our beers before we had to get to the movie. You could often just hang out on the stoop of one of the brownstone buildings and no one would even notice. I was about to sit down when he grabbed my arm and jerked me up. "What?" I said. Rob nodded in the direction of the avenue, where a police car had turned down the street. The siren wasn't on, but the lights were spinning, flashes of blue and red flickering across the dark brownstones. We didn't say a word, just ditched our open beers on the stoop and started walking back toward Third Avenue. My heart was pounding, my house keys clinking against the other bottle still in my pocket.

"What are we going to do?" I said.

"Just keep walking," Rob said.

If we could make it to the corner, I thought, we could disappear back into a store or the crowd, maybe jump on the bus. As far as I was concerned, we could forget about coming back to the East Side ever again.

Soon, the police car pulled alongside us, moving at the same pace. A bright light pointed in our direction and then the siren wailed loudly for a few seconds. We stopped as the car pulled over. Two policemen stepped out, an older white cop and a younger black cop. "We're going to need to chat with you gentlemen for a second," the older cop said. He was a burly man, like a cop out of a TV show, but his voice was so calm you could almost forget what was happening. Almost. "I'm going to ask you to place your hands on the back of the car and spread your legs," he added.

"We didn't do anything," Rob said.

"Then you don't have anything to worry about," the black cop said.

I put my hands on the car, the metal ice cold. Rob stood next to me.

"A young woman was assaulted nearby," the black cop said. "She described the assailants as male. One white, one black."

"We didn't do it!" I shouted.

The older cop patted me under my arms and around my chest,

my waist, and my back. He probably could feel my heart pounding in my chest. He stopped when he hit the bulky bottle in my pocket.

"What do we have here?" he said. He pulled the tall bag from my pocket, then removed the beer. The other cop did the same to Rob.

"You boys were thirsty," the black cop said.

The older cop held the bottle up and laughed. "Jesus, look at the size of this? Just looking at these makes me want to take a leak."

All around us windows started to light up and open, heads leaning out to see what was going on. I kept my face down as if someone might know me, but I could still see Rob had his head up, looking around, almost asking people to see him. The black cop pulled out Rob's wallet and started flipping through it. "Check this out," he said to the other policeman, holding up Rob's fake I.D. The older cop pulled out my wallet and I.D. "The 'Show Me' state," he said. "You're a long way from home, Mr. Bird." He looked over at Rob's I.D., and started laughing. "You too, Mr. White."

The policemen had us sit in the back of the car, shutting the door behind us with a heavy thud. The back of the police car was a jail—no door handles, a thick lattice of metal wire separating the front seat from the back. There were no seat belts, as if safety was the least of your troubles.

The two policemen got in the front seat. "Are we under arrest?" Rob asked, but the cops ignored him, talking on the radio to someone whose voice echoed through the static. "I want to call my lawyer," Rob added, his tone almost aggressive.

The younger cop turned and said, "You have a lawyer?"

Rob paused, before adding, "My father."

Both police officers nodded. "Don't worry," the older cop said. "We'll call your dad soon enough."

We started driving, headed north up Third Avenue. The car passed Eighty-Sixth Street and then pulled over behind a line of parked police cars. I couldn't imagine they were all for us. The avenue was alive with flashing lights, but it was oddly quiet, as if the outside world were suddenly far away. "You boys relax for a second, okay?" the older cop said.

"I can't believe this," I said when the police were gone. "We should never have come to the East Side."

"Just calm down," Rob said.

"Calm down? We're sitting in the back of a police car! Under arrest!"

"We're not under arrest," Rob said, not even looking at me. His eyes followed the cops outside as they talked to a group of other policemen. It looked like a whole precinct had assembled to get us. "Until they read us our rights, we're not technically under arrest."

I had no idea if he was right. All I knew was that my parents were going to freak out. They were never going to forgive me. "I don't want to go to jail," I said.

"No one is going to jail," Rob said. "We didn't do it."

"I'm sure that's what everyone in jail says. I'm sure no one innocent has ever been put away."

"Stop being such a baby," he said. "Jesus, why do I even hang out with you?"

He looked at me, pure disgust in his eyes. I felt like I didn't know him at all. It was as if all the weeks of time we'd spent together just disappeared and we were complete strangers. Then he looked out the window and started laughing. I said, "What's so funny?"

He shook his head. "I can't believe we stopped here." I looked out the window, trying to figure out what he was looking at. The East Side looked exactly like the streets around my apartment building on the West Side in so many ways—avenues lined with everything from delis and dry cleaners to restaurants and pizza shops, side streets with brownstone buildings—but it wasn't my neighborhood. I knew that. And those similarities only made it feel stranger, like I was in some kind of bad dream where everything felt familiar and yet I didn't know where I was. Rob pointed at a fancy high-rise apartment building on the corner. "Jessica lives there," he said. It was the first time he had ever mentioned her name around me. "I bet her dad would enjoy seeing me like this," he added, patting the cage between us and the front of the car.

I didn't understand what he was talking about and didn't care. My head was spinning, trying to compute what was going on— we were in a police car, on the East Side, maybe arrested. This was not good.

The car door opened and the police officers got back in. "Gentlemen," the older cop said. "Another unit just caught the perps over on Lexington Avenue. They've been positively I.D.'d by the victim."

I took a deep breath, my body starting to relax again.

"However," he added, turning to face us. "These fake I.D.'s are a problem. Manipulating government-issued documents is a crime." His expression was serious, his face screwed up the way my dad's sometimes got when I left the refrigerator door open.

My mouth dried up again. Just when I thought we were in the clear, another bomb was falling. Part of me knew this was coming. The I.D.'s had been too good to be true since we got them a month ago. We bought six-packs of beer and bottles of alcohol, inviting girls over to hang out at Rob's house because his parents were often away on weekends. Just the weekend before, Rob's parents had been away, so we had a small party and Rob invited some girls he knew from a school across town. I ended up talking to one girl named Hillary all night, bringing her vodka cranberries, even though she told me I looked like Mr. Spock from *Star Trek*. We ended up kissing on Rob's couch, pawing at each other through our clothes. Rob had been working on this one pretty blonde the whole night, asking her if she had ever been with a black guy. When I left at the end of the night, they were in Rob's bedroom.

Rob said to the cops, "Can't you just forget about the I.D.'s?"

"Can't do that, son," the black policeman said. "Technically we're supposed to bring you in, file a report. We'll have to contact your parents."

"Just throw us in jail," I said. "I'd be better off."

Both cops laughed. I didn't. It wasn't even the punishment I feared. It was that hangdog look of disappointment my parents got when I did something wrong.

The policemen discussed something quietly and then turned to us. "I tell you what," the older cop said. "You tell us where you got these and we won't call your parents. But we will have to confiscate the I.D.'s and the beer."

Rob didn't hesitate. "Times Square. This place called Over the Rainbow."

The policemen looked at each other and nodded, as if they expected us to say that. They didn't even write it down. "Yeah, we know it," the older cop said.

I felt like I should add something, so I said, "Mr. Quarters. His name was Mr. Quarters."

They offered to drive us home, and we agreed, but made sure they left us a few blocks from my house, just in case anyone we knew was around. Despite being in the back of a police car, driving through the transverse from the East Side to the West Side felt like coming home.

We decided it was time to get drunk. The plan was simple: Stop at my house to pick up some cigarettes and then run over to Rob's place to pick up the leftover vodka from the party, hidden away in his closet. Easy. When we got to my apartment, my parents were up, sitting in the living room, listening to a Broadway musical.

"Hey there!" my dad shouted over the music. "You guys are back early."

My mom got up, lowering the volume. "Dave called looking for you. He said you were supposed to meet him at the movies." I could imagine Dave's look of disappointment, the wounds growing deeper. Nothing was going as I had planned. My mom said, "What happened?"

I wasn't going to say anything, but the words just poured out of me like a confession. I told them about getting stopped by the cops and being frisked. I told them about the woman who was assaulted. Part of me thought they might be mad, but I left out the part about us buying beer and the cops confiscating our I.D.'s. I think I just wanted to hear that everything was going to be all right. Rob stayed quiet, his expression cautious, as if he wasn't sure how much I was going to say. "They made us sit in the back of the cop car," he finally said. My parents sat and listened, their expressions shocked.

"How's that for presumed innocent," my dad said, shaking his head. "It's like a fascist state."

"Are you okay?" my mom asked, standing and walking over. Her eyes were filled with concern, almost crying. She reached out and touched Rob's arm.

"I'm fine," I said.

Rob looked down at my mother's hand, his expression suspicious, and then nodded. My mom said, "Do you two want something to eat?"

"We're okay, Mom," I said.

"Is there anything we can do?" my dad added.

I said, "Let's forget about it, all right?" and my parents agreed.

When we left, we stopped at the deli to buy some juice to mix with the vodka. The Korean lady behind the counter knew us well. "No beer tonight?" she asked, smiling. "My best customers."

"Not tonight," I said.

Rob's mom and dad were up as well. I really didn't want to see them. I was usually good with parents, but Rob's mom was always very formal, asking probing questions about my life. His dad just plain scared me, looking at me suspiciously as if I was some kind of bad influence on his son.

Rob walked straight into the living room. "Hey," he shouted. His mom was sitting in a chair, reading a book, while his dad stretched out on the couch, watching a basketball game on TV, drinking a bottle of beer. I'd never seen them looking so relaxed. Most of the times I saw them they were coming from work, dressed formally and carrying leather briefcases. I wondered what his dad would say if he knew that, only a week ago, I had been dry humping some girl right on that couch.

"Hi, Marty," Rob's mother said, putting down the book. "Good to see you."

"Hello," I said.

"You two are home early," his dad added.

There was a long pause, and I hoped Rob would just head to his room.

"Tell me, Marty," his mom finally said. "Have you started to think about where you might want to apply for college?"

"A little," I said, which wasn't the truth. I hadn't given the college thing any thought. The whole idea of leaving didn't seem real. It was just this thing we talked about at school like any other subject. Next summer my parents and I were going to tour some schools, but that still seemed like a lifetime away.

"You see?" Rob's mother said to him, which completely surprised me. I just assumed he was headed to Yale.

"Not now, Mom," he said.

"I thought you went to the movies," his dad said. He clicked the remote, turning down the sound on the TV, and took a swig of his beer. I could practically taste it. "You guys want to watch the game?"

Maybe it was because he had heard me talk to my parents. Maybe it was because he needed to say something. I didn't know. But Rob started telling his parents what had happened, just as I had told my mom and dad. I stood behind him, silent and a bit uneasy. "'The assailants were male,'" Rob said, mimicking the voice of the young black police officer. "'One white, one black.'"

"That's terrible," his mother said.

His father stood, setting his beer on the coffee table and tossing the remote. "Did you get their names?"

Rob looked at me. I shook my head. "What about their badge numbers?" his father continued, his voice growing louder, his expression turning frustrated. "Did you at least get their badge numbers?"

"Dad..." Rob said, and I could see the look of regret sliding across his face.

"What have I told you?" his father said, marching across the room to a desk, and started flipping through a book next to the phone. "I'm going to call Evan down in the district attorney's office. This kind of shit shouldn't happen anymore."

"It's nine o'clock, Donald," Rob's mom said. "No one's going to be there."

"Dad, we're fine," Rob said. "I'm okay."

His dad listened in the phone for a second and then slammed it down. He looked at us, and then marched over to Rob, standing eye to eye with him. I rarely got to see them next to each other like that, but now I could see the similarities—the same broad shoulders, the same long, lanky runner's body, the same look of determination. It was startling, as if I could clearly see the man Rob would someday become.

"You don't get it, do you?" his father said. "It isn't okay." Rob's dad raised his hand to his forehead and pinched his brow, turning away from his son. He took a deep breath and looked at Rob again, sizing him up. "Maybe if you didn't dress like a homeless person this kind of nonsense wouldn't happen."

Rob took a step toward his bedroom.

"Robert, don't walk away from me," his father said.

Rob turned back, his expression stony. I could see Rob's father searching him with his eyes, his hands strangling the bottle of beer.

"Donald..." his mom finally said. The sound of her voice broke something between them, and his father took a breath. "When are you going to shave that foolish thing off your chin?"

Rob reached up and rubbed his fingers back and forth on his stubble. "Are we done here?" he said, and I could see the fight coming out in Rob again. His father shook his head and then sat back down on the couch, reaching for the remote control.

"Go ahead, honey," Rob's mom said. She turned to me, her expression uneasy. "Nice to see you, Marty."

Outside, Central Park West was quiet, just a few people strolling up and down the avenue. Empty cabs streamed by, slowing down as they passed us, as if we might need to get in. My mind was still stuck on what had happened upstairs. We hadn't managed to get the vodka. "I can't believe how pissed your dad was," I said.

"Welcome to my world," Rob said.

"He acted like it was our fault," I said. "Like we had done something wrong."

Rob started rubbing his goatee and then caught himself, digging his hands into the pockets of his overcoat.

"We were just hanging out," I continued, "not bothering anyone and—"

"Marty," Rob said.

"What?"

"Just let it go," he said, and I did, although I didn't see why my talking about it made him so annoyed.

We crossed the street, over to the park side of the avenue. Central Park loomed over us, this vast sea of darkness, like walking on the beach next to the ocean at night. It was amazing how the park could look so inviting during the day and then become something so menacing at night. We sat at a bench and lit a couple of cigarettes. "What was with the college talk?" I said, and then added, "Everyone thinks you're headed to Yale."

Rob took a deep drag, shaking his head. "My parents want me to go through the whole process," he said. "Applying. Visiting. Interviewing. They keep telling me I shouldn't take anything for granted."

I nodded, but it didn't make any sense. If he knew he could get in to Yale, I didn't get why they would go through all that. "What should we do now?" I said. Rob turned, looking over the wall into the park, as if he was searching for something. "I know what we should do," he said.

"What?"

"We should go in." He pointed down the path. We were right near the entrance to the park that led to the reservoir. It was the same entrance we were supposed to go through three times a week to run for the track team. We hadn't been here in so long. I couldn't see the track from where I was standing, but I knew it was out there, hidden by the inky blackness of the trees. "Yeah, right," I said.

He walked over to the entrance, where the cobblestones on the sidewalk shifted to the smooth pavement of the path into the park. "I'm serious," he said. "Let's go in."

"I'm not going in there," I said.

He didn't say a word, just studied the darkness. "Everyone's so scared of the park," he said. "Think it's so much safer out here."

He turned, looking across the street. "See?" he said, pointing to the sidewalk on the other side of the avenue. "Everyone's walking on that side."

He was right. There was barely anyone on our side, just one couple in the distance moving slowly toward us. "Yeah, so what?"

"It's not so bad," Rob continued. "There's nothing in the dark that isn't there in the daytime."

I didn't know what he was talking about. People were mugged all the time in Central Park at night, sometimes killed. You didn't need to be a genius to know it wasn't safe after dark. But something had gotten to him. The conversation with his dad had flicked a switch in him and he wanted to get into a battle with someone, maybe me. The couple walked toward us, coming within about twenty feet before they crossed the street.

"That's bullshit," Rob said, loud enough for them to hear.

"Maybe they were just going home," I said.

Rob shook his head. "They were scared."

"What're you talking about?"

"'One white and one black,'" he said, mimicking the officer again. "They probably thought we were going to attack them."

"Don't get all paranoid on me," I said.

"I'm not 'paranoid.'" He turned and looked me up and down. It was the same look he'd given me in the police car. "Whatever. You don't get it."

I knew there were things I didn't get. I also knew that Rob didn't have it that bad. From where I stood, he had a pretty good life.

"I'm going in," he said, and this time he didn't bother waiting for me. I didn't have to go in, and I certainly didn't want to, but

I also knew that if I didn't, something would change between Rob and me. I didn't want that to happen. Being around Rob had given me access to a world that was new to me, filled with fake I.D.'s and girls and skipping practice without consequences. I wasn't sure I wanted to give that up. "Wait," I said, walking in after him.

Inside, the park was quieter than the street. I could still hear the buzz of cars racing down Central Park West and crossing the transverse from the East Side to the West Side, but it was muffled, like being in the back of the police car. The light from the avenue slowly faded and disappeared behind us. I walked quickly, my body on alert. I focused on the row of lights around the reservoir that started to emerge in the distance. "Slow down!" I called out to Rob, still ahead of me.

I crossed the loop, a street that threaded through the park. During the day, cars and taxis used it, the lights changing from red to green like any other traffic light, but at night, with the road closed, the lights blinked yellow, only the occasional police car passing by. Right then, it was completely empty. I caught up to Rob on the other side of the street and we walked in silence, the sound of our footsteps falling in sync. "Wait up," I said.

"See? What'd I tell you?" Rob finally said. "Not so bad."

I noticed how my eyes were becoming more accustomed to the dark. Soon I could see the outline of bushes rising alongside of us like walls, the surface of the asphalt path beneath us changing slowly to gravel. We walked up onto the path that circled the reservoir. The chain-link fence that separated the path from the water was a dark grid against the sky. Rob walked to the fence, lacing his fingers around the metal, and stared out at the water. For a long time, we didn't talk, just listened to something you rarely heard in New York—quiet, just the distant murmur of city life, as if we were the only people around. "Jess *loved* being in the park at night," Rob finally said.

He had never spoken of her before, and that night he had already mentioned her twice. I didn't know what was going on for him. The only time I'd actually seen Jess other than in the hallways of school was just a week ago, at one of the parties at Rob's house. She'd arrived late, when everyone was gone and I was on my way out. My parents wanted me home by one. Jess threw her arms around Rob, whispering things in his ear, kissing him, although she stumbled around, clearly drunk. I'd never seen her so out of control. "See you later," I called out, and they both looked over. "Who's that?" she said, and Rob whispered something in her ear. She laughed, and then they disappeared inside his room.

Even after this, it was still tough to imagine Jessica Minkus, the banking princess, strolling through Central Park at night. "That was her *thing*," Rob said. I could see him look at me in the moonlight, his eyes lit up and smiling. "Stretched out on the grass in the North Meadow. Up against the reservoir fence. Had to be somewhere the whole world could see. Crazy."

I was still a virgin. The idea of sex, let alone sex out in the open, seemed unimaginable. I stayed quiet, my eyes turned to the reservoir. The whole park felt like a place where there were more secrets than I had ever known. The moon slipped out from behind a cloud, lighting up the water, and then went dark again as the clouds moved in. "So what happened?" I said. He'd brought it up, so I figured I could ask.

"Somebody from the building saw her one night," he said. "Saw *us*. Somebody walking their dog. Told her dad. He freaked." He pushed off the fence and started walking down the track. "Guess whose idea he thought the park was? Jess didn't argue. Whatever. It's history now."

I stood in the middle of the track, digging my feet in the gravel. We were right at the point on the track where a series of turns rounded into a long straightaway. I remembered how satisfying this part of the track was, how you could just kick into autopilot and not think about anything except moving ahead, almost falling forward.

Rob turned back and forth, staring in opposite directions down the track. "I know what we should do," he said.

"What?"

"We should race."

I laughed. "Right. Maybe we could do intervals."

He turned to me, his eyes gleaming in the moonlight. "No, serious," he added.

"What are you talking about?" I said. "I don't want to race."

"Why not?"

"Well, for one, it's nighttime."

"So what? It's not bad at all. You can see fine."

He was right. My eyes had adjusted to the dark and I could see everything clearly—the fence, the water, the leaves on the trees, even the rough texture of the gravel on the ground. The world seemed almost clearer here than it did on the sidewalk under the harsh streetlights. It didn't make any sense, but it was true—everything was sharper, as if there was less to distract you under the night sky.

"C'mon," I said. "It's been a really long night."

Rob looked out, down the path. "It's just a straightaway, right to the first house. Not even a hundred yards. You could run it in your sleep."

"You're crazy," I said.

"I'm wearing boots," he said, that familiar look of determination in his eyes. He pointed at these calf-high combat boots we'd gotten in the East Village. They were badass, but I wouldn't want to run in them. I was in a pair of old Chuck Taylors, not exactly running shoes but at least they were sneakers.

"I don't want to race you," I said, but that wasn't completely true. Part of me wanted to race him, if only to shut him up. Until he had joined track, I was the fastest kid on the team. With him wearing those boots, maybe I could win.

"I tell you what," he said. "If you win, I'll buy us new I.D.'s. Not those cheap-ass ones either. Real ones. The good ones."

He had the money. I knew it. And I wanted that I.D., but both of us knew I couldn't afford it. I said, "And what if you win?"

Rob thought for a moment and then shook his head. "Nothing," he said. "You don't have to do a thing."

At that moment, it was clear that I didn't have anything he wanted. This wasn't about racing at all. It was about beating me. "I'm not racing you," I said.

"C'mon!" he shouted.

"Will you fucking stop it?" I said.

"Stop what?" he said. "I want to race. I need to run."

"Go ahead," I said. "Run. Sprint. Run around the fucking whole reservoir, for all I care."

"It's no fun if there's no one to race against," he said, and there it was—that sense that everything was a battle, that everything was a fight to be won or lost.

"What's your problem?" I said, recognizing that we weren't friends at all, at least not the way I was with Dave and Max. Maybe he just let me hang around to feel better about himself.

Then again, maybe I was doing the same. I looked around, the light of the East Side to one side of me, the West Side on the other. The city split in half. "You know what?" I said. "I don't have to be here." I started walking, heading back the way we came, trying to find the path.

"Marty!" he called out.

"I'm going home," I said, approaching the street that threaded through the park, the light blinking a cautionary yellow.

"Don't be like that," he said, but I just kept walking, anxious to make it out to the avenue again before he said something he couldn't take back. I knew he had it in him.

"Marty," he said, one last time, and I thought about turning back, even stopping and giving him a second chance. This was just a bad night. But then a police car came flying up the street that ran through the park, the lights spinning, the siren screeching, breaking the silence of the park like glass shattering. I turned and saw Rob across the street as the police car passed in front of us. The officer on the passenger side looked out at me, sizing me up from head to toe, before driving on, not even stopping. I turned back to Rob, expecting him to be there watching as well, but he was gone, nowhere in sight.

fortress

Dave and I were in Central Park, perched on the Fortress of Solitude, debating which of the *Star Wars* movies was the best, when Max showed up with his girlfriend.

"What's up, boys?" he said, pushing his way through the thicket of bushes. We had named the place in sixth grade after Superman's hideaway—a secret clearing, buried behind trees, on top of one of the massive black stones that edged the park. From here, you could see the entire world below. People coming and going, never knowing they were being watched. "Hi, guys!" Annie Gottlieb said, following behind Max.

Dave turned to me, disbelief all over his face. "What's she doing here?"

Max shook his head. "The park is public," he said, stretching out along the edge, his feet dangling off the side. It was only the end of February, still winter, but the temperature was warmer than usual, a thick, fertile scent in the air. Spring trying to push through. The noise of cars and buses and taxis rushing up and down the avenue surrounded us and then faded. Annie crouched next to Max, up on her heels, as if she thought she might have to leave at any moment.

"Dave is making his *A New Hope* over *Empire Strikes Back* argument," I said, trying to change the subject.

"You're crazy," Max said. "*Empire* is the best. Han in carbonite? C'mon."

Dave shook his head. "Without the first one, the rest don't matter. It's all about where things began."

"What are you guys talking about?" Annie said. We all turned to her, silent.

"Seriously?" Dave said, looking at Max and then me.

They'd been a couple for just over a month. Annie hadn't been on any of our radars freshman and sophomore years because she dressed like a middle school kid, wearing baggy overalls and tee shirts printed with animals, a complement to her Coke-bottle glasses and braces. Then she came back from Christmas vacation with her braces off, contacts in, and a new wardrobe. Max knew her already from synagogue, so he asked her out immediately. The two of them had been attached to each other ever since. Dave and I were still getting used to having her around all the time, hanging out with us between classes, sometimes coming over to one of our houses in the afternoon. Still, we never thought he'd bring her to the Fortress. It had been our place, just for the three of us.

"Who's out there today?" Max said, trying to change the subject. Dave didn't answer him. I walked over to the edge, peering down. People walked down the path below, headed in and out of the park. Nobody ever bothered to look up. We'd seen it all from here: sophomore Ben Benedict selling weed to a group of freshmen; junior Amy Sorrento, the quietest girl in high school, giving a blow job to one of the track team stars behind a thicket of trees; but today it was just the regulars. "Smokers," I said, referring to the line of kids from our school gathered behind the wall, a thick white cloud of cigarette smoke hanging over them, barely moving. I turned to look the other way, down the path, and saw someone sitting on a bench. "Mr. Jansen's in his usual spot," I said.

Jansen was the youngest member of the faculty, a former lacrosse star at the school back in the day. Now he taught history and was an assistant coach on the team. I wouldn't have paid him any attention, but he was also the yearbook advisor and I had joined the staff after Ms. Rafi, the college counselor, told me I needed to boost my extracurriculars. Of course, the main reason anyone talked about Jansen these days was because he was at the center of the biggest scandal to ever hit the school: an affair between two teachers. And not only was it an affair between two teachers, but the other teacher was Dr. Reubens, the biology teacher—an older, married man. It was so outrageous, it was almost hard to believe. On one side was Jansen, good-looking and athletic, the favorite son returned home. Girls swooned over him. And then there was Reubens, middle-aged, thinning blond hair, always in short sleeves and clip-on ties. The definition of uncool. Before the scandal broke, we often saw the two of them sitting together on the park bench down the path, chatting away. Since the story had come out in January, Jansen continued to come to the bench, but alone. He'd sit there for almost an hour every day, no matter how cold it was, his eyes fixed on the entrance, occasionally checking his watch, as if he expected Reubens to show up at any moment.

"I heard Reubens's wife already moved out," Annie said.

This wasn't true. I knew because I was Dr. Reubens's go-to babysitter. My mom had set it up—they lived just around the corner. I had no love for little kids, but it was still kind of fun playing Monopoly and Life, hide-and-seek and tag, all the games I hadn't played in years.

"Reubens failed me on my bio test," Max said. "I hope he gets canned."

There had been rumors about one of them losing his job, but nothing had happened yet. Annie let out a big laugh that echoed off the trees. "You're so mean," she said. Max made a fake pouty face. "Come here," he said in a low whisper. He was still shorter than me and Dave, but his voice had hit this low register in the past year that made him seem more of a man than any of us. He and Annie started kissing, slobbering over each other as if there was no one else around.

"You two need to get a room," Dave said.

Max separated himself from Annie for a breath and gave us a mischievous look before going back to Annie.

"Let's get out of here," Dave said, standing up tall and grabbing his backpack.

I hesitated, thinking we should stay. We could just ignore them. The sun had slipped out from behind a cloud. I could feel the warmth on my face. Then I saw Max trying to wind his hand under Annie's sweatshirt. "I'm right behind you," I said, waving goodbye to Max and Annie as if they would have noticed.

———

The next day, I had a yearbook meeting right after school. I'd joined late, missing the first few meetings when they handed out assignments, so I ended up in charge of faculty, the job no one wanted. You had to corner every teacher, take their picture, and then gather some interesting or personal fact about them, like their favorite color or breakfast food. From what I'd heard, I might as well have asked for a kidney.

To make matters worse, I had to have it all done in three weeks, when the last remaining pieces of the yearbook went to the printer. "The faculty can be a tough bunch," Mr. Jansen said, his sleeves rolled up in workmanlike fashion, his tie hanging loosely around his neck. I wondered if he was speaking from personal experience. He handed me passes to get into the faculty lounge. "Take Jenna with you," he said, pointing to a girl sitting by the window.

Jenna Bayles was the main photographer for the entire yearbook, in charge of all the student and faculty pictures as well as candids. It was a pretty important job, particularly for a freshman. Then again, her photos already lined the hallways of the high school, arty black-and-white shots of bicycle wheel shadows, little kids running at the playground, close-ups of flower petals. They reminded me of those games I'd loved as a little kid in magazines like *Highlights* and *Ranger Rick*—pictures zoomed in so close you couldn't tell what you were looking at. They were impossible to figure out—how could you know what the skin of a grasshopper actually looked like?—and yet there was always this thrilling sense of amazement when you saw the full image and couldn't believe you didn't recognize it for what it was.

Jenna herself was tough to figure out at any distance. She was a jumble of styles, dressed in long floral dresses and a jean jacket, stomping around in black leather combat boots. She might have been pretty, but no one could tell. Her face was almost always covered by her wavy brown hair, which hung like a curtain over one eye. Her most distinctive feature was her camera, slung over her arm. Every time I had seen her, she was snapping a picture— in the hallways, during assemblies, in study hall, out in front of school—and the habit had earned her the nickname "Flash" among many of the students. Then again, she didn't seem to care what people thought of her. During the only other yearbook meeting I'd attended, she had suggested we make the pages perforated so that people could tear away anyone they didn't want to remember.

"Let's meet at the faculty lounge tomorrow," I said to her that afternoon.

"Like seeing Oz behind the curtain," she said.

"Right," I said. "Be there at noon."

"See you then," she said, and then held up her camera and took a picture of me before I had a chance to react. The flash blinded me. I blinked, and by the time the blur had cleared, she was gone.

⌒

I went to the Fortress after the meeting. Dave and Max were both there, but no Annie. For a moment, it seemed as if things were back to normal. "Where have you been?" Max said.

"Yearbook," I said.

Dave started laughing. "I can't believe you joined yearbook."

"Screw you," I said. "Ms. Rafi said it would help with college."

"Right," Max said. "Taking pictures of the janitor is going to get you into Harvard."

"I hate to say it," Dave said, "but he's right, Marty."

I walked to the edge and looked down. I saw the smokers. Some couple was making out against a tree. Mr. Jansen was at his bench, alone. And then I saw someone hiding behind the park wall, looking up at me through a camera. It was Jenna.

"Shit!" I screamed, and dove down next to Dave.

"What is it?" he said.

"Flash," I said in a whisper.

"She's so weird," Max said. "Like that camera is attached to her face."

"Did she see you?"

"I don't think so," I said, although I knew she had. Her lens had been pointed directly at me. I even saw the flash going off several times. In spring the leaves on the trees surrounding the Fortress shielded us, but for now, the branches were still bare.

"Let's just lay low for a while," Dave said, leaning forward, his hair falling around his face. He'd grown it long this year and it often fell over one of his eyes, as if he was just peeking at the world.

Soon, we were all lying on our backs, stretched out on the flat slab of rock. Above us, the world was a dome of white, as if there was no such thing as blue sky. Dave pulled out a cigarette and was about to light it when Max stopped him. "Are you crazy? We don't need to send up signals," he said.

Dave sighed, putting away his lighter. "We need chewing tobacco," he said.

Max laughed. "Remember that time at soccer camp in seventh grade? When we all tried it?"

I moaned, rolling on my side, remembering how we'd stolen a container of tobacco from some senior boy's bag. We'd gone behind the dorms, packing wads of the stuff in our mouths, not bothering to read the instructions on the pack. I remembered how sick I'd felt, how it had knocked me out all morning. "You puked, didn't you?" Max said to me.

"I did not!" I said, sitting up. "Did I?"

The two of them smiled at me, and then I remembered throwing up right after we tried the tobacco and again, later, on the field during our afternoon scrimmage. "Shit," I said, and they both burst out laughing.

"That stuff is gross," Dave said.

"Nasty," I said.

Max laughed. "Annie says she could never kiss a guy who chewed tobacco."

Dave leaned forward, bringing a cigarette to his lips again. He peeked over the side. "Looks like the coast is clear," he said, lighting it and blowing out smoke. Max stood, looking over the edge. "Annie should be here by now," he said. "I wonder where she is."

"I have no idea," I said, looking over the edge with him, as if I was actually trying to find her.

—

"This place is miserable," Jenna said, as we walked into the teachers' lounge the next day. She was right. It was even more depressing than I had imagined—a windowless room with a threadbare couch and a bookshelf lined with old textbooks and paperbacks. A tiny old fridge sat along a wall with a coffee maker sitting on top, the power switch glowing orange despite the fact that the container was empty. Two round tables were set in the middle of the room. At one table sat two French teachers, chattering *en français*, eating salad out of plastic containers.

"Yearbook," I said, flashing my pass.

They both rolled their eyes, taking silent bites of their salads.

At the other table was Dr. Reubens, sitting alone, eating a sandwich and reading the newspaper. His tie was unclipped and lay on the table next to him. He dabbed a napkin across his mouth and stood up. "Where do you want us?"

I turned to Jenna. She hadn't said a word about seeing me on the rock, which felt oddly disappointing, as if I almost wanted her to call me out on it. She looked around, sizing up the space, her expression pure disgust. "How about outside?"

I shook my head. "Let's try in front of the bookshelf."

Jenna took photos of the French teachers first, neither of whom laughed when she said, "Say *fromage!*" before each picture.

I asked them their favorite food, movie, or place to vacation.

"*Za besh,*" one of them said.

"What?" I said.

"*Besh, besh!*" the other shouted, clearly annoyed. "You know, *la plage?!*" They stormed out of the room before I could ask what they were talking about.

"The beach," Jenna said. "She was talking about the beach."

"Right," I said.

When it was Dr. Reubens's turn, he moved in front of the bookshelf, reclipping his tie. I don't know if it was the color of the room or the fluorescent lights, but his face looked sallow, dark circles sagging below his eyes.

"How's the school year going, Marty?"

Truth was, it was the most difficult year I'd ever had. My classes were impossible. The only thing my parents or teachers really wanted to talk about was college. I didn't have a clue. I was supposed to take some kind of SAT prep course, but I had been putting it off. For the first time ever, my friends and I weren't all getting along. And about what? Some of it seemed to be about Annie, but I got the sense that it was more than that coming between us, that what we wanted wasn't the same anymore. Dave wanted things between us to stay as they had been when we were younger. Max was moving into something new. Me? I wanted both, but that was starting to feel impossible. "Kind of sucks," I said, surprising myself. I had no idea why I was being honest to Dr. Reubens, an adult. Maybe I thought he was one person that might understand, given what he was going through. He nodded and smiled sympathetically, and for a second I believed he knew exactly what I meant.

"Say cheese," Jenna said. The room flashed several times.

"You still good for this weekend?" Dr. Reubens asked.

Plans had been made for me to babysit, but I didn't know if anything had changed. "I guess," I said, looking up. "If you are."

"Yep," he said. "All good."

He gathered his stuff and headed toward the door. "Dr. Reubens?" I called out, startling him. It looked like it took all he had to hold himself together.

"Yes, Marty?" he said.

"Favorite food, movie, or vacation spot?"

He smiled, looking relieved. "How about *Casablanca*," he said, and left.

Jenna folded up her tripod. "Date with Reubens this weekend?" she said.

"I babysit his kids," I said. I looked down my list, checking off the names. "Three down. Twenty-six to go."

Jenna leaned in to look at the list, her face inches from mine.

I could smell chemicals from the lab around her, a vinegary, sour smell I remembered well from the one photography class I had taken. The smell had lingered on my fingers for weeks. "It's a movie," she said, pointing at one of the entries.

"What?" I said.

"*Casablanca*," she said. "'Play it again, Sam' and all that."

I looked down at my list, wondering how many other ones I'd gotten wrong. "Great love story," she added, and when I looked up, she snapped another picture of me before sweeping out of the room and leaving me all by myself.

On Saturday night, I was a prisoner in a fort made of sofa cushions.

"We've got to reinforce it," Kyle, eight years old, said as he peeked at me through a small opening in the roof. Next to him, Alex, only five, was bouncing up and down, shouting "More pillows!" over and over again. He grabbed one and threw it over my last remaining lookout, blocking out the light. "Careful," Kyle said to his brother. "You're going to bring down the whole thing."

"Knock it down!" Alex shouted, eager for the best part. I couldn't argue with him. I remembered how amazing it felt when I was their age to burst out of a fort like some kind of monster. Dave and Max and I had built forts for years, some of them large enough to hold all three of us. We'd sit in there as long as we could, until the desire to bring the whole thing down was too much to resist.

Then again, there was something incredibly relaxing and

peaceful about sitting in the fort right then, warm and surrounded by darkness, the only sounds those of the two boys negotiating how to keep me trapped. There wasn't much quiet in my life these days between Max and Dave arguing, schoolwork, yearbook stuff, and my parents pushing me to get going on college applications. Just the night before, they had thrust the phone at me after dinner, my cousin Evie on the other side. She was a junior in college down in North Carolina. I quickly understood that they had called Evie, asking her to talk to me about college. "What do you want to know?" she asked, as if I had a list of questions ready. In the background, I could hear music and voices. "What's it like?" I said. "College, I mean."

"Great," she said, and then added, "Terrible. Depends on the day."

"I don't get it," I said.

"I don't know what to tell you, Marty," she said, her voice pointed, growing frustrated, a tone as familiar as anything I knew about Evie. "I thought the noise would disappear when I left, but some days it's only louder."

"What noise?" I asked.

"I thought getting away from my mom and that world would change everything," she said, ignoring my question. "Wrong."

"Why?" I asked, but she said she couldn't talk anymore right then and that I should call if I had other questions. I didn't know where to start.

But in the pillow fort that afternoon with the boys, surrounded by the quiet, I thought of what Evie had said, and wondered if this was what she meant about the noise disappearing. For a moment, it was as if time stopped and I could stop thinking about everything I was supposed to do. Above me, the fort trembled as Kyle and Alex spread blankets over the top, re-inforcing it. I could just make out their whispers, faint but clear. "Say it," Kyle said to his brother.

"What?"

"You know! Say it!"

There was a pause, and then Alex shouted, "He'll never escape now!"

That was my signal. I started to rise, shaking the walls of the fort. The boys shrieked in delight. We'd been doing this for an hour since their parents left, and I'd already destroyed three forts.

"Red alert!" Kyle shouted.

"Red alert!" Alex repeated.

"The prisoner is trying to escape!"

"Get him! Get him!"

I burst through the top of the fortress, destroying it in seconds. The boys were on me, climbing on my back, pinning me down with a pillow until I gave in.

After that, we played Life. The boys both loved the game, although Alex never really spun the wheel; he just turned it to ten every time so that he could fly along the path as quickly as possible. He was inevitably done before Kyle and I were halfway through. I was having a run of bad spins, seeming to land only on squares where I had to pay money, pushing me further into debt. When it came time for Kyle to get married, he decided he wanted another blue peg in the car.

"Two boys can't be married," Alex shouted.

"Girls are gross," Kyle said.

"But it's not allowed," Alex said.

They looked at me, as if I had some kind of answers. "It's just a game," I said.

Just then, I heard keys turning in a lock and the creak of the door opening. "Hello!" Dr. Reubens called out.

Kyle and Alex jumped up and ran over to him as he came into the living room. I started picking up pillows, putting cushions back on the couch. "Marty, please," he said. "I'll be the prisoner as soon as you leave."

Dr. Reubens sent them off to put on their pajamas and brush their teeth, promising to finish the game. He paid me and then booked me to walk the boys home from school for the next two days. "The Game of Life," he said, looking down at the table. "I hate it. All about making money, getting married, and having children." I nodded, although that seemed pretty much like what adult life was like—family and work, maybe getting a car.

"I'm not very good at Life," I said. And although I believed it, I had no idea why I was telling this man.

He smiled and then said, "Who is?"

Alex came running in, wearing pajamas with colorful dinosaurs all over them. He ran to his dad, raising his arms. Dr. Reubens picked him up with ease, hoisting him on his hip. "Bye, Marty," Alex said.

"See you tomorrow then?" he said.

"Tomorrow, yes," I said, and left quickly.

———

"I can't believe he abandoned us," Dave said at lunch the next day. We were both looking at Max, who for the first time ever had decided to sit at a table across the cafeteria, wedged between Annie and one of her friends. He was laughing and smiling and looked genuinely happy.

"He's such a jerk," I said.

Dave said, "He'd better not tell everyone about the Fortress."

"He wouldn't," I said, and looked over at them, cozy at their table, and wondered if that was true anymore.

"Who wouldn't what?" someone behind me said, and I practically jumped out of my seat. Jenna was sitting next to me, out of nowhere.

"You scared the shit out of me," I said.

"I get that a lot," she said, smiling. "What are you two grandmas gossiping about?"

Dave looked at me and said, "What is she doing here?"

"Nice to see you too," she said, taking a french fry off my plate and eating it.

Dave shook his head. Jenna held up her camera, snapping Dave's picture. "Yearbook business," she said.

"Don't ever do that again," he said. "We can't even eat lunch in peace anymore." He stood, grabbed his tray, and made his way toward the garbage.

"Dave!" I called out, but he wasn't coming back.

"He seems nice," Jenna said. She smiled and laughed. For the first time, I noticed that she was actually wearing makeup—lipstick and something on her eyes—although it was faint, as if she wasn't sure she wanted people to know. I figured girls only wore makeup to attract boys, and that seemed like the last thing on Jenna's mind. "What are you doing here?" I asked.

Jansen had told her about a faculty meeting after school in a few days where we might make a lot of headway on the faculty photos. "It could be a gold mine," she said.

She was right. It was the only way we were going to meet our deadline.

"Okay," I said, "let's hit the lounge for the next few days at lunch, and then see what we can get at the faculty meeting."

She held up her camera. "Smile for the birdie," she said, snapping one more picture of me before she left.

That afternoon, I picked up Alex and Kyle and walked them into the park, headed to their house. Spring had pushed through, the air warm, people shedding clothing like layers of skin. I carried the boys' parkas while they picked up sticks and dueled each other. We were just about to pass the secret entrance to the Fortress when I heard raised voices behind me. I turned and there were Mr. Jansen and Dr. Reubens, walking into the park. The two men were far enough away that the boys didn't notice, but I could see clearly that they were fighting—Mr. Jansen shouting, waving his arms around, while Dr. Reubens leaned forward, deflated, his hands up around his neck. I had to act fast. "Want to see something cool?" I said, and the boys nodded.

"I can't believe you brought them here," Dave said, when we emerged from the bushes onto the Fortress. Annie and Max were stretched out on the flats, their arms wrapped around each other. I held the boys' hands, refusing to let them get anywhere near the edge.

"Wow," Kyle said, his eyes wide.

"This place is so cool!" Alex shouted.

"Seriously, dude," Max said. "Are you insane?"

"I had to," I whispered, pointing over the edge.

Max and Annie looked over. Dave just shook his head.

"Is this your secret clubhouse?" Alex said.

"That's right," I said.

Dave added, "Not much of a secret anymore."

"Shut up, dude," Max said. "Quit acting like you own this place."

Dave turned away from Max, peering over the edge. "Hey look, Marty," he said. "There's your girlfriend. Why don't we invite her too?"

Annie and Max immediately peered over the side again. Alex and Kyle tried to move to the edge as well, but I held them back. Kyle called out, "I want to see!"

"Jenna Bayles?" Annie said. "You like her?"

"I do not," I said.

"I want to see!" Kyle repeated, trying to pull away from me.

"Who's Jenna?" Alex said. "Is she your girlfriend? Are you going to marry her?"

"No, she's not my girlfriend," I said. "No, I'm not going to marry her."

"I didn't even know you were dating," Max said, slapping my back.

"Aw," Annie said. "You guys are such a cute couple."

"Jesus," Dave said, disgust in his voice.

"We are not a couple," I said, holding tightly on to the boys' hands. "We are not dating."

"Who are you dating, Sport?" a voice said behind me, emerging from the bushes. Jenna, of course. She looked around. "Nice hideout."

"I can't believe you told her," Dave said.

"I didn't," I said.

"Seriously?" Dave said. "Maybe we should invite the whole school to the Fortress."

"'The Fortress'?" Annie said. "I like that."

"Like the Fortress of Solitude?" Jenna said, smiling. "From Superman?"

Of course, she knew. "We were in sixth grade," I said, making excuses.

"Who else is going to come up?" Dave said. "Maybe Mr. Jansen needs a new spot. Or Amy Sorrento."

"I hear she's slept with the entire track and field team," Annie said.

"Like a sleepover?" Alex said.

Everyone looked at me. Jenna was laughing. "Yes," I said. "Like a sleepover."

"Maybe we can all hold hands and play a game," Dave said. "Like duck duck goose or something."

"Yeah!" Kyle shouted.

"Chill out, dude," Max said.

"Kids. Girlfriends," Dave said, and then pointed to Jenna. "Her."

"You don't own this place, Grumpy," Jenna said, and the boys both laughed. She walked to the edge and cautiously looked over. "And look at the view," she added, holding up her camera and taking pictures from the edge. "Students killing themselves on nicotine? Teachers behaving badly?" she said. "It's a candid gold mine."

"That's enough," I said.

Dave stood up and grabbed his bag. "Where are you going?"

"I'm done," he said.

"It's no big deal," I said, although I could see in his eyes that he thought it was.

Max shook his head. "What's with you?"

Dave didn't say a word, but the two of them shared a look

that showed the stress in their friendship at that moment. Jenna broke the silence snapping a picture of the two of them. That was it. Dave dropped his bag and moved toward her as if to grab her camera, but I stepped in between them. "Dave," I said, holding him back. He looked at me as if he didn't know who I was. "What the fuck!" he screamed, and then grabbed his bag and pushed his way through the bushes.

"Dave, wait," I said.

"Let him go," Max said.

Kyle pulled at my arm. "Can we go home now?"

"That boy is very mad," Alex said.

"He's being a jerk," Annie said. "He'll get over it."

I walked over to the edge and looked down. Jansen and Reubens were gone. The path was empty until I saw Dave appear, his backpack slung over one shoulder, his head down, not heading toward the exit but deeper into the park.

"So much drama, Sport," Jenna said, raising her camera at the boys. I put my hand up in front of her camera lens, shouting, "Stop it!" The sound of my voice echoed around the Fortress. Jenna looked at me, startled, and then lowered her camera. "C'mon boys," I said, and led them out onto the path again, headed home.

Jenna and I met outside the faculty lounge the next day. She looked different—her hair pulled back in a way that let you see her whole face—and she was dressed more like all the other girls, like Annie, in a long skirt and sweater. I almost didn't recognize her. "You look weird," I said, and I wanted to take back the words the moment I said them. The smile she'd had on her face when she saw me disappeared.

"Flattery will get you everywhere," she said.

I peered through the door window and saw them—nearly all of the faculty, sitting around the table, leaning against the walls, listening to the principal talk. Surprisingly, they looked a lot like we often did in classes—tired, a little bored, not exactly pleased to be there. Still, this was our chance. We could practically finish the faculty section when they came out.

The meeting, of course, went late. I kept looking at my watch, hoping it would end before I was supposed to pick up Reubens's kids. I realized that this meeting was probably why he wanted me to pick up the boys. I bounced between looking through the window and pacing in front of the door. "You're making me nervous," Jenna said.

"It's taking so long," I said, looking at my watch. "I've got to get the boys."

Jenna pulled out whatever had been holding up her hair, and it all fell around her face. "Just go," she said, grabbing the clipboard out of my hands.

"What do you mean?"

"I can take care of this." I wasn't sure if she felt bad for what had happened the day before at the Fortress or if she was just being nice. "It's not rocket science. Take a picture, ask a question. I got it."

"You sure?"

She looked at me like I was an idiot. "Thank you," I said, and ran to get the boys.

By five thirty, neither of the parents had come home yet. The boys and I had already played two rounds of Life. In the first game, I was a hairdresser with four girls. In the second I was a doctor until I lost my job and ended up becoming a salesperson. The boys kept suing me for all my money. I lost both games. We moved on to building couch fortresses soon after. I suggested we make the biggest one ever and their eyes lit up. We dragged in every pillow we could find—from the sofa, bedrooms, and closets—stacking them carefully like an igloo. It was pretty fragile—pushing any part of it could bring the whole thing down—but inside, they could both stand up. We smiled at each other, marveling at what we had built together.

"This is awesome," Kyle said.

"It's like a real house," Alex said.

I looked at them and raised my eyebrows. I knew what they wanted to do. I wanted to do it as well, maybe even more than they did.

"The prisoner is trying to escape!" I shouted.

We jumped up, sending the pillows flying in every direction. The boys were shouting in delight, and so was I. We were up to our knees in pillows. Right then, the door opened and the boys' mom appeared.

"Marty?" Mrs. Reubens said. "What are you doing here?"

I froze, thinking she knew. "Dr. Reubens asked me to walk the boys home."

She shifted her eyes around the room, searching. "Of course," she said. "Let me pay you." She went to her bag, digging through it. Then the front door opened again and Dr. Reubens came in, out of breath, as if he had run up the stairs.

"Hi," he said to Mrs. Reubens, his expression startled, as if he was surprised to see her.

"I didn't know Marty was picking up the boys," she said.

"I had a faculty meeting," he said. "It took longer than expected." Then he turned, looking around the living room, at the massive pile of pillows, his expression suddenly concerned. "What's happened here?"

"Just a little fort building," I said, walking over to the boys and putting my hand on each of their shoulders.

He put down his briefcase, shaking his head. "This is too much," he said, his voice pointed. Kyle picked up a pillow, hugging it to his chest. Alex leaned in closer to me. "Are those from my bed? Do you know how much those cost?"

"I'm sorry," I said, holding the boys tightly.

"You're supposed to make sure the kids don't destroy the place, not join in."

"Richard," Mrs. Reubens said.

"This is really disappointing, Marty," he said.

"Richard!"

"We pay you to be responsible—"

"Enough!" Mrs. Reubens shouted, cutting him off. The boys looked at their parents, and then at me, as if I knew what to do. There weren't enough pillows in the room to protect them from this. Dr. Reubens sighed, running a hand through his thinning hair. "Here, Marty," Mrs. Reubens finally said, reaching into her bag. "Take this." She pulled out a wad of bills, far more than I was owed. "Say goodbye to Marty, boys," she added. "And then we'll clean up." The boys hugged me and then started grabbing pillows and throwing them onto the couch, making a game of it. Dr. Reubens took a step as if to join in, and then stopped, checking himself, as if he wasn't allowed. He unclipped his tie, looking at me for a second, his expression uncertain. Then he turned, retreating to the bedroom, and I left as quickly as I could.

At the yearbook meeting the following week, Mr. Jansen was in a terrible mood, complaining about everything the staff had done—the way the layout looked, all of the seniors who hadn't gotten their photos taken...you name it. When it was our turn to present the faculty photos and info, Jenna laid out the pictures on the table. "These are great," I said, and it was true. They were artfully done and made most of the teachers look better than they actually did in real life.

"Thanks," Jenna said, smiling.

"Did you get the teacher facts?" Mr. Jansen said.

"That's me," I said, handing him my clipboard of facts. Almost everyone was filled in thanks to Jenna.

"There are still a few missing here," he said, scrutinizing the list. "Ms. Ogilvie, the life sciences teacher. Mr. Hermann, English."

"I figured I could get those tomorrow," I said.

He nodded, saying, "I suppose." He took a big sigh. "What about the candids? Let me see those."

That was Jenna's other job. She brought over her portfolio and opened it, pulling out hundreds of pictures, spreading them out on the table. I'd never seen so many pictures gathered together in one place. They were genuine candids in every sense of the word, people caught unexpectedly in transparent moments: A boy sitting in class, his arms folded across himself, looking bored. A teacher looking at a girl with pure confusion on his face. Two girls laughing at something like it was the funniest thing they had ever heard, their faces twisted awkwardly. Some of the pictures were so realistic they were almost uncomfortable to look at. Mr. Jansen shook his head. "This is not some kind of art project, Jenna," he said. "They're going in the yearbook, for godsakes."

He continued flipping through her pictures, and I started to notice how many of them were of me—ones I knew she had taken in the lunchroom, in front of the faculty lounge, on the Fortress, but others as well: pictures of me across a hallway, walking out of school, when I had no idea I was being photographed. "If Marty were the only person at the school, we'd be in good shape," he said. He leaned over to me and said, "I think you have an admirer."

It was a cruel thing to say, as if he was trying to embarrass her. Jenna's shoulders slumped. "You want to tell a story," he said, grabbing last year's yearbook and opening up to a candid picture of Mr. Wilson, the math teacher, talking to some middle schooler. "This," he said, holding it up, "this is about learning."

"And this," he said, flipping to a picture of three high school girls laughing together. I knew them. They were all mean, probably plotting someone's humiliation. "This is about friendship." He looked down at Jenna's pictures. "These…" he said, picking up a few of her candids. "These don't tell a story."

Jenna straightened up, standing tall, staring down Mr. Jansen. Her eyes studied him, as if she was trying to understand something about him. Then she reached into a pocket of the portfolio and laid out a few new pictures. "What story do these tell?"

They were all of Jansen and Reubens—in the park, walking down the street, even in the hallways, despite the fact that I had never seen them together in school. "Jesus," Mr. Jansen said. "Where...How?"

Jenna didn't look at him, just grabbed her jacket and headed out the door, leaving her portfolio. He turned to me, then ran his hands through his hair in clear frustration, although I didn't know if it was with us or himself. "Jenna, wait," Mr. Jansen said, running out the door after her.

I looked down at the photos. One was a picture of the two of them walking side by side in the park. Dr. Reubens was smiling, looking into the distance at who knows what. Mr. Jansen was also smiling, but he was staring directly at Dr. Reubens. And for the first time, I could see it in Jansen's face—this sense that everything that mattered to him in the world was right there in front of him. I'd never been able to see it before in real life, but there, frozen in time, I could see it clearly.

I waited for them to return, but no one came back. Eventually, I collected all the photos and put them back in the case, taking the portfolio home so nothing would happen to it.

The next few days I kept a close eye out for Jenna at school, but I couldn't find her anywhere. I hadn't opened the portfolio once; I certainly didn't want to see pictures of myself, let alone anyone else at the school, but it also felt wrong, like I was spying on her. It made no sense—they were her pictures of *other* people—but I couldn't do it. Instead, I just lugged the thing around school, trying to find her. I suddenly wanted to see her, as if I had something to say, although I wasn't sure at all what that was. Sure, we needed to track down the last few people on the list or we wouldn't get our names in the yearbook staff listing, but that wasn't it. Not completely.

I found Ms. Ogilvie and Mr. Hermann in the lunchroom. When I told them Jenna would be finding them to take their pictures, they told me she'd already done it. "When was that?" I asked.

"A few days ago," Mr. Hermann said. She'd already gotten the personal fact as well.

"Good," I said, acting as if I already knew. "Great."

I was headed out of the lunchroom, when I heard my name called. I turned around and there was Dr. Reubens. "I just want to apologize for my behavior the other day with the kids," he said. "I was out of line."

"It's no big deal," I said.

"Well, I was wrong," he said. "There's just been…a lot going on."

I nodded. I would never have thought that I shared anything with this middle-aged man, but I felt it as well—this unsettling sense of things in motion that I couldn't stop.

"Anyway," he said, "I hope you won't hold it against the boys. You're their favorite sitter."

I thought about how much fun they had doing just about anything. It was all so simple.

Dr. Reubens looked down at the portfolio I was carrying. "I didn't know you were a photographer."

I shook my head. "It's a friend's," I said, and Dr. Reubens nodded and went back inside, just as Max and Annie were coming out.

"Marty! Where you been?" Max said, fake punching me in the stomach.

"Around," I said, although in truth I had been avoiding them.

"What did Reubens want?" Max said. "To ask you out?"

Annie laughed. "You're so bad."

"Nothing," I said. "Just babysitting stuff."

"Did you hear?" Max added. "About Jansen."

"What?"

"He quit. Left the school."

"Serious?" I said. Max nodded and then added, "Too bad. He was a cool guy."

"And super cute," Annie added.

Max growled at her and put his arms around her. "Is that Jenna's?" Annie said, pointing to the portfolio in my hand.

I nodded.

"Carrying your girlfriend's stuff around?" Max said with a smile.

"So sweet!" Annie said.

"She's not my girlfriend," I said.

"Right," Max said. "See you at the Fortress later?"

"Sure."

I found Jenna sitting on the wall of the park, by the entrance. "I think this belongs to you," I said, handing her the portfolio.

"My hero," she said. She handed me a big envelope. Inside were the last faculty pictures with the facts on the back. "You hear about Jansen?"

"Yeah," I said. "Sucks. He seemed like a nice guy."

"Well, you know what they say about nice guys." She jumped down off the wall. "You headed up to your tree house, Christopher Robin?"

"What?" I said, totally confused.

"Your spot above it all," she said, looking up toward the sky. "Fortress of Solitude," she added, her voice dramatic.

"Think so. I told Max I'd meet him," I said, before adding, "And Annie." I realized I might have to think of them that way from now on.

"Have fun, Superman," she said.

I looked down the avenue toward the entrance to the school. I saw the entire school pouring out—kids being picked up by babysitters and nannies and parents, kids getting on school buses, and kids headed out to team practices. Some played handball against the wall in front of the school or lingered on the street in packs. Everyone going somewhere or doing something. Then I saw Dave standing across the street, his lanky tall body looming above a group of middle school kids, waiting at the light to cross toward the park. He saw me as well. The light changed to "Walk," but he didn't move. I turned to Jenna. "Want to come up?" I said, nodding into the park.

"I don't know," she said. "I think that friend of yours was ready to toss me off."

I looked back toward the street, where Dave had been standing. He was gone, nowhere in sight. "He's not coming," I said.

We walked up the path and then cut through the woods. The sounds of cars whooshing down the avenue mixed with all the screaming voices of everyone leaving school.

"It's through here, right?" she asked.

I pushed aside some branches, opening the path even wider. "This is the only way to get in," I said.

the castle or the wall

I HAD JUST BOMBED my on-campus interview at Colton when I found my mom and dad waiting for me in front of the admissions building. My mom was crying, my dad holding her hand.

"What's going on?"

I stood on the stairs, looking around. The quad was dotted with students stretched out on the grass, reading books, playing hackysack, like some kind of ad for college life. A banner for an Amnesty International pancake breakfast from a few days ago sagged between two trees. "We just got some terrible news," my dad said.

For a moment, I thought it was Grandma. It was a wonder she had stayed alive so long, given her drinking and smoking and the strokes and her general disdain for humanity. She was like some kind of crotchety old superhero. But then I reminded myself that it was my mom crying. She had never been sentimental about my dad's mother. "What is it?" I asked, a sinking feeling in my stomach.

"It's...your cousin," my mom said. "Evie. She's..." Her voice trailed off.

Evie. Evie was gone. My body tensed and went cold. I wasn't

sure what to say. It didn't make any sense. A day ago Evie had been in the world, and now she wasn't. The only other person I had known who died had been her father, but I was so young it barely registered. Evie was different. We didn't talk much, but I still believed—or maybe wanted to believe—that she was at college, living her life. Maybe they were wrong and nothing had changed. Maybe it was like when we played hide-and-seek as kids over the summer in Cape Cod and she was just tucked away inside a cabinet or under a couch, waiting to come out when someone finally called after her. I said, "Are you sure?"

My parents looked at each other, their expressions uncertain, as if they didn't know how to answer my question. "We just spoke to Beth," my dad finally said.

Classes must have come to an end, because students began filing out of buildings, moving in waves onto the quad. I had to clear off the stairs to make room. It was an overwhelming sight—all these people appearing out of nowhere, as if the world had been asleep and come back to life all at once.

"Does this mean we're not going to Boston?" I asked, surprising myself with the question. My mom folded into my dad's arms, her body trembling as if she were cold, never answering my question.

We were on our college tour, visiting schools around the area before applications were due by the end of the year. Most of my friends had done their tours last spring or over the summer, driving around Pennsylvania and Connecticut and Massachusetts, flying to the Midwest, even going out as far as California in some cases. I had put it off as much as I could, despite my parents' nagging and the prodding of my college counselor. I didn't want to think about leaving. The plan was to apply to five or six schools, mostly close to New York, maybe as far as New England. I was still narrowing my list. The only application I'd gotten in so far was one to my parents' alma mater, a big Midwestern state school where they had met. I hadn't visited, but then again all their stories were enough to make me feel like I'd been there. I wasn't even sure I wanted to go there, but sending in the application kept them off my back. The fact that it was their college made me less interested in it anyway. The only school I was excited about was Colton, a liberal arts college in Rhode Island where a dozen of the coolest kids at my school went every year. My college counselor made a point to remind me that the students who went to Colton also had GPAs much higher than mine, a full battery of extracurriculars, and typically some kind of alumni connection. I had none of these. And I had totally screwed the campus interview. Things were not looking up.

And now Evie was dead.

The last time I'd seen Evie was over Labor Day weekend, a few weeks ago. She'd stayed at our house, although no one had seen her the first night. She'd gone out with friends, staying out all night and then sleeping the whole next day. Her mom must have gotten upset with her, because the next night she offered to go out with me and Max. She took us to a dive bar in the East Village, where there was a mini pool table, a jukebox with songs in Russian, and a row of empty booths. The only other person in the place was an old woman behind the bar, sitting on a stool, listening to the radio. She glanced over at us occasionally, but her eyes were glazed over white, as if she were blind.

"I'll tell you the key to making girls like you," Evie told us that night. Max and I were on one side of a booth, Evie on the other, her legs stretched out, her white Chuck Taylors hanging off the end of the seat and glowing in the dimly lit room. "It's not complicated," she said, turning to us with a serious expression on her face. "Shut the fuck up."

The old woman at the bar hooted loudly, slapping the bar. A talk radio station played in the background, the voices in a language I didn't understand. I wasn't sure if she was laughing at what Evie had said or at something she had just heard.

"Excuse me?" I said.

"You heard me." Evie took a big swig of her beer and gave Max and me a stern look. It was the look of an adult, chastising children for something they'd done wrong. "Most guys just talk talk talk," she continued, shaking her head. She took a sip and slammed her beer down. "Listen. Shut the fuck up and listen."

"Shut the fuck up," Max repeated. I nodded. It sounded so easy, so obvious.

On the subway home that night, nearly one in the morning, Evie slumped down in her seat, her head falling on my shoulder. Max had already gotten off at Forty-Second, switching to the local. She said, "Marty?"

"You're awake?" I said.

"Are you okay?" she asked. I'd only had one beer, working at the label more than the beer itself. She'd drank one after the other, standing them in a row on the table like a wall of glass between us. It was a wonder she could stand, let alone ask how I was, but it was clear she was practiced at drinking in a way I wasn't.

"I'm fine," I said. We were on the express train, speeding

through local stops in a blur. The subway darkened as we passed between stations, the lights flickering on and off like a strobe. Evie tucked her hand under my arm like a pillow, making herself more comfortable.

"None of this really matters," she said. I could feel the heat of her body against my shoulder, the sound of her breathing matching the rhythm of the train.

"None of what?" I said. My heart started to race. It happened a lot lately—this unexpected anxiety sweeping over me for no reason, like my body was kicking into flight mode. I mentioned it to Max once and he nodded, saying, "My mom's always saying 'Breathe, one, two, three.' I mean, all the time. Some kind of mantra her shrink gave her when she gets all wiggy."

That night, on the train, the weight of my cousin's body sinking into me, I said "Evie?" even though I knew she had fallen asleep, and I hoped my voice, now just a whisper, could somehow draw her back to me.

⟡

We cut our college tour short and drove home that afternoon. Halfway home, my mom asked me if my Colton interview had gone well. "Sure," I said.

I had been rehearsing for weeks, my college counselor prepping me for the interviews like a lawyer with a client. She told me how to answer questions about classes, sports, my family. She told me to phrase questions about the school as if I was interested. She told me it was a performance, like acting on the stage. "Play the part of the curious student," she said, as if I wasn't.

At the first few schools, I had done just that. The interviewers, older men and women who looked as wooden as the desks they sat behind, smiled and cooed their approval at my articulate and thoughtful answers.

At Colton, however, the interviewer was a student, a pale young woman dressed in black who held a cup of coffee in her hand like an extension of her body. Her whole body slumped to one side, as if she were thoroughly bored. "Why don't you ask me questions today," she said, paging through my file with a kind of glazed attention I recognized all too well. I nodded, but her request threw off my game. I had a couple of reserve questions designed for the end of the interview, when I was inevitably asked what I wanted to know, but these were questions about class size and time with the professors, nothing substantive. I went through those in about five minutes, and then she said, "Anything else?"

My mind went blank. "I can't think of any," I said.

She took a sip of her coffee, looked at her watch, and then stood. "Thanks for visiting Colton," she said, extending a small bony white hand. "Best of luck."

Back home, I called Jenna.

"Surprise," I said.

"College boy?" Jenna said. "Where are you?"

"I'm home."

"I thought you weren't back until Sunday. I'd better tell my other boyfriend to cancel our weekend plans."

"Don't bother," I said. "I'm busy."

"That's a relief," she said. "He's really hot."

Jenna was two years younger than me, a sophomore at our school. After becoming friends on the yearbook staff, we had turned into a couple this past summer. The shift had been seamless, as if being in a romantic relationship was just an extension of what we already were. The fact that she was younger didn't make any difference. She was the first person other than my friends that I wanted to be around all the time. The only stumbling block in our relationship was the fact that we'd been together for nearly six months now and hadn't had sex yet. Jenna was scared, preferring to fixate on picking the right opportunity, the best time of day, the ideal music that would play in the background. Maybe I was a little scared too, but it wasn't like I didn't want to. Still, the longer we waited, the bigger the issue seemed to become. This thing. The plan had been to do the deed the following weekend, but now there was a funeral planned.

"You want to come over?"

Jenna lived just a few blocks away. New York was strange that way. It was this giant city but sometimes you felt like it was a small town and everyone you knew lived within arm's reach. The idea of going to see her sounded perfect, like exactly what I needed, but my mom and dad were camped out with Aunt Beth in full grief mode. I could hear Aunt Beth sobbing, this low moan rising and falling from the living room. Leaving to visit my girlfriend didn't seem like an option.

"I can't," I said.

"How about later?"

"Maybe," I said. "I don't know."

There was a pause on the line. "College boy, are you breaking up with me?"

She was joking, but there was a part of me that thought I

could do it. Right then and there. Trash the only good thing in my life. I knew it wasn't the smart thing to do, but the possibility lay like a lever I just needed to reach out and pull. I told her about Evie.

"Oh, shit. I'm so sorry," she said, her voice filled with genuine concern. "Are you okay?"

The thought hadn't occurred to me that I wouldn't be. I was alive. Evie was dead. This wasn't about me. Still, my heart started to race. I thought of Max's mom. *Breathe, one, two, three*, I told myself.

In truth, I didn't know what I was. I knew I was supposed to be upset about Evie, but her death was like college—somehow far off and intangible. "The funeral is Saturday," I said. "I've got to hang around the house for now. All my family is here."

"Okay," she said. There was a long pause. "How was your interview?"

"Not good. Like bad."

"That's okay," she said. "Education is overrated. You should just fail your classes this year so you can come back to school with me."

"That sounds like a great plan," I said. She laughed, although part of me knew she wished it could be true.

―――

Back at school the next week, I had an appointment to see Ms. Rafi, the college counselor. She was on the phone when I walked up to her office, but she waved me in, pointing at the chair in front of her desk. Her eyes moved back and forth like one of those cat clocks that look different ways with each ticking second. Totally creepy. She moved her hand over her curly red hair, as if she was checking that it was still there, and patted it twice. "Excellent," she said, smiling to no one but herself. "I'll pass on the news."

When she hung up, she looked at me. Her expression changed, growing concerned, although it looked a bit like she smelled something funny. "Martin, I heard about your loss," she said. "I'm very sorry."

I nodded, unsure how to respond. Were you supposed to thank the person? Were you supposed to just agree? Ms. Rafi raised her eyebrows, adjusting her oversized glasses. It seemed like a signal that she was done discussing my loss and was moving on in a new direction in the conversation. "I just talked to the admissions people at Colton," she said. She pointed at the phone as if they lived inside it. "They completely understood why the first interview went…" and then she paused, searching her mind for words. "Why it went the way it did." She smiled again.

"The interviewer was this girl barely older than me," I said, shifting in my seat. "She didn't have any questions. She wanted *me* to ask the questions."

Ms. Rafi stared at me, her expression confused. Then she shook her head, as if to dismiss the whole idea of it. "Yes, well, you were undoubtedly distraught at that moment," she said, her eyes widening.

I understood. "Yeah, I was," I said, not bothering to tell her how I'd found out about my cousin after the interview.

"Good," she said. "Now, your parents told me you could head back up that way next week. I wasn't able to set up another on-campus interview, but I was able to set up an alumni interview with someone in Boston. He went to our school and then to Colton."

"It's like me in the future," I said. Ms. Rafi didn't even blink.

"He'll call you in the next week or so to set up an interview," she added, right before her expression turned gravely serious. "I just want you to understand one thing," she said, bringing her hands together and batting the tips of her fingers against one another. "You should think of Colton as your 'reach.'"

Ms. Rafi had expressions that we all knew: Advice to "boost your extracurriculars" meant your grades weren't good enough. "Accentuating the way you add to the school's diversity" meant you should dig up the non-American in your family history and write your essay on that person. Thinking of something as your "reach" was the most common one. Translation: You won't get in to that school. She encouraged us to apply to one "reach," telling us it was important to think big, but for her the choice to do it was like buying a lottery ticket: The odds against you were astronomical.

"Thanks," I said, getting up, giving her back one of her own smiles. She seemed to recognize it, and looked taken aback. "I'll expect his call."

———

The funeral was the following Saturday. Everyone was there. Aunts and uncles, cousins and friends, all these people I barely knew who had descended on a funeral home on the Upper East Side, which I'd supposedly been to once when I was three and my grandfather died. I didn't remember any of it. I stood in a hallway next to my dad, wearing one of his black suits. I was already taller than him, so the pants and suit jacket were a bit short, but the waist was so big I had to add an extra hole to my belt to hold them up. People kept coming up to us, shaking our hands and telling us how sorry they were. I'd slicked my mop of wavy brown hair back off my face for the funeral, and my mother came over to me, cupping my cheek in her hand. "I love seeing your face," she said, as if she had never seen it before. After that, she stood next to Aunt Beth, feeding her tissues, until the whole scene had become too much for my aunt, and my mom shepherded her into the chapel.

Max arrived, and to my surprise, Dave was with him. I hadn't hung out with Dave in nearly a year. Last I'd heard, he was hanging out with another crowd and had a girlfriend.

"Hey," he said, throwing his arms around me. "Max told me what happened."

"Sorry about your cuz, dude," Max said, grabbing my shoulder. "She was cool."

It was so strange to see them all dressed in suits, standing together. Max had been growing a beard all summer and now it was thick and full like his father's. Dave was even taller than I remembered, his hair long and gathering around his shoulders. They were both thoroughly recognizable as the friends I'd known most of my life, but new, young adult versions of themselves, still rough at the edges. I wondered if that's how I appeared to them. I often still felt like the little kid who built fortresses out of furniture cushions and collected baseball cards.

"How are you doing?" Dave asked.

"Me?" I said, digging my hands in my pockets. "I'm fine."

Max leaned in, whispering, "Did she really off herself?"

"Jesus, Max," Dave said. He turned to me and said, "Just ignore him."

"Don't worry," I said to Dave, smiling. "I always do."

All of a sudden it was as if nothing had changed between the three of us, as if we could just step back into our friendship with ease. Still, Max's question about Evie hung in the air. "Honestly, I don't know what happened," I said.

The doctors had reported that Evie died of an overdose, but people were vague about whether it was accidental or not. My mom kept insisting that she couldn't imagine Evie would kill herself, but I suspected that my mom's version of Evie was stuck a decade in the past. Whenever she talked about Evie and me, she talked about what we had done as kids on the beach. I started to wonder if that's what death did—it locked a person in time for you, as if they only existed in small windows of memory. I had my own set of memories of Evie—eating pizza backwards, playing hide-and-seek, swimming underwater, kissing me in a hotel room—but the most vivid now, the one that kept coming back to me, was the last time I'd seen her, smiling at me over a row of bottles like a fence between us.

As we walked in, I turned to Dave and said, "I'm sorry we haven't hung out more."

"It's no big deal," Dave said.

"No, it's my fault," I said, and I realized how much time I'd spent blaming him although I was equally responsible. I could have made an effort. "I was a dick," I added, and looked up at him.

He turned. "Yeah, you were," he said, giving me a gentle shove.

Jenna came by herself before the service began. She had never met Evie, but she said she wanted to be there for me. She hugged my mom and dad and then came over, squeezing into the seat, taking my hand in hers. Inside, the chapel hummed with a quiet echo, the only sounds the occasional cough and the clank of pipes expanding and contracting. Someone had brought a baby, and I could hear it starting to whimper and cry somewhere behind me. The priest, an old friend of Aunt Beth's who still lived upstate, talked about Evie's spirit, her love of reading, dance, and the beach—an Evie checklist. I figured Aunt Beth or my mom had fed him all the material. Aunt Beth sat in the row ahead of me and seemed oddly stoic throughout the service, her expression dreamy, almost lost, as if she was on something to make it through the day. Jenna leaned over to me at one point and said, "It's okay if you want to cry."

"Gee, thanks," I said, and Jenna turned away. Maybe crying would have been the best thing, but all I knew was I didn't want to be there any longer. "You can cry for me," I added.

"I will," she said, and eventually she did. I stayed silent the whole way through.

After the funeral, people came over to our apartment for a reception. My parents often had parties at the house, and this had the feel of one of those, hors d'oeuvres spread out on tables with white tablecloths, half-drunk glasses of wine dotting the tables, people in every room. The only difference was that everyone wore dark colors and spoke in hushed tones. In a short time, though, whether because of the wine or because the service was behind us, people seemed to relax. Voices grew louder, and you could occasionally hear laughing. I took three beers from the fridge, opened them in front of everyone in the kitchen, and handed them to my friends.

"You sure it's okay?" Dave said, hiding his beer inside his jacket. Max clutched his beer in both hands, his expression equally suspicious.

"Absolutely," I said, although no one had given me permission. "Cheers." I raised my beer, clinking so loudly with my two friends you would have thought the glass would break.

Pretty soon I was on my third beer and getting buzzed. Jenna pulled me aside, dragging me into the hall closet, the only free space. It was pitch black inside, the sound muffled by thick winter coats. I could feel her wind her arms under my jacket and around my back.

"You're cold," she said.

"No I'm not," I said.

"Okay," she said. "Then I'm cold." We stood there, silently leaning into the coats. I could hear voices outside, people walking by the closet on their way to the other end of the apartment. Jenna said, "I miss you."

"I'm right here," I said.

"No you're not," she said. "But it's okay."

We started to kiss, gently at first, then I moved my hands up her sides, and then under her shirt. "Marty," she said, a hint of protest in her voice.

"What?"

"It's a funeral," Jenna said.

"So?" I said, pulling her tighter.

"For your cousin."

"She won't mind," I said.

I dragged my hands all over her body, kissing her neck. Jenna sighed, although her body coiled in protest, pushing me away.

"Wasn't this the plan? This weekend?"

"I know, but not now."

"How cool would it be if we just did it here, now, while everyone around is talking about death?"

"This is not really what I had in mind," she said, but I was barely listening any longer. My hand slid down the front of her skirt.

"Marty," she said, trying to push me away, but I held on tight. My hand slipped inside the band of her skirt, sliding inside her underwear, my fingers reaching.

"Don't!" she shouted. She grabbed a handful of the flesh of my arm and dug in her nails with all her strength. I cried out in pain, pulling out my hand. I couldn't completely see her in the darkness, but my eyes had begun to adjust, and I could make out her outline, searching the door for the handle, trying to escape. Before she could get it, the door swung open. My dad was standing there. "What's going on in here?" he said.

Jenna ran out. My dad looked at me. "Marty?"

"Nothing," I said, the light in the hallway a bright shock to my eyes.

⌒

"We talked to Ms. Rafi," my dad said the next morning at breakfast. "We're going to head up to Boston on Wednesday to do some more interviews. We made an appointment for a Colton alumni interview."

"Can't wait," I said, as I slathered butter on a bagel.

My mom stood at the kitchen counter, sipping her coffee, staring at me as if she was trying to figure me out.

"What?" I snapped at my mom. "Don't we have any cream cheese?"

My mom's expression looked unconvinced. "It's okay to be upset," she said. "I am. I'm sad. Confused." She paused, letting out a sigh. "I'm angry."

I looked at her, at the dark circles under her eyes from not sleeping because she was taking care of my aunt. Beth was living with us for now, although I wasn't sure if she had any plans to leave. I said, "That's it? Any others?"

I didn't know why I was being such a jerk. I was just sick of everyone asking me how I was feeling. My mom and dad shared a look.

"Fine," my mom said, raising her hands in defeat. "You just be whatever you're going to be."

"Thanks," I said, taking a bite of bagel.

"We wanted to ask you a favor," my dad said, walking up to stand with my mom. "Aunt Beth is having Evie cremated."

I knew what it meant. Evie reduced to ashes by fire. I didn't believe in souls or an afterlife or anything like that, but I couldn't help but wince at the mention of it, as if she would still feel pain. "What do you want me to do?" I said, putting down the bagel. I wasn't hungry anymore.

"Beth wants to take Evie to Cape Cod and spread her ashes at the beach. We were wondering if you wouldn't mind if she came along on the trip. We could take her out to the Cape after your interview in Boston."

I tried to imagine the four of us in the car together the whole time. Correction, the five of us: me, my mom and dad, Aunt Beth, and Evie's ashes. "Seriously?"

My parents looked at each other. "Beth wants you to be there, Marty," my mom said. "She says Evie would want it that way."

I sighed, leaning back in my chair. I was tempted to say that Evie didn't want anything anymore, but I stayed quiet. "I don't want to share a hotel room with her," I said, pausing before adding, "Meaning Aunt Beth. Or Evie. Or both of them."

My parents nodded in sync. "Fine," my dad said.

Jenna stopped by the next day unexpectedly. I was glad she came by, but I couldn't look her in the eye. "I'm sorry about the other day," she said, although I didn't know why she was apologizing. I was the one who had been a jerk.

"It's okay," I said.

She had other things on her mind. She opened her bag and pulled out a calendar. She flipped it open to November. "This is it," she said, pointing to a Saturday early in the month.

"This is what?"

"The date. When we're going to do it."

"What are you talking about?"

"The nasty. Get funky. Mattress magic. Sex, dipshit."

I laughed. "It's okay," I said.

"No, it's not," Jenna said. "My parents will be away. We'll have the whole place to ourselves. No scented candles. No lotions. Those aren't my thing." She paused before adding, "Maybe a little Barry White would be appropriate."

"You don't have to do this," I said.

"That funeral got me thinking," she said, and started moving around the room, picking up random things, studying them, and then putting them down. A baseball. A stapler. "It was all about regrets. Living life. I don't want to regret anything. Fact is, in less than a year, you'll be gone and I'll still be in school." She stopped in her steps and looked toward the ceiling, shaking her head. "I can't believe I have two more years to go in that place."

"Time goes faster than you think," I said, like some kind of stupid fortune cookie.

"I started to think," she continued, "about who I wanted to…you know…do it with…and who I would want to think back about doing it with…and the only person I could come up with was you."

"I'm flattered."

"Don't you get it? This is an important milestone. It's our first time. With anybody. We'll remember it for the rest of our lives."

I nodded, although my stomach dropped. Truth was, I wasn't a virgin. I'd lost my virginity last year in Max's parents' bed with some friend of his sister's who was visiting from out of town. We were both drunk. All I remembered about it was her asking me if I had a condom—I did, although it had been in my wallet for two years and was as flat as my learner's permit next to it—and how quickly the whole thing went. When it was over I rolled off her and she looked at me, her expression a bit disappointed, and said, "Maybe we should put our underwear back on." I never told Jenna because I figured it would only make the whole sex issue even weirder between us.

"I want this moment to be special. That's why I picked that day," she said. "It's some kind of Mayan fall harvest day. Or planting. I can't remember. Whatever. Of course, we'll be damn careful not to plant any seeds."

I looked at Jenna in her Lou Reed tee shirt, with her crazy brown hair. I didn't see it before but at that moment she looked a little like Evie. "I don't know," I said, my heart racing again. "Maybe this is just not the right time."

Jenna paused. "What do you mean?"

"Maybe we shouldn't force it."

"No, I want to do this," she said.

I knew she just wanted us to be as close as possible. And part of me did too. But my heart was beating so quickly my fingers were pulsing. My throat felt like it was swelling and closing up. "I'm away next week," I said, "back on the college tour. And then I've got all the applications to do. I'm going to be really busy."

I could see her expression sink. "What are you saying?"

"I don't know," I said. "Maybe we should just cool it off for a while. At least until everything settles down."

"'Cool it off'? What does that mean?"

I took a deep breath, trying to calm myself down. "Just that."

"Are you saying you want to break up?"

"No," I said. "Yes. Maybe. I don't know."

Jenna stared at me, stunned. "Wow," she said. "This is not how I saw this going."

"Jenna—"

"I'm such a fool," she said. "I'm glad we decided this before we had sex. Your being too busy to lose your virginity and all that."

I watched her pack her calendar back into her bag, trying to make an exit as quickly as possible. I said, "I'm not a virgin." She looked up at me again, a look of shock on her face. "I never said I was," I added.

She said, "Because you never told me you weren't."

"You just assumed," I said. *Breathe, one, two, three.*

Jenna looked at me with disbelief, tears welling in her eyes. "I think I should go," she said.

"Wait," I said, and what was remarkable was the calm that washed over me, as if the anxiety that had surrounded me lifted like a fog. Jenna started to cry. "Please wait," I said.

"Everything's changing," she said through her tears. "I get it. You're leaving. I'm not. People are dying. It's crazy. But that doesn't mean you have to trash everything good in your life."

"I'm not trashing anything," I said, reaching out to take her hand. "I don't know what you're talking about."

"Don't," she said, pulling away. "Just…don't." She started for the door and then turned, her eyes fixed on me. "You're scared. I get it. I'm fucking scared." She paused, taking a breath, before adding, "I guess I just didn't realize how much of a coward you are." She picked up her jacket and walked out before I could have stopped her, if I had tried.

My aunt barely spoke on the drive to Boston. She sat in the back seat next to me, staring out the window. Every once in a while she'd make a comment about driving in the area at some point in her life, but then the conversation would steer toward Evie in camp or college and she would go silent again. Her head leaned against the window. She'd always been fragile, compared to the sturdiness of my mother, but at that moment it seemed a bump in the road could shatter her completely. Evie's ashes sat at her feet in a square white box, like a wedding cake. It was unthinkable to me—an entire person reduced to something so small, like some kind of sick magic trick.

My mom had a file full of brochures from a few small liberal arts colleges and universities in the Boston area. There were tours we could go on almost every day and a few interviews set up, but now, actually back on the road, I didn't want to go on any of them. "What if I don't want to go to college?" I said.

My mom turned from the front seat, her expression pure disbelief. "What are you talking about?" I could see my dad's eyes fix on me in the rearview mirror.

"We always hear about all these great people in history who became famous and never went to college," I said. "Why is it the only choice?"

"Most of those people probably didn't have the opportunity," my mom said. "You do."

"College is the best," Aunt Beth said, and then started to tear up again.

"I mean, you go to school for what—thirteen years? Then you go to school for four more?" I said. "I don't get it." We were on I-95, headed north, the road packed with traffic creeping out of the city. My view out of any window was blocked by a wall of 18-wheelers. "Who decided that's what you *have* to do?"

My mother looked at my father, searching for his help. He was focused on the road, which was narrowing down from three lanes to one. Cars and trucks jockeyed for position, trying to squeeze into the only open lane. It was madness.

"College is where you figure out who you are," my mom said. "Who you want to be."

"And what if that doesn't happen?" I said. "What if I can't figure it out?"

I looked at my mom, but she wasn't looking at me. She was staring at Aunt Beth, whose eyes were fixed on the box at her feet.

My dad slipped into the open lane, and we slowly started to move forward again. "You're going to college," he said, and with that, the conversation, if it ever was one, ended.

―――

I had three interviews the next day and they went exactly as the others had gone before the disaster at Colton. Same questions, same smiles at my rehearsed responses. At the last interview, at a decent university in the heart of Boston, the interview was going so perfectly that I thought there was nothing I could say that would mess it up. The interviewer, a woman who looked like a clone of Ms. Rafi, asked me why I wanted to go there. "It's a good school. I know people who went here," I said, my eyes drifting to the window. Outside, leaves were swirling in the breeze, spinning in circles, rising up and then falling back down onto the ground. "I thought I could probably get in here."

The morning of my alumni interview with the Colton guy, my mom and Aunt Beth decided to go for a walk through the neighborhood while my dad and I went out for breakfast at a diner near the hotel. We sat in a booth eating sunny-side-up eggs and hash browns that were greasy and delicious. "You nervous about today?" he asked, dragging a piece of toast through his yoke.

"Not really," I said, although I was worried that the same

thing would happen again—someone just asking me if I had any questions. Ms. Rafi had given me a list of things I could ask, but I still didn't think it was enough for a whole hour.

"You'll do great," he said. "Besides, there's always the ol' alma mater," he added with a wink. I raised my eyebrows suspiciously. He knew his school wasn't my first choice, and he tried to act like he didn't care, but even I knew that he would have been thrilled for me to go there. There was nothing wrong with it—it was a great school, a big sprawling university in the Midwest, just a plane ride away. I knew it through descriptions in college directories, from photos in brochures, from stories my dad had told me over and over again about his time there. The tiny dorm room he shared with a farm boy from Michigan. The statue in the center of campus that freshmen were told not to touch or risk failing their first class. The football games at the stadium that were as important as any religion to many students. Still, at that moment the idea of going halfway across the country, that far away from my life in New York, seemed more impossible to imagine than any of the other schools I was considering.

"How's Jenna?" he asked. "I feel like we haven't seen her in a while."

I hadn't told them what happened. I hadn't told anyone. I didn't know what there was to say. "She's good," I said.

My dad sipped his coffee. "Your mom and I think she's great," he said. "Smart. Funny. You guys make a great couple."

"Yeah," I said, although my stomach sunk. *Idiot*, I thought to myself. *I'm a fucking idiot.*

"Listen, I wanted to talk to you," he said, putting his coffee cup down. I realized right then that this breakfast and my mom's walk with Aunt Beth hadn't been spontaneous at all. "Your mom's worried about you."

"Mom worries about a lot of things," I said.

He grinned. "That's true," he said. "She just thinks you have…" He paused, searching for the right words. "She thinks maybe you might want to talk about Evie. About what's happened."

My dad leaned back, putting his arm across the top of the booth, trying to look relaxed. He didn't. He looked about as uncomfortable as he could get. I said, "What's to talk about?"

"How you're feeling about it," he said. "What's going through your mind. Whatever you want."

"It's not about me."

"She was your cousin, Marty," my dad said. "You guys used to be like brother and sister."

"That was a long time ago," I said, and then I added, "It's not like we were close anymore." The words fell hard between us, and I could feel the silence that followed like a weight on my chest. My dad, the consummate lawyer, seemed to recognize that there was little he could do to change my mind. He sighed and nodded, then raised his hands to signal for the check.

My parents dropped me off at a café in Cambridge. I don't know why I expected someone in a suit and tie, but maybe it's because that's what all the other college interviewers had worn. Instead, he was a young guy in a tee shirt and jeans, with thick hair and a half-grown beard. "Marty?" he said, smiling.

His name was Nick. He had graduated from Colton three years ago. He asked me a lot about what I liked to do, not at school but for fun. I talked about my friends, going to horror movies, playing baseball. "Yankees or Mets?" he asked.

"I don't know," I said, although that wasn't true. I was just afraid it was going to make a difference to him. "Actually, I love the Mets. I hate the Yankees. Everything about them is evil. If Yankee Stadium went up in flames, I'm not sure I would care."

Nick laughed, holding up his hands defensively. "Okay, okay," he said. "As a Red Sox fan now, I'm completely with you."

He told me about how he taught English at a private school in Cambridge, not unlike my school. He was an assistant track coach as well. We talked about our experiences at my high school. It turned out that we both had almost all the same teachers. Nothing had changed in a decade. Rafi had even been his college counselor. "We used to call her Bug Eyes," he said, opening his eyes wide.

"Yes!" I shouted.

He told me he didn't have any idea what he wanted to do when he graduated. That sounded familiar. Later, when he paid the check, he said, "I heard about your cousin. You doing all right?" It was the question everyone seemed to want to ask. My heart started to race, that closing-up feeling surrounding my throat. *Breathe, one, two, three.*

"Not really," I said, surprising myself. "I don't know. It's all so surreal. College. Moving. Leaving New York." I didn't understand why I was telling this guy so much, but once I started I didn't want to stop. "My cousin offing herself," I said, for the first time acknowledging what I suspected was true. I looked at him and he looked a little uncomfortable. "I just broke up with my girlfriend and I have no idea why."

He nodded, his expression sympathetic. "Your cousin...that's heavy stuff. And your girlfriend. I don't know what to tell you on that." He looked at me slyly. "But all of this stuff...where you go to school... which city..." he said, waving me closer, as if what he was going to say had to stay a secret. "I'll tell you something."

I leaned in to meet him.

"None of it really matters," he said. It was the same thing Evie had told me that night on the train. "Just don't tell Bug Eyes that I told you that."

I sat looking at the street outside the window of our café. The sidewalks were packed with people moving in every direction, headed somewhere. "So what matters?"

Nick stood. "That's the question, right?" he said.

"I don't understand," I said, and I really didn't.

"You make choices. They work out or they don't," he said. "It's not that complicated."

We shook hands and he told me he'd write me a stellar recommendation. I thanked him, but also knew even a recommendation wouldn't make a difference. I wanted to call Jenna and tell her she still wasn't getting a sweatshirt. I wanted to call her to tell her I was sorry. I wanted to call her to tell her I was a fool, even though I figured she already knew that.

⟵

The next day, we all drove out to Race Point. It was the beach at the end of Massachusetts, where the arm of Cape Cod swung into a fist. The water was fierce, rougher than I remembered it, whitecaps roiling, waves breaking in successive crashes. The tide was low, leaving a low swath of beach where rocks and shells were exposed like skin rubbed raw.

We parked the car and the four of us got out. I wasn't sure what the plan was. My hope was just to sit on the hood of the car and watch the water. It was October, so the beach was pretty much empty, just a few people strolling up and down the shore, toward the point where the ocean and bay came together. Two little kids were standing with their parents by the water's edge, running from the water as it rolled up the shore and screaming with delight. Out along the horizon, I could make out enormous ships, a line of them, some heading toward the Boston bay, others headed into open water.

Aunt Beth started down the beach toward the ocean, my parents and I following behind. Not going along didn't seem to be an option. We passed from the soft sand that hadn't been touched by water to damp sand, still wet from the earlier tide, where my sneakers sunk in, sticking with each step. A mist of water swept over us from the ocean's waves. Aunt Beth stopped before we got too close, and sat on the ground, clearly unconcerned about getting wet. The box was still in her hands. She looked up at me. "I remember how the two of you could play on the beach all day," she said. "From morning until night. We had to pry you away to leave at the end of the day."

My mother laughed. "I remember," my dad said with a smile.

"We'd come down every hour or so and have to pull you out of the water or make you stop whatever game you were playing so we could slather you with suntan lotion," she said.

"You two *hated* that," my mom said. "You would have thought we were torturing you!"

"Do you remember?" Aunt Beth said, looking up at me.

I kneeled down, digging my hands into the ground, the wet sand coarse between my fingers. "I remember making sand-castles with her right here, on this beach," I said, and I did remember. I had a clear image of us sitting on the ground, digging and digging, my skin taut from baking in the sun. "All Evie cared about was building the wall. She didn't care about the castle. Not at all."

"She didn't," Aunt Beth said, agreeing.

"What kind of person cares more about the wall than the castle?" I said, and Aunt Beth shook her head, laughing between her tears.

I said, "I remember how she would position us close enough so that we could get a little water in the moat around our wall, but not so close so that it would get destroyed. She would spend forever finding the right spot before we could even start digging. Nothing upset her more than when we would come back hours later and find her wall knocked down."

My mother and father looked at each other, my mom touching my father's arm. "I think we'll wait in the car," my mom said. Aunt Beth nodded, smiling.

They walked back up toward the car, my mom's arm threaded through my dad's for support. "I hate the beach," Aunt Beth said, surprising me, when they were out of earshot.

"You do?"

"Always have. But Evie...her dad...They loved it. It's where they were happiest. So I went along."

She was right about Evie. Her whole personality seemed different near the beach, as if every time she got there she found a missing piece of herself.

"That's all I wanted," Aunt Beth said. "For her to be happy."

I tried to think of a time when Evie had been happy. It just wasn't a word I associated with her. At that moment it occurred to me that maybe it took more work to be happy than to settle into one's sadness. Maybe Evie just didn't have the strength anymore. I looked at the box sitting next to us and remembered again that it wasn't just a box, but all that was left of her. "What do we do now?"

Aunt Beth sat up on her knees. "What do you say we build her the best wall ever?" she said.

The two of us began to dig. We dug a deep trench in the sand, pulling armfuls of sand out of the ground, not caring that it was freezing out or that our clothes were getting soaked. She was a better builder than I would have thought, and pretty soon the mountain of sand stood over a foot high. I kept piling handfuls of sand and then patting it down, trying to make it as solid as possible. That was how Evie had always done it: adding layer after layer, fortifying each time with a combination of wet and dry sand. We didn't have tools—no plastic shovels or pails, and the bits of seashell around us weren't useful at all. Soon, my fingers grew raw from the coarse wet sand. At one point the water rolled in, filling the moat, but the walls held.

Aunt Beth clapped in delight. "Weathered the storm!" she shouted.

When we were done, Aunt Beth opened the white box. Inside was a clear plastic bag filled with white and gray ash and tiny stones. I couldn't believe that was all that was left of Evie. Aunt Beth dug a hole in the sand behind our wall. Then she opened the bag, reaching in and taking out a handful, careful to shield it from the wind. She dropped what she had in the hole. She held the bag up to me. I reached in, taking a handful as well. The ash and stone were colder than I imagined it would be. Emptying my hand felt like water slipping through my fingers. Then she closed the bag and put it back in the box. She didn't want to let it all go right there. We covered the hole with wet sand and patted it down. Aunt Beth let her hand linger on the spot where we'd buried the ashes.

The little boy and girl playing nearby came running over, each maybe five or six years old. They looked at us, as if we were doing the most fascinating thing in the world.

"What are you building?" the little girl said.

"A sandcastle," I said, although all we had was a wall.

"Cool," the little boy said, and the two of them ran to a spot not far away, and started to build their own castle.

Aunt Beth smiled, turning to me. "Let's go," she said, picking up the box.

We stood and walked toward my parents. In an hour, we would pack our bags and check out of the hotel and head back to New York. The next week, I would call Jenna and tell her how sorry I was, that I was a fool. She would agree, forgiving me far more easily than I deserved. A month later, I would come home from school one day and find an acceptance letter to my mom and dad's alma mater, as well as three rejections, including one from Colton. Jenna would come over, taking my hand and leading me to the bed where we would have sex without any planning or talking or Barry White, just a slow consideration of each other as if we were into something new and something was also coming to an end. After, she would look at me and say, "I wish we were ten years older." I wouldn't understand what she meant until I was finished with college and back in New York. I would be on my way one evening to meet Dave and Max for a drink when I would run into her and her college boyfriend on the street, and I could see she had moved on. "You look happy," she would say. I would say "I am," and I believed I was, although I was (and I am still) haunted by moments when the world seems to press down on me from all sides as if I am underwater. I would eventually get used to these incidents, learn to live with them, like a family member you put up with because you have no choice. They are simply part of who you are.

But that day on the beach with Aunt Beth, walking into the dunes and onto the parking lot, I looked back at the castle, waiting to see if any waves threatened the wall we'd built for Evie. Nearby, the kids worked on their own creation, shouting out instructions at each other and crying when the waves rolled in and knocked down what they had started. They were far too close to the water, and eventually they would figure it out. A few times, the water rolled in, filling our moat, but the wall stood tall, at least for now. Eventually the tide must come in, and I knew everything we'd made would be gone. No one would ever know what had been there. I thought about Evie's ashes mixing with the sand and sea, how part of her would live there forever. I listened to the sound of waves breaking and crashing and striking the sand like explosions, and heard the high-pitched laugh of children rising above it all.

acknowledgments

So many people to thank for bringing Martin into the world. All the great folks at Grand Central Publishing for their care and attention at every step. A huge thanks in particular to my editor, Karen Kosztolnyik, and her assistant Elizabeth Kulhanek for their insights on the book and for guiding me through the process in the kindest, most supportive possible way.

To my agent, Mitch Hoffman, the greatest advocate for the book that I ever could have imagined. Each and every person I meet in the publishing industry who knows you tells me that I've got the best agent. I can confirm that this is absolutely true. Huge thanks to the brilliant Irina Reyn for introducing us and for being my sounding board all along the way. Soup is on me. Thanks as well to Danielle Svetcov for her advice as I navigated the maze of the publishing world. And my deepest gratitude to Julianna Baggott for your willingness to help, listen, and advise on just about everything.

To all the teachers, students, and staff at Warren Wilson College's Program for Writers, particularly my mentors Rob Cohen, Wilton Barnhardt, Janet Peery, Debra Spark, and Peter Turchi. Thanks to my friends and teachers at the Fine Arts Work Center in Provincetown, Bread Loaf Writers' Conference, and Tin House Writer's Workshop, where many parts of this book took shape.

To the editors at *Columbia Journal*, *North American Review*, and the *Blue Penny Quarterly* for taking a chance on the first pieces of this book.

To Craig Bernier, Karen Dwyer, and Jim Zervanos, the best reader-teacher-writer friends. You three spent almost as much time with Martin as I did. Grateful doesn't even begin to express my feelings.

To the friends and family who have given me so much support, as well as the occasional place to hide away and write: Michael Annichine, Saul Anton, Greg Barnhisel and Alison Colbert, Robin Black, Steph Burt, Marc Cozza, Martin Cozza, Daniel Eisenberg, John and Diana Engel, James Engel, Seth Greenberg, Garth Green, Paula and Neal Holmes, Kari Jensen and Michael Seaman, the KAS crew, Magali Michael, Katherine Mosby, Nick Pachetti, Elaine Reichek, Beth Roper, Jim Shepard, Adrian Slobin and Mary Trull, Jared and Elisa Smith, Sanford Smith, Dan Watkins, Jeff Williams, and Gary Zebrun. A special thanks to Amy and Hemi and the awesome staff of Make Your Mark in Pittsburgh, my home away from home.

To all my colleagues and coworkers at Duquesne University and Macalester College. I particularly want to thank Jim Swindal, Chris Duncan, and the late Al Labriola for their institutional support as deans. And an enormous thanks to all my students, past and present, who keep me on my toes and inspire me with their passion and creativity.

To my siblings Libby, Paul, and Sarah. Thanks for leading the way and making me smile and laugh. And of course, Barbara and Shelly, my mom and dad, for giving me, well, everything.

Lastly, to the three people who make every day a joy: my boys, Emmett and Henry, who teach me more than I could ever teach them. And Laura, my first reader, my best friend, my heart.

reading group guide

discussion questions

1. What are some of the key characteristics of a coming-of-age story, and where do you see these represented in *The Martin Chronicles*? How do you think the novel's beginning and conclusion relate to Marty's journey?

2. *"There's no 'base' in real life, Marty. There's no 'time-out.'"* What are some rules that Marty and his friends have that disappear as they grow up? Do they gain any new rules in the process?

3. Turning thirteen is often viewed as a significant milestone of becoming an adult, which is reflected in the tradition of bar mitzvahs like Max's. How else do you see the transition to adulthood marked in *The Martin Chronicles*?

4. How do Marty's relationships with Max and Dave develop as they grow older?

5. Consider Marty's relationships with the adults in his life. How do those relationships vary, and how do they evolve as Marty matures?

6. A line is drawn in the sand while Marty is at camp and is made to choose between Carter and his new friends. At what other points in the book is a line drawn in the sand, where a choice needs to be made? How do the stakes get higher as he gets older?

7. When Marty goes to the beach with Evie, he observes, "*I stood knee-deep, the dumbest place to be, neither in all the way nor out.*" How else is Marty trapped between places throughout the book, and is he eventually able to move on?

8. *The Martin Chronicles* opens with the line, "*Girls invaded our school two months into sixth grade.*" Girls "invade" in different ways throughout the book, from Evie to Max's girlfriend Annie. How does Marty's reaction to these intrusions change?

9. At one point during his friendship with Rob, Marty says, "*I knew there were things I didn't get.*" In what ways is Marty's perspective limited, and how does this affect your reading of the book?

10. Marty remembers that when he and Evie built sandcastles together, "*All Evie cared about was building the wall. She didn't care about the castle,*" and asks, "*What kind of person cares more about the wall than the castle?*" How do you think this observation characterizes Evie?

11. Marty comments on the games in children's magazines featuring "*pictures zoomed in so close you couldn't tell what you were looking at. They were impossible to figure out—how could you know*

what the skin of a grasshopper actually looked like?—and yet there was always this thrilling sense of amazement when you saw the full image and couldn't believe you didn't recognize it for what it was." Are there other elements of Marty's life—or the novel itself— that are too "zoomed in" to be easily understood or immediately recognized?

12. What do you think is the significance of Ray Bradbury's *The Martian Chronicles*, which Marty repeatedly struggles to read beyond the first page?

13. How did the 1980s setting affect your reading of the book? Do you think this story would have evoked the same emotions in you as a reader if it had been set in a different time period?

14. What feelings of nostalgia does *The Martin Chronicles* bring about for you when reading it? What events do you recall from your own childhood and adolescence that now seem relevant to you in shaping the adult you became?

a conversation with john fried

What first inspired you to write *The Martin Chronicles*?

After I completed my MFA, I had a really hard time writing for a while. There were too many rules and too much advice floating around my head from teachers and mentors and fellow students. I was fixated on developing my "authentic voice" and sounding literary, but everything I did was forced and, well, terrible. Often, I couldn't get anything on the page. So I just decided to block out all the voices and focus on the kinds of stories I liked to read, which were slightly more plot-driven stories with a mix of humor and pathos. And somehow that led me to Marty. The first piece of it was the chapter called "Birthday Season." After that, I wrote a lot of different kinds of stories about other characters, but I just kept coming back to Marty. I started to see a shape and an arc revealing itself in the different pieces of his story, and I recognized that there was a book here about Marty's transformation from adolescent boy to a young man. I didn't write the book chronologically, but much of the second half of the book emerged later in the process. And I was evolving and growing as a writer as I worked on it. Although the last few chapters weren't necessarily easier to write, at least I felt a tiny bit more confident as a writer when I wrote them—like 50 percent sure the book was going to become something, instead of 20 percent. And that was unexpected and completely exciting.

Did your own experience of growing up in New York City affect how you wrote Marty's character or developed the plot?

Absolutely. New York City is a world I know very well. And it's certainly one that I drew on in constructing the setting that Marty inhabits. That said, I'm not Marty and there's no one person I knew growing up that exactly matches a particular character in the novel. I've borrowed from different people, from myself, and fabricated a whole lot simply in the interest of telling a good story. My hope is that while New York City figures largely in the plot and Marty's life, the reader doesn't have to know that environment to appreciate what he goes through. Marty is just a kid, trying to navigate the world as best he can, and that's true no matter where you're from.

Did writing from Marty's perspective as a boy and then teenager present any challenges for you?

I think writing from the perspective of a young narrator—particularly in the first-person point of view—is hard. You have to be aware of little things, like syntax or phrasing in how he speaks and even thinks. At the same time, there's this question of narrative stance. The book is told primarily in the past tense, but the question is, how far is Marty from the actions he's describing? I've always thought it's not that far. He's got a little distance, which allows him to reflect on what's happened and offer as much insight as he is capable of offering given his age, but it's not like he's an old man with a lifetime's worth of wisdom looking back on his childhood. Being conscious of that part of his voice was something I had to consider the whole time I drafted and particularly when I revised the book.

Much of this book feels like a timeless coming-of-age story, but it is nevertheless infused with a strong sense of time and place. Why did you choose 1980s New York for the setting? Did you ever consider having Marty grow up somewhere else?

There was something really great about being a kid in New York City at this time, because you had so much independence. There were no cell phones tethering us to our parents and friends, no Internet to occupy our time. There were other distractions, no doubt, but it was simply quieter. That's my memory of it. That freedom and solitude was definitely exhilarating, but it could also be scary. That's something I try to show in Marty: how he's often left alone to make sense of the world. As far as setting it somewhere else, I tried, but it just seemed like I was avoiding the obvious about Marty. He's a New Yorker. All my images of him involved the terrain of New York—walking the streets, in the park, in the subway—and I just decided to trust my instincts on it. That part of the story comes straight from me.

In "The Castle or the Wall," Marty says, "I started to wonder if that's what death did—it locked a person in time for you, as if

they only existed in small windows of memory." Was this idea of preserving memory present elsewhere in the book or in your wish to write it?

As the structure of the book became clear to me—that it was going to be episodic in nature—I think I just bought into the idea that you could paint a picture of someone's whole adolescence by showing these different key moments. Several people very close to me—family and friends—had passed away right around the time I was finishing up that particular chapter, so I think that idea was fresh in my mind. I had given a few eulogies at funerals and listened to many other people talk about death and life, and I noticed how everyone picked these moments to zoom in on as a way of letting us know who that person was and their relationship to them. Then again, I could also say that I stole that idea from Virginia Woolf and her whole idea of "moments of being," which has stuck with me since reading about it in college.

What are some of your favorite coming-of-age stories?

This is such a hard question. When I was young, I read everything by authors like Judy Blume and Paul Zindel. I remember reading *Catcher in the Rye* and *A Separate Peace* and *The Outsiders* in school and being in awe that you could create a story about someone that age. And then there are the "coming-of-age" books I've read as an adult like Stephen Chbosky's *Perks of Being a Wallflower* or Tom Perrotta's *Bad Haircut* or Susan Minot's *Monkeys* that became almost models for Marty's story once I understood what I was trying to do. When I teach fiction writing, I discuss a lot of coming-of-age stories, whether it's

Charles Baxter's "Gryphon" or Julie Orringer's "Pilgrims" or ZZ Packer's "Brownies," partly because I really like them but also because I think they are such good models for new writers. These transitional moments in life make rich material for stories. But I often struggle with the expression "coming-of-age story" in general because it seems to reduce the writing to such a simplistic idea. It almost sounds cute, like a little kitten you pick up and play with for a few minutes. This is going to sound like a total cop-out, but I've always wondered if most stories couldn't be considered some kind of coming-of-age story. Obviously not every story is about someone young becoming an adult, but most stories center their conflict on a character struggling with the transformation from one state to a next (or their failure to do so).

Why did you choose to structure the narrative in an episodic format? Were certain episodes easier to write than others, and did any chapters not make the final cut?

Once I had two or three chapters of the book from different points in Marty's life, I started to see the arc of a narrative emerging, which centered on his growth from age eleven to seventeen. I started to believe I could tell his whole story that way. So in a lot of ways, I didn't necessarily choose it as much as the structure revealed itself to me. But yes, some episodes were definitely much easier to write. There were no full chapters that didn't make the cut, only a few scenes that, in revision, were unnecessary or bad or insane or simply didn't move the story forward. But that's pretty much true with any writer I know.

Marty has so many firsts and lasts, as well as beginnings and endings. Were there any moments like these in his life that you particularly wanted to focus on?

I never started a chapter thinking, oh, this is going to be the one about Marty's first love, or this is going to be the chapter about race or sexuality. I always started with an image or scene or idea in my mind and let it see where it would go for me. The image of Marty driving the elevator as a young kid. The idea of Marty talking to his grandmother when she believes she sees her dead husband. The scene of Marty trying on the girl's stolen retainer. (That scene, in particular, had been around for a long time attached to no story or character, just this idea of the perverse things kids do that are vastly more complicated than they appear to be. I remembered reading it in a workshop once. Some people loved it. Others looked as if they were terrified of me.) All the scenes were the triggers that got me going deeper into a particular moment of his life, but I never knew exactly what they would become. If I had gone into a story trying to write about a specific touchstone moment, I think it wouldn't have worked at all. It had—and still has—to be organic on some level. No matter what I write I always feel a sense of reassurance when the characters take over and surprise me. When the story, in other words, becomes something different than what I imagined.

When did the idea to incorporate Ray Bradbury's *The Martian Chronicles* and name your novel *The Martin Chronicles* occur to you?

I love science fiction and I read a lot of it growing up. Bradbury's book, along with Asimov's *I, Robot*, and a few other sci-fi classics were incredibly important to me. Marty, on the other hand, isn't much of a reader. Anything he was going to read was going to be done begrudgingly—forced upon him by his mother or school. I don't know if my love of Bradbury's book played subconsciously on me, but once I saw the connection between his name and the book, it was as if I'd been given a gift.

VISIT **GCPClubCar.com** to sign up for the **GCP Club Car** newsletter, featuring exclusive promotions, info on other **Club Car** titles, and more.

@grandcentralpub   @grandcentralpub   @grandcentralpub

about the author

John Fried teaches creative writing at Duquesne University in Pittsburgh. He received his MFA from Warren Wilson College's Program for Writers. His short fiction has appeared in numerous journals, including the *Gettysburg Review*, *North American Review*, and *Columbia Journal*. Prior to teaching, he was a magazine writer and editor in New York, and his work appeared in various publications, including the *New York Times Magazine*, *Rolling Stone*, *New York*, *Time*, and *Real Simple*.

YOUR
BOOK
CLUB
RESOURCE

VISIT
GCPClubCar.com

to sign up for the **GCP Club Car** newsletter, featuring exclusive promotions, info on other **Club Car** titles, and more.

 @grandcentralpub

 @grandcentralpub

 @grandcentralpub